All S

MW01097044

Letting Go Series

Book Two

By Nicole Deese

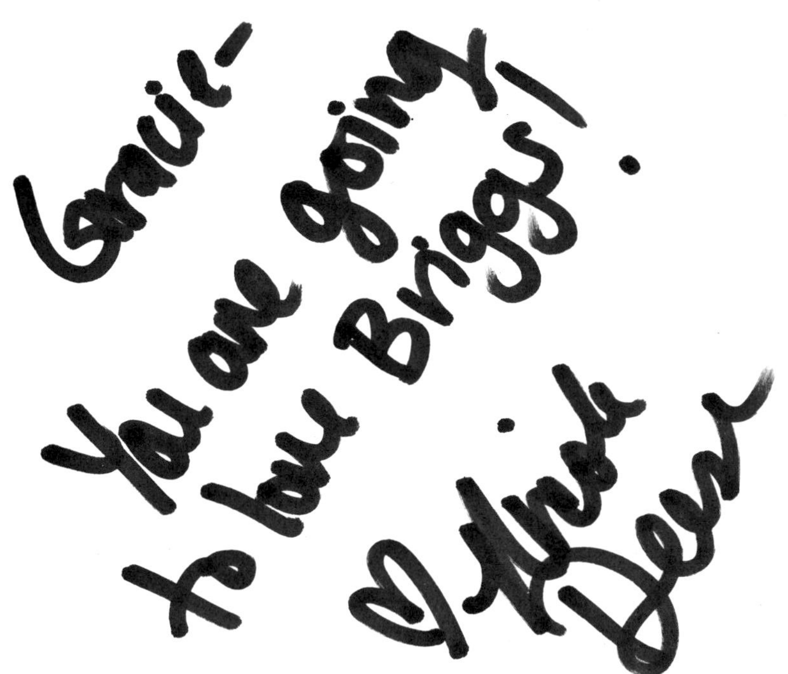
Gracie-
You are going to love Briggs!
♡ Nicole Deese

Okay Creation Cover Designs
© Sarah Hansen
www.okaycreations.net

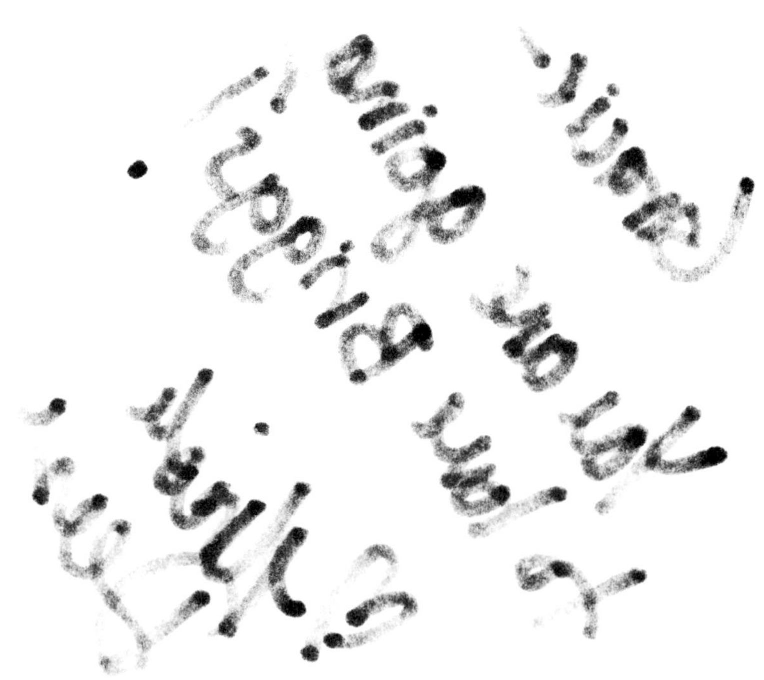

Dedication

This book is dedicated to my dad and mom.
Without you my passion for the arts would not exist.

I love you.

Prologue

Charlie

I used to pray for amnesia.

The irony of how some memories refuse to be erased while others could so easily slip my mind—like sand through a colander—was not lost on me.

Even with years of therapy, I still choked on the word that defined my childhood. It remained trapped somewhere inside my head, yet the feelings it provoked were unrestricted. It was almost as if time had chosen to skip over those memories completely, denying me the ability to forget.

I could remember everything—all the details that my five-year-old brain should not have been able to recall. I remembered the smell of the carpet, and the stale hot air that festered in our run-down flat. I remembered the dumpster in the parking lot, and the children who played near it round the clock. I remembered my tangled hair and the never-ending hunger that gnawed at my belly.

But most of all…I remembered *her*.

She liked the quiet, yet she cried incessantly. And when she wasn't crying, she was sleeping. I was old enough to see that she was broken, and desperate enough to believe that I could fix her—that I could make her well, that I could make her smile, that I could make her love me.

The day I heard the music, was the day I thought I had finally found her cure.

The delicate piano notes were a whisper on the wind, calling to me. I crouched below the open window so I could listen to the woman play. A fire ignited in my chest as the sound filled me; it was the sound of happiness.

Maybe music could make my mama happy, too.

I ran.

I ran through the parking lot, past the dumpster, up the stairs to the blue door with the chipping paint. I threw it open, running to the bed where my mama lay. I stroked her hair softly, careful to keep my voice low as I tried to rouse her from her sleep.

Mama didn't answer me though.

I spoke louder the second time, and louder still the third.

But mama never woke up that day.

When I went to live at a new house, with a new family, nothing was familiar to me. There was no dumpster with free stuff, no parking lot littered with kids, and no darkness lurking in the corner. It did have one thing though—the one thing I wished she could have heard, and the only thing that dulled the pain she left behind.

Music.

Chapter One

Charlie

"What did you say?"

"I'm revoking your scholarship. You've failed to keep up your GPA, which breaks the guidelines of your scholarship," Dean Thomas repeated.

I stood up from the plush leather chair and slapped my hands down on the shiny mahogany desk in front of him. "You can't be serious! Maybe you haven't heard, but my fiancé just dumped me! Doesn't the committee ever look at life circumstances, or are they just a bunch of cold-hearted-"

"Don't finish that sentence, Charlie. Your engagement ended last December. It's April now. We've given you more than enough grace to resolve your personal drama. There are students who are working extremely hard out there—trying to earn the scholarship you were granted. We cannot keep overlooking your grades. It reflects poorly on the University," he said.

Fireworks were going off inside my head. *This can't be right…they can't just do this to me without any warning. I'll get a lawyer; some big, hotheaded Texan that loves to sue stuck up Universities for wrongful termination—or whatever this could be classified as.*

My scowl intensified as I sat across from the old man with salt-and-pepper hair. Tears blurred my vision. Our stare-down lasted several long seconds before he finally broke the trance and scribbled something on a piece of paper in front of him, handing it to me hastily.

"What's this?" I snapped.

"That," he said, pointing to the document in my hand, "is the second chance I'm not convinced I should give you."

"Okay?" I questioned, carefully.

"I want you to take the rest of the term off. Go home; get your life straightened out. I'll hold your scholarship until fall term starts...but that's it, Charlie. No more chances. When you come back, there will be no more grace to give, are we clear on that?"

"Crystal."

I stared at the paper, knowing I should feel grateful, but the words refused to come out. I wasn't going to *thank him* for my suspension. That was stupid. I may be a lot of things, but stupid wasn't one of them. I mustered up the humility I needed to nod my head once before I turned to leave.

"Miss Lexington?"

"Yes?" I said, reaching for the doorknob.

"I had a nice long chat with your father about this today. He is expecting your call."

"Well, that's just excellent. Thank you for being so thorough, Dean Thomas." The words were like poison dripping from my lips.

"Anytime."

I closed the door hard as I exited.

Of all the schools I could have chosen! Why did the blasted Dean have to know my father!

As I reached my dorm room, I was relieved to find that Sasha wasn't there. It wasn't that I wanted to avoid my roommate per se, but I needed to do a little venting first. And that needed to be done alone. I screamed into my pillow until I felt light-headed, then I marched across the room—all ten feet of it. I picked up the picture I had refused to trash (along with the rest of the swag from my broken engagement) and threw it hard against the wall.

Shards of glass flew everywhere, but the photograph lay unscathed on the floor.

I stared at it. His sultry smile, his dark hair, and his laughing eyes, all taunted me. What a fool I'd been to believe he loved me. A single tear slipped down my cheek, I wiped at it impulsively.

I was *so sick* of crying over Alex Monroe; loving him had screwed everything up.

My phone buzzed in my bag. I reached for it instinctively, throwing my head back in frustration when I read the name.

Of course…daddy.

His timing was impeccable.

Briggs

"Briggs! My office—now, please," Chief Max bellowed.

I stood abruptly as my name echoed within the concrete walls of the fire station. I hadn't the foggiest idea why I was being summoned, but I moved quickly regardless. He wasn't a man to be left waiting—that is—unless you liked urinal duty. I happened not to.

"Yes, sir?" I asked as I reached his open door.

"Come in and close the door, please. Have a seat." Chief rested his elbows on his desk, massaging his temples. I entered. It was obvious something was wrong, but while not being the best at reading emotions, I decided to wait for him to address me further.

He took several deep breaths before breaking the silence. Finally, he looked at me. "I need your help."

"Anything, of course. What's up, sir?" I asked.

"Julie and I are scheduled to leave next week on our anniversary cruise to Greece," he began; I nodded as this was not news to me, "but we have run into a bit of a snag."

Probably forgot to find a dog-sitter. I like dogs. No problem.

"You need someone to watch Rocco?"

He lifted his head and stared at me as if re-assessing his need—or perhaps the solution to his need.

"No. I wasn't exactly looking for a dog-sitter, Briggs; I have one of those already. That's the least of my concerns at the moment."

He took another deep breath, drumming his thumbs on his desk in a thoughtful rhythm.

Whatever it is…it sure has him worked up.

"Charlie's coming home from school this weekend—for a while—and I need someone at the house to keep things in order while we're gone."

Charlie? Hmm…why did I think Chief had a daughter?

"Okay, like in what way, sir?" I asked, confused why a college-aged boy couldn't keep a house in order for four weeks.

"Charlie's gotten into some trouble at school. Too many extra-curricular activities, and not enough time hitting the books, if you get my drift. I need you to keep an eye on her while I'm gone. And the only way you can do that is to stay at the house."

Her? I nearly choked on my own spit as I swallowed.

"Charlie's a-"

"*Charlotte* is a young woman, yes. I thought you knew I had a daughter, Briggs?"

"Uh, right…of course I did," I said, clearing my throat.

"So, it's settled then? You'll stay at the house and make sure she follows my rules? I knew I could count on you."

I looked behind me instinctively.

Um…

The firehouse was filled with candidates much better qualified for a job like this.

"Sir, I think you might be better off with Kai—or Evan," I protested

"Kai's getting married in six weeks, and Evan is flying back home for his brother's military graduation."

Oh…so I'm third on his list. That makes way more sense.

Glad to know he's not losing it entirely.

"Julie will get the apartment above the garage all set up for you. I know this is a lot to ask, Briggs, but Julie won't go on this cruise unless we know Charlie's in good hands. She's a little spitfire for sure—always has been, but she needs consequences for her poor choices. She may have just turned twenty-one, but I'm still the bank that funds her life."

Chief Max smiled a bit at his last statement.

"Well, I guess…"

"Great. Thanks again, Briggs. I'll leave some instructions for you both while we're away. I've set it up for her to come to the station during the day and do some office work for me. Other than that, she is not to leave the house unsupervised."

"What—you mean like house arrest?" I asked incredulously.

"You got a problem with my parenting, Briggs?"

"No sir, it's just that you said she's twenty-one…won't she want to go out with friends and-"

"What she *wants* and what is *best* are two very different things. She has lived how she's wanted to for the past six months. Not only did that get her suspended from school, but her current taste in friends is nothing short of repulsive. So no, she can't go out, not until I'm back from my cruise," he said sternly.

"Got it. No going out. But what about my shifts, sir?" I asked, thinking about my schedule.

"She will come to the station when you do, and she will leave when you do. Obviously she won't be spending the night here, so figure out how to make your hours work around her. She's the priority here, Briggs. She's still my little girl—and the most precious person in my life short of my wife," he said, sighing, "I just can't trust her right now."

I nodded, though I was still having a hard time computing his paranoia. I stood to leave, as it was clear to me that he was finished. When I turned toward the door, he cleared his throat, drawing my attention back to him once more.

"I trust you won't let me down, Briggs."

I nodded.

His eyes communicated more than his words. He knew me—the real me, and yet he *trusted* me. There were guys at the station who assumed my past was still my present, but not Chief.

I wouldn't let him down.

Charlie

"Dinnertime, Charlie!" my mother called from downstairs.

Great. Just what I need: A family dinner to discuss my life choices.

"Be down in a sec!"

I threw the last of my clothes into my dresser and kicked my suitcase inside my closet. The one plus about moving back home was that my room here was nearly three times larger than my shared dorm room was. The downside was that Sasha wasn't here with me. She was four hours away, in Austin.

I walked down the stairs, glancing at the pictures on the wall. Smiling, happy, gag-me, pictures of a family that had been anything but connected as of late, stared back at me.

"Hello Charlie."

My dad's voice was unmistakable. It was a strange mix of authority and kindness—a combination I'd never heard duplicated.

"Hi Daddy," I said as he pulled me in for a hug.

"I'd like to say it's nice to see you, sweetheart—under different circumstances it would be." His tone could have been labeled, "The Disappointed Father".

"Unbelievable," I said, pulling out of his grip. "It hasn't even been a full minute and already you're reminding me of what a disappointment I am."

"Sweetheart, *you* are not a disappointment…your choices are," he said calmly.

I rolled my eyes, "Please Daddy, if that is your version of the 'love the sinner—hate the sin' conversation…I'd rather skip it."

"Sit down, Charlie; we have a lot to talk about."

I pulled out the dining room chair and sat down hard, deflecting the glare of my father by smiling at my mom instead.

"Please don't put your elbows on the table, Charlie," my mom said.

I re-adjusted, sitting up straighter. My stomach grumbled loudly in response to my mother's southern cooking. She was a phenomenal cook—deemed the Firehouse Mother a long time ago. She reveled in the joy of providing homemade pies and cobblers for the men at the station. I did not acquire that same skill set, or joy when it came to cooking.

"Let's say grace."

After bowing my head, I waited for the *amen*, my mouth salivating. I hadn't eaten lunch, refusing to stop for fast food during my four-hour drive home to Dallas. No amount of convenience was worth putting that garbage into my body.

After listening to some pleasantries from my mother about the latest on-goings in the neighborhood, my dad leaned back in his chair, indicating he was ready to get down to business.

"Your mother and I have decided that we are not going to postpone our cruise on account of your suspension, Charlie."

"I would hope not." I shot back, after taking a bite of salad.

"Charlie, don't talk with your mouth full," my mother said softly.

I rolled my eyes.

What was I—a first grader?

"Do not roll your eyes at your mother, Charlie!"

I put my fork down and leaned back slowly. Obviously, there was more to this conversation. He never snapped at me like that. I waited anxiously for the other shoe to drop.

"The reason we have decided to leave is because I've thought of a compromise."

He smiled; I did not smile back.

"And what might that be?" I asked.

"I've arranged to have someone come and stay with you while we're gone. They'll hold you accountable to the rules I told you about during our phone conversation last week."

"*What?* You have got to be joking! Who…who did you possibly arrange to *watch* me, Daddy? Old Lady Watson—or maybe Aunt Jo?" I couldn't help but laugh at the idea of either of those old women playing the role of babysitter for me like they had when I was in elementary school.

"Actually, it's one of my men."

I stopped laughing.

He was serious—dead serious. I gaped, words escaping me for the first time since I'd been home.

"Speechless? Well now you know how your mother and I felt when we got the call last week from Dean Thomas. We aren't playing games here, sugar. Things have to change with you…there are consequences for your actions. And it's our job to-"

I threw back my chair from the table, standing so quickly that my drink splashed over the rim, soaking the tablecloth.

"It's not your job, Daddy! *I* am not your job anymore…I'm an adult!"

He laced his fingers together, as if unfazed by my outburst.

"Really? Does an adult go out dancing till the wee hours of the morning? Does an adult get caught in the school parking lot drunk with their roommate after curfew? Does an adult get suspended from their scholarship because they stopped caring about their grades? That sounds like a rebellious child to me, Charlie—*not* an adult. I still provide for you financially-"

"Money? Is that what this is about? You think you can control me because you still pay for some of my bills while I'm in school?"

My arms waived wildly in the air as if they were no longer attached to my body. The explosion of rage going off inside me was unlike anything I had ever felt. I was losing it. The slow tick of a bomb that had been set months ago had finally found its mark.

I could do nothing to stop it.

"Charlie, please calm down. We understand that you've had a difficult season with the break-up and all, but we can't sit back and watch you self-destruct any longer," my mother said, adding to the conversation for the first time.

"Don't bring him into this, Mother!"

"Why not? He's at the crux of this whole charade, isn't he? Your mother and I told you our thoughts on Alex the first time we met him, and yet you still chose to say *yes* to his proposal—against me, against our blessing!"

I could hear the hurt in his voice, but I couldn't bring myself to let it soak in. I carried too much hurt of my own to let anyone else's in.

"I know what you think of him, Daddy! But can't you just for one, tiny minute, think about me? Think about what it was like for me to wake up to a note that left me without a fiancé, without the future I had planned with him? I loved him!" My hands shook as they covered my face. I felt a sob jolt through my entire body as I said the words again. "I loved him…and he *broke* my heart."

It was my mother's arms that encircled me as I cried. The grief that washed over me felt as fresh as it had the day I found his note. The rejection was just as overwhelming. I heard my dad stand, and an instant later I felt his heavy hand on my shoulder.

"We leave the day after tomorrow, Charlie. Briggs will stay above the garage, and you will follow the rules I have laid out for you while I'm gone."

He didn't need to add anything else to his last statement. He was done with this conversation, and there was nothing I could possibly say to change his mind. He had no compassion when it came to Alex. He despised him, for reasons I did not understand. If anyone had the right to hate Alex…it should have been me.

But it wasn't.

The night was long as I cried myself to sleep for the millionth time, my thoughts on the wedding that would have happened in just twenty-five days.

Briggs

Duffle bag in hand, I climbed the steps to the garage apartment. I still couldn't believe I was actually going to be babysitting a twenty-one year-old. *Who does that?* I wasn't a pushover, but saying no to Chief Max was like saying no to God…if I didn't end up in the belly of a whale, it would be equally as consequential for me. I unlocked the door with the key Mrs. Julie had given me and opened it. The inside smelled like a mixture of lemon and pine. I looked around the large space and smiled in approval.

Maybe this isn't going to be as bad as I thought.

The flat screen TV called my name, as did the couch and leather recliner. The kitchen was stocked with food, both in the pantry and the fridge, and the bedroom was larger than the current room I occupied at my shared apartment with the guys. There was a walk-in shower, double sinks and a closet that could have been called a spare room. I was all over this.

Now to go and make nice with Chief's daughter.

I was sure we could reach a mutual understanding. As long as she agreed to follow the rules Chief had outlined, I would stay out of her way, and she could stay out of mine. It was simple.

After putting my clothes away and flipping through a couple of sports channels (I needed to make sure everything was in proper working order), I headed down the stairs toward the house. I had seen a copy of the rules on the breakfast bar in my new apartment, but after glancing through them briefly, I figured this girl was old enough to sort them out on her own.

I wasn't some crazy dictator after all.

I knocked on the house door several times. When no one came, I turned the knob. I assumed Charlie was home since I'd just come from the station. Chief Max had reminded me again before he left that if she was not doing office work at the station, she was to be at home or with me. Case closed.

I walked inside, trying to make as much noise as possible.

"Hello?" I called through the house several times. I tried to ignore the fact that I hadn't been invited in.

This is my job. I'm just doing my job.

"Anybody home?"

Okay…so she's M.I.A on my first day.

Awesome.

I heard something then—coming from the back of the house. I made my way there slowly, still feeling more like a trespasser than an employed boarder. I reached a hallway that seemed to lead to the source of the sound. I stopped for a moment, listening.

It was music: muffled notes of a piano, I was pretty sure.

I walked down the hall until I saw a set of French glass doors that led into a room I'd never seen before when I had visited Chief Max's home. A baby grand sat inside, on the middle of the hardwood floor. My eyes swept over the piano until I saw her, or at least a part of her.

Charlie.

Her hair was the color of strawberries and cream—the wavy locks falling just below her shoulders. As I made a move to knock on the glass, she jumped in her seat, startled by my presence. I took two steps back, though there was still a closed door between us. I didn't want to scare her. She stared at me through the glass, as if calculating something, then slowly sauntered over and pulled it open.

"So, you're the manny, huh?"

Her face was…*wow.*

Her face was wow.

"I uh…the what, now?" I asked, my brain seemingly stuck on that one word: *Wow.*

"The manny…the man-nanny?" She said again—slower, as if she was dealing with someone who's elevator didn't make it all the way up to the top floor. "You're here to watch over me while my parents are off gallivanting in Greece, right?"

Okay, so she's funny.

"Yes, I guess that would be me," I said flashing a smile at her.

"Great…well let's get something straight, shall we? I don't need a babysitter. I won't cause you any trouble and you won't cause me any either, that sound good to you?" she asked, batting her eyelashes.

I was lost again momentarily in a sea of turquoise.

Was that even a real eye-color? Turquoise?

"Hello?" She waved her hand in front of my face, breaking the spell.

"Uh, yeah. That sounds good and dandy to me. Your dad left a copy of the rules in my apartment," I laughed casually, "So as long as you're good on those…I don't think there will be any issues."

"Perf," she said.

"Perf?"

"Perfect…see ya around, Manny," she said closing the doors and strolling back toward the piano.

I stood there, dumbfounded.

Well, that was easy.

I walked back down the hall and out the front door, locking it behind me on my way out.

Guess Chief Max is more paranoid than I thought. She seems reasonable enough.

Back at my new headquarters I made a frozen pizza and watched the highlights on ESPN. With no one to wrestle me for the remote, and a kitchen stocked with my favorite foods, I decided I would relish every minute of living in this lone bachelor pad.

I smiled to myself as I pulled the lever on the recliner.

This could quite possibly be the best four weeks of my life.

Chapter Two

Charlie

Well, that was easy.

After finishing up some work on my latest compositions, I made my way upstairs. Careful to turn off all the lights in the house, with the exception of the interior hall bath, so it would appear the house was asleep.

The house might be, but I'm sure not.

I smiled at myself in the mirror. My black mini skirt and heels complimented the purple sequin tank I had on nicely. Though the weather was still fairly cool, the club would be humid from all the packed-in bodies. I had texted Jackie earlier. Naturally, she was more than willing to assist me with my plan of escape. She was two years older than me, so technically this was our first time going out together since I had turned twenty-one. I hadn't thought ahead enough to park my car away from the garage where the manny was staying, so she had agreed to pick me up at the end of the street.

It was ten o' clock; the night was young.

Sasha had taken me to my first club—which was post-breakup. Though I'd always loved to dance, the idea of being around so many guys looking for a hook-up had kept me away from those scenes in the past. She assured me though, that as long as I was smart, I would be fine. So far that logic had proven true. I never accepted a drink from anyone, I never sat a drink down and returned to it later, and I only danced with the friends I arrived with.

She had also taught me a few good lines to get a Pervy Pete to move on.

I leaned into the mirror, painting on my lip-gloss before throwing my hair up into a twist. If I didn't put it up now, it would be stuck to the back of my neck all night. I grabbed my purse and slowly crept down the stairs—realizing a minute later the absurdity of my stealth-like movements when no one was home. I exited through the side door, doing my best to stay in the shadows and avoid the moonlit areas of the driveway. I didn't need Manny catching me on the first night of this hellish month to come.

I made a beeline toward Jackie's car, throwing my head back against the seat the second I was inside. My heart was racing. It was stupid to be this worked up—I was twenty-one for cryin' out loud! I shouldn't have to sneak-out anywhere. I forced my heart rate down, as Jackie laughed at me unabashed.

"What's got your panties in a bunch?"

"Nothing. I just needed to get out of there. I've been stuck inside that house since I got here three days ago. Dancing sounds like heaven right about now."

"So who do they have playing the role of guardian over you while they're away?"

"Oh…just some guy from the station," I muttered under my breath while she drove.

"What? You're hiding a hot fireman inside your house and you want to go out dancing?" She looked at me like I had just sprouted a third arm right before her eyes.

"It's not like that—he's old and creepy."

Okay, so maybe that was a little far-fetched—or a lot.

If I were being honest, he would fall on the opposite side of ugly when it came to the Hottie Spectrum, but I wasn't going to be honest. I couldn't be honest with Jackie, not with that type of information. *She can think he looks like a warthog for all I care.* If Jackie started coming around the house, I'd never have peace again. I'd witnessed her games with men *many* times, and I wasn't interested in watching that for the next four weeks in my own home. No thanks.

No man could resist the temptation that was Jackie. With her long, blonde hair and her model height, she was a Siren, calling to men without even having to open her mouth. Where Jackie went, men followed, and I didn't need Mr. Manny what's-his-name to be hanging around. In fact, I didn't need him at all.

"Bummer," she sighed as she flipped her hair to the side.

With the club in sight, I felt my body relax.

This is just what I need: to lose myself in the beat of the music.

Briggs

It was nearly two in the morning when I awoke from my dead slumber.

At first, I wasn't sure why, but then I noticed the beacon of light streaming in through the bedroom window. I shielded my eyes against it, which was like trying to block the sun with a leaf. Stumbling out of bed, I made my way over to the glass and peered out into the darkness, beyond the spotlight. It had obviously been triggered by movement.

I felt a cold chill cut through me as I rubbed at my eyes—taking in the sight with new interest.

There, tip-toeing through the driveway in bare feet, heels in hand, was little Miss Strawberry Shortcake herself. I could practically see her cursing at herself as she tried to avoid the motion detector, but there was simply no place for her to hide. When she glanced my way, I ducked back into the shadows.

"So daddy was right about you after all…well, two can play at this game, Shortcake," I said to the empty room.

Okay, now I'm talking to myself. That's not crazy at all, Briggs.

I went back to bed with my mind fully engaged. I should've known better than to trust a woman—especially one as strikingly beautiful as Charlie Lexington. She would most likely hate me by the end of this four-week stint, but that didn't matter. Chief Max was counting on me. That was all that mattered.

He'd given me a chance when he had hired me—taken a risk on me—one that frankly I hadn't deserved. I was not about to let him down now.

I was a lot of things, but a failure wasn't one of them.

Charlie

The manny offered me a ride to the station in the morning, but I had politely refused. Gathering up the supplies I would need, I shoved each of them into my satchel before slipping my heels on. My black capris would make for comfortable work attire for the day, but I wasn't about to dress-down my feet. Heels were about the only thing that made me feel older than a fourteen year-old. At barely five-foot, a girl had to do what she could.

I layered a cardigan over my light-blue tank and made my way to the front door a second later. I smiled as I walked to my Chevy convertible. Though it wasn't quite warm enough yet to have the top down, that day would be here soon. I loved to drive. It was one of my favorite things to do. Driving to my parent's lake house with the top down, wind in my hair, was the very best way to spend a sunny afternoon.

I sighed as the cool wind nipped at my exposed ankles. I cut my daydream short and hurried to my car, gearing myself up for one long, boring day.

The station was just as I remembered it.

I realized on the way over that I hadn't been back since I was in high school. Even still, it hadn't changed at all. The smell of rubber and disinfectant filled the air—a strangely comforting scent. I strolled in, ignoring the gawks and head-turns that followed me. Firemen weren't my thing.

I knew all about the life of a fireman: their priorities, their schedule, their sacrifice.

No thanks.

I made my way to my daddy's office and unlocked the door. He had left a key for me next to one of the many "rule lists" back at the house. After putting the key in my pocket, I had trashed each copy of said list.

I flicked on the light and looked in horror at the stack of files and paperwork he had taken out for me to organize and log into the computer.

"You have got to be kidding me," I grumbled.

There seemed to be random stacks of paper covering every square inch of desk space—although with daddy, nothing was ever random. Next to each pile was a sticky-note detailing what he expected me to do with each type of file. I couldn't help but wonder why, if he had taken the time to write each of these bright and annoying notes, couldn't he have just logged the files himself?

I put my satchel down and shut the door behind me. I would deal with the piles in time, but first, I would do a proper cleanup—my way.

This, after all, would be *my* work environment for the next month. I might as well make it cozy.

For the next two hours I cleaned—and by cleaned, I do not mean I broke out the Windex and dust rag. I simply mean I picked up trash, which he had obviously left for me—as per a bright pink post-it-note. I also moved several filing boxes, stacking them so as to open up the floor space even more.

When I went to search his desk for a pen, I accidently pulled the top drawer out with too much force. Everything fell out—including a pile of his personal receipts, which I'm sure were in some kind of order prior to their current demise. When I stepped back to assess the new mess I'd just created for myself, I had to laugh.

It looked like the aftermath of someone who had just come in and "made it rain"—that was one of Sasha's favorite phrases.

Too bad it's receipts and not cash.

I scrunched my nose up as I looked around. *Something smells rank in here.* Tomorrow I would bring candles—the air could really use some fresh and fruity.

Toward the end of the day, I finally found the fowl-smelling contributor. As I looked behind one of the large metal file-cabinets, an old coffee mug lay on its side—a science project growing inside it.

I trashed it—there was no way I was going to wash that nasty thing.

Heaving a large, black hefty bag over my shoulder like Santa Claus in one of those freaky Tim Burton movies, I made my way through the station, heading for the dumpster.

Briggs

"I'm telling ya Kai…this girl's a con artist," I lowered my voice as I told him my latest conspiracy theory—only this one was completely factual.

Kai smiled wide, "What? Are you *afraid* you may have lost your edge—nervous you can't stay one step ahead of her?"

I punched him in the chest. He laughed.

"Of course I haven't lost my edge! I *am* edge! She's just-"

I stopped mid-sentence, as every head around the lunch table seemed to turn at once, focused on something in the parking lot. My eyes followed suit.

There she was, carrying a garbage bag that was wider than she was tall. Before Kai could comment, I was on my feet, trailing after her.

"Can I help you out with that?" I called as I jogged over to her. I took the bag from her before she could protest and threw it into the dumpster—the dumpster which towered over her by at least two feet. Mathematically speaking, there was no plausible way she could have made that shot—unless of course, she possessed some secret Olympic high-jumping skill I wasn't aware of.

She flashed a quick smile, but before I could fully register it, it was gone.

She took several strides in the direction of the station before throwing me a "thanks", over her shoulder.

"I was thinking we could order Chinese tonight? What do you say?" I called after her.

Her quick, easy stride halted abruptly. I felt a tug of nerves pull at me as she turned.

She shook her head. "I don't think so, Manny. That could be considered a conflict of interest, and I wouldn't want to break any of my daddy's rules," she cooed.

Okay little Miss Shortcake, if that's how you wanna play it, then that's how it will be played.

I crossed my arms in front of my chest, smiling like a Cheshire cat, "Suit yourself."

She drew her eyebrows in, as if questioning my response, but her puzzlement didn't deter her long. She disappeared inside the station a second later.

I chuckled softly to myself.

It's gonna be a fun night…

Charlie

I texted Jackie to let her know I had solved my car issue from the night before. This time, I had parked on the street, far from the garage and the annoying motion-detector. Avoiding any and all attention was my only goal for the evening.

I won't make the same mistake twice—that stupid prison-break-light can be seen from the moon.

Jackie*:* I can be there in 20!

Me: PERF!

Jackie: :-)

I walked carefully along the far side of the fence, making my way toward the street, smiling as I approached my car. I glanced into my purse, digging around for my keys. But just as my fingers made contact with the cool metal, I nearly had a heart attack.

A man jumped out from behind my car.

"Going somewhere?"

I screamed.

The manny!

As I fought to remain standing while clutching my heart and panting like an old lady who had just lost at hide-and-seek, he laughed at me.

"I tried to play nice," he said, "I even gave you the benefit of the doubt…but this is how you repaid my generosity." He shook his head dramatically while pointing at my car. "Unfortunately, what you failed to realize was that I wrote the book on defying rules, Shortcake. In my day I ruled-the-roost."

I put my hand on my hip. "Oh, in *your* day, huh? What are you, eighty-five?"

He laughed again—heartily.

I wanted to deny that his laugh held within it the most contagious quality I'd ever heard, and how it transformed his entire countenance into a snapshot of joy. But most of all, I wanted to deny the fluttering.

My insides felt like the release at The Butterfly Kingdom exhibit.

I bit my cheeks to keep from encouraging whatever twisted campaign he was about to reveal.

"You're funny, Shortcake," he said, grinning from his mouth to his eyes.

I stood there—void of all emotion, thinking hard about my next move.

"Okay, so you caught me, but I'm totally fine with pretending you didn't. Let's just go back to our own little worlds of make-believe and my daddy will never have to know any of his precious rules were broken." I pushed him aside, making my way to the driver's side door.

"That only solves half the issue," he said pointing to himself, as if indicating that he was the other half.

"Tell yourself whatever you want to—you're conscience isn't my problem."

As I pulled up on the door handle, two things happened at once: One, his arm had magically snaked itself under my elbow, turning me around fully in less than half a second. Two, my keys were no longer in my hand, they were in his.

"Yeah, that's not gonna work for me, nice try though." He looked past me then, staring at my car with lustful eyes. "I've always wanted a convertible."

I was seriously contemplating punching him—hard—in the throat.

When I pulled out my phone to check the time, my frustration peaked. "Look, I don't care about whatever stupid arrangement you made with my father. I have to go. You've made me late."

A wave of panic washed over me as I saw his hand tighten around my car keys.

"And just what are you *late* for?"

Is he speaking that slowly on purpose? Unbelievable.

I couldn't leave Jackie at the club alone—that would be like throwing a package of raw steak to a group of hungry pit bulls.

She needed me; we needed each other. That was the first rule of clubbing: Never go alone.

"I have to go meet a friend, she *needs* me. You could be jeopardizing her safety if you don't let me go," I pleaded, hoping he would take the bait.

He crossed his arms over his chest, considering me, "Where?"

"None of your business," I challenged.

"Suit yourself, see ya." His long strides had him halfway up the driveway before I could react.

Seriously?

"Urgh! Manny—wait!" I stomped my foot like a tantruming toddler. He stopped immediately, turning around to face me again. "I'll tell you, but I still have to go regardless of what you think about it, ok?"

"I'm listening." He raised one perfectly arched eyebrow.

"The Dive—on Jefferson Street, it's a-"

His face darkened. "Oh I know exactly what it is, Shortcake, and if you think for one second that I am going to let the Chief's daughter go off to some booty-call club, then you've pegged me for the wrong kind of manny."

Though he had practically spit each word out in disgust, I felt my earlier resolve start to buckle at the mention of his now self-proclaimed title. No amount of cheek biting could hold it in this time. I laughed, the tension between us broken, at least for the moment.

He joined in almost immediately.

After I finally pulled myself together, he stared at me. "Do you *really* have a girlfriend that's supposed to meet you, or is that just another ploy?"

I sighed. "Yes, I *really* do have a girlfriend meeting me there, in fact, she's probably there already."

"Text her. If she doesn't respond in two minutes, I'll drive you."

I looked up at him, a fresh argument ready to launch off my tongue. But maybe it was time to switch gears. If he was willing to *try*—even though the reality of my current situation was completely asinine—then I could *try* as well.

Five minutes later we were driving toward Jefferson Street, in his old, restored '67 Chevy truck.

Briggs

When Charlie laughed, she glowed. Her eyes were intense—both deep and fiery at the same time. And the *sound?* I wanted to bottle that sound.

Immediately after she climbed into my truck and secured her seat belt, she reached for the radio, turning it on.

"Um…what do you think you're doing?" I asked.

"What does it look like?"

"It looks like you're being a little too handsy with my truck." I patted the dashboard for effect. "She'll need to warm up to you a bit before you start putting moves on her like that."

Out of the corner of my eye, I watched her decide whether or not to take me seriously. I smiled when she leaned back and crossed her arms in front of her, a smirk twisting her lips as she spoke.

"And what kind of warm-up might she need?"

Ah, now I'm getting somewhere.

"The usual I suppose—small talk first. She's rather particular, not just anyone gets to ride in her cab," I replied. I leaned over as if to tell her a secret and whispered, "She's the jealous type, so you might want to put her at ease."

"And fairly high maintenance it seems," she whispered back, "Is this where I declare my intentions?"

I laughed, "Nah, but conversing with her driver seems to work well."

"Well, let's see," Charlie started, "how long have you worked at the station, Manny?"

"Six years."

"How old are you?"

I smiled, "Not eight-five—shocking, I know!"

She laughed, "Really…how old are you?"

"Twenty-six."

"Why did you agree to be my manny for the month?" Her tone had quickly gone from sweet and playful to sour and testy.

I glanced in her direction before responding, "Because I like your dad. He's a good man—even if his rules seem extreme at times."

"So you agree this whole shenanigan is extreme, huh?" She asked, her voice noticeably warmer than five seconds prior. "That's five points to you, Manny."

"I get five points for agreeing with you on something? Wow, that's…generous. How many do I get for driving you to the booty-call bar?" I asked.

"Two."

"Two?" I turned my head toward her, laughing in surprise. "Please explain how the points went *down* for driving you across town in the middle of the night to help your friend ward off a sexual assault."

"Let's see," She held her little hand out, ticking-off a finger for each point-deduction. "You busted my escape, stole my car keys, and ruined my plans for a great evening."

I laughed. *Feisty little thing she is.*

A second later we pulled into the parking lot for *The Dive*—which was exactly how it looked, like a run-down hole of a business.

I put my arm out to stop her before she could open her door, "Do not leave my side tonight, Charlie. Taking your keys away is nothing compared to what I could do…if the need arose, got it?"

Chapter Three

Charlie

I stared at him for a long second, searching his face for any sign of humor. There was none to be found.

"Fine." I rolled my eyes as we made our way through the parking lot. "But I don't need a bodyguard," I mumbled, letting the music drown-out my words.

After showing my ID to the bouncer and paying the cover charge—which interestingly enough had been waived the night I didn't show up with the manny—we made our way through a sea of sweaty bodies.

"You're really cramping my style," I said flatly.

Naturally, he found this funny and laughed me off.

I checked my phone every couple of minutes. Jackie had yet to respond. I stood on my tip-toes and searched for her through the crowd.

"So, what does this girl look like?" Manny asked as we slid behind a group of rowdy women.

"Like a celebrity. Tall, blonde, thin…and gorgeous."

For once he had no comeback.

I texted her again.

Me: I'm here. Where are you?

After twenty minutes of walking around playing detective, I told Manny I was going to check the restroom.

"Okay, but I'm going with you."

"No way!" I balked, "You're not coming with me to the ladies room—that's *weird.*"

"Do you know where the majority of assaults happen in places like this, Shortcake? In. The. Restroom." He leaned in close so that I could hear him over the booming bass. His warm breath on my neck caused goose bumps to work their magic down my arms. "So yes, I *am* coming with you. Two minutes should be all you need to check the stalls."

Swallowing hard, I could only nod in response.

True to his word, he stood directly outside the door to the ladies room while I went inside to look for Jackie. *He's almost as bad as my father.*

The narrow bathroom housed at least twenty stalls and reeked of urine and body odor. I scrunched my nose up, determined to breathe only when it was absolutely necessary. I always did my best to avoid public bathrooms, so the two-minute time limit set by the manny seemed far too generous.

"Jackie?" I called, my voice echoing off the grimy tile walls and floors. "Jackie, are you in here?"

"Charlie—that you?" The last stall door swung open to reveal all five-foot-nine-inches of her statuesque body at once. Jackie tugged at her mini skirt as she stepped out, smiling down at me.

"I've been looking all over for you," I said, defensively.

"Well, I've been looking for you too!" She huffed back at me. "My phone died on the way over and my stupid brother took the charger out of my car—again! I just walked in here a second ago to use the restroom…we must have ESP or something." She shrugged, making her way over to the trough-style sink, as if to dismiss the worry I'd felt over her for the last twenty minutes.

That was irritating.

"Charlie? Is everything okay in there?" A distinctly male voice called into the bathroom, straining to be heard over some techno beat.

I rolled my eyes. *Great.*

"Yep. I found her, give us a sec alright?"

The music muffled again suddenly as I looked at Jackie, who was smiling at me like I was about to hand her a new puppy. She raised her eyebrows. "That your guardian man out there? He doesn't sound so old and creepy to me, Charlie."

"Yes, well…I may have exaggerated a tad," I mumbled. "Come on, let's get out of here…it smells."

Manny stood post like a guard, waiting attentively for us outside the restroom door.

Jackie pushed me aside to step in front of him, reaching her hand out to make her introduction. A bitter taste filled my mouth as I watched the interaction. I couldn't hear what she said to him, the music was too loud, but I could see his cheeks flush as she bent her head back and smiled. The bitter taste grew more and more acidic with each passing second.

He was *her* type—heck, he was any woman's type.

His dirty blond hair was a messy kind of gorgeous—longer on top and perfectly groomed on the back and sides. Some sort of wax product must have held the look together somehow, but nothing about it looked unnatural. His tall, lean body had to be a tad over six-foot as he towered over the majority of people who passed by us. With eyes the color of rich chocolate, it was no wonder why women stopped to ogle him when we had entered the club. Whether he didn't notice, or didn't care, it was a constant occurrence nonetheless.

"I'm gonna hit the floor," I called out over my shoulder as the two love birds continued their intimate conversation.

I made it about ten feet before I felt a strong grip on my shoulder—a familiar voice accosting my ear, "I thought we had a deal, Shortcake."

I turned dramatically, staring straight into his eyes as I nodded in the direction of Jackie. "Looked like you were busy, and I want to dance."

He narrowed his eyes at me, "You have thirty minutes. Use them wisely."

Briggs

Every one of my five senses was screaming for relief.

Not only was the smell of this grand establishment equivalent to a middle school locker room, the last fifteen minutes alone had made me want to flush my eyes out with disinfectant.

I checked my phone again for the time as I leaned against a metal railing.

Charlie and Jackie were dancing just a few feet out from where I stood, yet my eyes continually scanned the crowd around them. I had a knack for predicting the behavior of others—one that had been carefully honed after nursing dozens of black eyes, broken ribs and bruised organs. Fighting had created many opportunities for me to sharpen my observational skills.

It wasn't that I thought Charlie was stupid—in fact, I believed the opposite to be true, but this evening had seriously made me question her judgment. It bothered me more than I cared to admit that she had been in places like this before with only the protection of *friends* like Jackie. I shook my head remembering Jackie's soft-spoken words that held the venom of a cobra. Her not-so-subtle invitation had supplied me with all the information I needed.

Her face was equal parts surprised and curious after I had turned her down.

I wasn't into casual sex—at least not anymore.

A particularly vulgar group of males was on the move, stalking their prey like a pack of hungry wolves. I straightened; my jaw clenching tight as I focused my attention on one in particular who had made his way over to where a certain redhead was dancing. I was in motion a good ten seconds before he even touched her shoulder.

As I pushed through the sweaty mass, I saw her turn toward him, a look of evident disdain on her face. I saw her lips move quickly as he began to close the gap between them, it was then her eyes found me. But as I reached her, the creep had already backed-off. Whatever she had said to him had apparently been received.

For being the size of a Keebler Elf, the girl was no lightweight when it came to her tenacity.

The rigidity in my shoulders relaxed as she smirked at me and shrugged.

"It's time," I said tapping my invisible watch.

She rolled her eyes, but surprisingly, she complied. I watched as she pulled Jackie away from some dude who had practically tattooed himself onto her thigh. She was none-to-pleased, but she followed after Charlie regardless.

As we parted ways with her in the parking lot, Jackie blew me a very dramatic kiss. I ignored her, which apparently did not dissuade her.

"Hope you don't keep the hottie all to yourself, Charlie!" Jackie bellowed through the parking lot.

Charlie waved without comment and then looked at me incredulously.

"You gonna tell me what that was about—*hottie*?" She asked, sarcasm dripping from her last word.

"Are you gonna tell me what you said to that creeper in there?" I challenged back.

"Ladies never kiss and tell."

I laughed. "Well, if that is your idea of kissing, then your daddy has nothing to worry about."

She smiled, looking out the window without saying another word. Perhaps we both felt the events of the night had filled our quota for social stimulation. I wondered how long my ears would keep ringing from the hideous excuse for music I was forced to endure.

The silence was greatly appreciated.

I walked her to the front door after parking my truck in the driveway. I pulled out her keys, which had been in my pocket all night, and unlocked it for her.

"Thanks."

I nodded, knowing it was meant to cover much more than that simple gesture.

After I watched her enter the foyer I called to her. She turned.

"Here," I said, tossing the keys at her. She raised her eyebrows in surprise as she caught them.

"Am I free from my house-arrest so soon, Manny?"

"No," I laughed, "but if you find yourself itching to leave this house again, I want your word that you'll tell me first."

She held my gaze as if analyzing each word I had spoken before answering, "Okay."

She closed the front door a second later, re-locking it. I hopped off the porch and headed up to the garage apartment. A curious satisfaction filled my chest.

What an interesting night it had been.

Charlie

Several candles and other miscellaneous decor filled my arms as I made my way to daddy's office. Trying to adjust the largest candle under my chin so that I could maneuver my keys in the lock was proving a difficult task. It was then that I was offered help from a paramedic who looked like he'd just walked off an exotic island. He swung the door open for me.

"Thanks," I said, laying down my treasures on the desk, "if only I had a few more arms."

"Whoa…you've made quite a dent in here." He looked around the office in surprise, "I saw the work he left for you—this is impressive."

"Yeah, well, it's not quite up to par with extinguishing fires or saving lives…but someone has to fight the war against clutter."

He laughed, holding out his hand for me to shake, "I'm Kai Alesana, I'm sure you don't remember, but we met years ago at a Christmas party."

I shook my head, sheepishly. There was hardly a fireman here I did remember—it had been too long.

"Well, I hope Briggs isn't irritating you too much."

Briggs?

"Oh…you mean Manny, nah he's alright," I replied as he released my hand.

"Manny?" Kai asked, confused.

"Yeah...that's what I call him anyway." I shrugged, "He's my man-nanny."

Before I could even give my explanation in full, Kai was bent over, cackling. Two other guys came into the office then, asking what was so funny. Between broken breaths Kai repeated what I had just said. I smiled as the men responded in much the same way.

Each time I walked through the station to grab something I needed from the supply closet or kitchen, I heard the phrase swirling about. I hadn't seen him yet today—*Briggs, now that will take some getting used to*—but I was sure he was around.

The alarm had sounded several times during the morning, but I was never alone for long. Men popped in and out of the office to see what the cleaning-fairy had been up to, each introducing themselves as they entered. I understood now why my dad always spoke so highly of them—they were a fun bunch.

With the surfaces streak-free, windows open and candles lit, I started to sort through the piles. I reached into my satchel and grabbed my reading glasses. My dad's script was tiny. Each document not only needed to be re-categorized, but also needed to be logged by date.

Oy Vey.

I couldn't help but wonder if all these papers had been mixed up on purpose, but my father liked efficiency too much to do something that extreme. With all the work ahead of me, I'd be lucky to have it finished within the timeframe he allotted.

While bent over a file labeled "equipment updating", I felt something hit the top of my head, before falling onto the desk. I glanced up.

A french fry.

"You missed lunch, Shortcake," Briggs said, putting a bag of fast food down in front of me.

I wanted to tell him I didn't eat fast food and that I found it quite repulsive that anyone did…but I didn't.

"Oh…uh, thanks," I said.

"Although, I'm none-to-pleased that you out-ed me this morning." Briggs' eyes were full of amusement as it dawned on me what he was referring to.

"If only I'd known you wanted to keep it as a pet-name between us," I mocked in my best southern-belle accent, "I never would have told them."

He laughed, pulling a chair up to sit down opposite me at the desk. Suddenly, I was nervous.

What is he doing?

He pushed the lunch sack closer to me as if my lack of chowing-down was due to proximity of the bag, and not the contents inside it. I opened it slowly, the overpowering aroma of greasy fries filling the air. My stomach growled.

Oh shut up, stomach! Not all food is created equal…

I placed the fries and chemically altered chicken sandwich on the desk and waited for him to say something more.

Nope. Nada.

Okay, this isn't awkward…

I ate a couple of fries and my stomach growled again in response.

"So, I was thinking..." Briggs began.

"Yes?" I reached for another couple of fries.

"You like cards?"

"Uh…that's not random or anything," I said.

"Random—maybe, but a very simple question nonetheless. Do. You. Like. Playing. Cards?" He emphasized each word like I was unfamiliar with the English language.

"Depends."

"On?"

I leaned back, assessing him carefully, "What's at stake."

His laugh was low and deep, "You're a girl after my own heart."

I felt a jolt of electricity charge through me at his words. Of course he was only joking, naturally, but the uncomfortable tension seemed to hang in the air like salt at the beach.

"What do you think about having a couple of my friends over tomorrow night—for poker?" He leaned in, putting his elbows of the desk as he waited for my response.

"Is this a new tactic to get me to stay away from the *booty-call clubs*?"

Smiling, he pushed his chair out slowly and stood, "That's ten points to you, Shortcake."

And then he was out the door.

I shook my head, biting my bottom lip as I tried to restrain my ridiculous grin.

****

The cool feel of the ivory beneath my fingers was *home*.

There was nothing I knew better than the keys of a piano, nothing more natural for me to give my life to. With each press of my fingertip I could orchestrate a piece of time and space. The melody was mine alone, responding only to my creative impulse and desire.

And in this ever-shifting world, that type of control was unmatched anywhere else in my life.

I grabbed the composition I had been working on during the last two semesters and played it over and over, getting stuck at the same bar each time through. I could hear the notes somewhere in the far corner of my mind…yet it just wouldn't transpire correctly when I tried to mimic it.

I thought of my favorite music professor—Mr. Wade—and smiled. He always had some crazy story about finding his latest muse; I was suddenly very envious of him.

I missed school.

Despite how awful the last six months had been, or how hard it was to show up for class and complete my assignments, I *fit* there. The students, the staff, and even the classes had all felt tailored for someone just like me.

Yes, I had been angry when the Dean suspended me for the term, but if I was honest with myself, the anger I felt was not toward the scholarship committee. I had never been one to slack off in school. I'd always had plenty of drive to push through the temptations of the social world, but that was all before Alex.

Alexander Monroe had swooped into my life almost as fast as he had swooped out of it.

He was a drug to an addiction never satisfied.

I could still feel the way his eyes had watched me during my audition last summer. He had followed me into the parking lot afterward, and I had known it was him before I ever turned around. His very presence was intoxicating, and I was drunk on his charm after just one sip. With him in focus, every line had been blurred. And within only a few days I had offered him my very soul.

I was desperate to be loved by him; he was all I wanted.

Yet no matter how he had spun it, no matter what he promised, only one fact remained:

Alex Monroe didn't want me.

Chapter Four

Briggs

"Did you get my birthday invitation, Uncle B?" Cody asked.

"Sure did—hey, are you calling to un-invite me?" I teased.

My nephew laughed. "No way! You're the only one who knows the rules for water wars."

I had made the game up three years ago at Cody's fourth birthday. Each year I threw in a new twist to make it more exciting than the year before, thus insuring my indisputable place-hold at the birthday party.

"Ha, right! And don't you forget it," I said.

"Okay, Mom says I gotta go do my homework now—I really *hate* homework!"

"Yeah, well, she used to get on my case about that too, bud, but she's right," I countered.

"I know, I know. Bye Uncle B."

I hung up the phone, shaking my head and chuckling to myself. I loved that kid more than my life, and I missed seeing him like I used to.

I closed the hood of my truck, wiping my hands on an old towel scrap I'd shoved into my back pocket.

Up until a year ago, Angie and Cody had lived five minutes from me. I saw them several times a week, but when Angie was offered a job as a floral shop manager, she convinced me that moving was the right decision for them. My anxiety over the distance between us had not lessened with time. An hour drive was likely insignificant to most people, but Angie was not most people to me. With the horror I'd watched her live through, an hour felt like a continent away some days.

I had warned her not to marry Dirk—begged her even, but she was blinded by desperation. Marriage wasn't the rescue plan she had hoped for—instead, it became the thing she needed to be rescued from the most. Her lies, excuses, and avoidance could only last for so long before the truth finally surfaced, just like her bruises had.

Angie's pregnancy was the reason we left Colorado, to leave the demons of our past behind us. But when Cody was nearly three, Angie's ex-husband found her again. If I hadn't gone back to the house that night to grab my wallet, she wouldn't have survived.

I probably wouldn't have either.

My phone buzzed in my pocket.

Kai: What time tonight?

Me: 6?

Kai: Sure. Tori's off today. Pizza?

Me: Sure, thx. I'll buy drinks.

Kai: K

I smiled then, thinking about what Kai would say if I texted back my new vocab word of the week—the one I'd learned from Charlie: *Perf.* I was pretty sure in order for me to pull that off though I would have to look and smell like a sorority girl. Not gonna happen.

Why was I even thinking about her?

After taking a shower, I left to go grab a few more things from my old apartment before hitting up the store. I thought about telling Charlie I was leaving, but I hadn't seen her all day. She probably wouldn't even notice I was gone.

Charlie

As I cleaned the kitchen, I heard him leave. *Where was he going?*

Wait—why do I care? I don't.

I scrubbed the sink and pretended not to feel his absence. Though we hadn't talked since yesterday in the office, I had seen him this afternoon working on his truck in the driveway. I had also seen him talking on the phone.

Did he have a girlfriend?

If he did, she had better be pretty secure in herself—he was a flirt, yet even as I thought it, there was a dramatic difference between his kind of *charm* and the charm that Alex possessed. Manny—Briggs, was light-hearted, fun-loving and a pain in my side, while Alex breathed seduction.

I glanced at the clock after vacuuming. It was 5:15. Briggs had failed to communicate a time to me for when this *game extravaganza* would commence, but I figured since he was still gone, that it would be a bit.

Time had never passed as slowly as it had since I'd been a shut-in. I had a whole new appreciation for those with agoraphobia. I grabbed my zip-up and walked out to the back deck. I made a mental note to tell Manny that I wanted to go to the bookstore soon since this was to be my life for the next few weeks. I hadn't read a good fiction masterpiece for a while—music theory hadn't really allowed for much pleasure reading.

I leaned back and let the cool April breeze float across my face. I closed my eyes, letting the smell of pine needles take me away.

****

I had seen Jenny's dad carrying a small pokey tree with funny branches into their apartment once. She had lived next door to us. The smell of it was strong, and I wondered what he was going to do with it once he brought it inside. Jenny said it was for Christmas.

I didn't know what they meant.

Mama was awake on the bed when I went back into our apartment. She glanced at me briefly before rolling back over onto her side. I approached her quietly—curiosity at the forefront of my mind.

"Mama, what's Christmas?"

"Where'd ya hear that word?"

"From Jenny—she lives next door."

"It's a holiday."

"What does holiday mean?"

"It's just something for rich people."

I thought about that for a second, wanting it to mean something to my four-year-old brain.

"Are we rich, Mama?"

She laughed, but there was nothing happy about it.

"Hardly. Now stop asking me questions, Charlotte. Can't you see I'm trying to sleep?"

"Sorry, Mama."

I left the room, and never asked about it again.

****

I opened my eyes and searched the sky.

When I came to live with Max and Julie Lexington, my life had been drastically altered. The paperwork for my adoption took less than nine months to finalize, and I had lived with them under the guidelines of foster care until the courts deemed us an official family.

I didn't question their love for me, but I did wonder at times…

They had been so *desperate* for a child, the same way I had been desperate for a home. They would have loved any kid in need that was brought to them. It wasn't like they had asked for me specifically; I was just next on the list of broken, rejected children.

They were good parents though, no matter how I treated them.

I knew I had hurt them when I accepted the proposal without their blessing, but I also knew that they would ultimately forgive me. They were, after all, the ones who had taught me that *family forgave.*

The risk had seemed so minimal when I chose Alex over them—but now? Now, I didn't even know how to start to repair the damage I'd done. All I knew was that it was there, like a piece of glass that had been smashed by a rock. One tiny movement in any direction could shatter it completely.

The disappointment I saw in their eyes when they looked at me was almost as painful as the isolation I felt from them.

"That's minus three to you, Shortcake."

I spun around in my chair. Manny was walking across the deck in jeans and a red fleece pullover. My insides squirmed as he approached. I didn't want to admit, even just to myself, how good he looked in red.

"I don't think you understand how the point system works." I rolled my eyes at him before turning back toward the yard.

"It would have been plus three if you had stayed in the house, but since it took me a good ten minutes to find you…it's a minus." He pulled out a chair for himself. I could feel his eyes on my face, but purposefully avoided them.

"So when does this shindig start tonight, anyway?" I asked.

"Any minute. Just waitin' on our guests—consequently, they have our dinner, too." He laughed, leaning back in his seat and kicking his legs out in front of him.

Our guests?

What would it be like to be an "our" with Briggs? I shook the thought away quickly.

"Please tell me it's not fast food."

"Nope…even better, pizza!"

I couldn't help but laugh then, his child-like enthusiasm was catchy.

Briggs

A gnawing feeling in my gut overwhelmed me the second I saw her sitting outside.

I've never been good at guessing emotions. They were messy, uncomfortable and complicated to boot. But a woman's emotions? Forget it. That was the kind of jigsaw puzzle that was missing pieces before it ever left the factory.

But still, something about the look on her face *called* to me.

I studied her for several seconds, and for whatever reason, I was reminded that I needed her number—in case of an emergency. I grabbed her phone off the patio table and scrolled over to her contacts. She looked at me incredulously, but didn't make a move for it.

Hmm…does she trust me?

"If you wanted my number, you could have just asked me for it."

"Nah, this way is better," I said, grinning.

"Whatever, just bring it inside with you—it's cold out here." She stood and walked toward the house, leaving me alone with her phone in my hand.

The snoop in me wanted to do a little investigation work, but she had just taken all the fun out of that. If she didn't care what I might find, then there was probably not much to find.

I plugged my contact info into her phone and then texted myself so that I could save her info in mine. The purple, glittered phone buzzed in my hand then. I looked down as a calendar reminder flashed on the screen.

April 7th - 6pm
Wedding Countdown…21 days!
Call Tux Shop- confirm fitting time.

What?

Today is April 7th—but what is this about?

A twenty-one day countdown?

I closed the reminder and went into her calendar, ignoring any feeling of wrong-doing. There, in the square for April 28th were the words that deflated my airway like a popped-balloon.

My Wedding Day!!!

The doorbell rang.

Charlie

I reached the front door as Briggs came inside the house, sliding the back door closed with a bang. He flew past me at a pace that could have won a gold medal, and handed me my phone. There was nothing gentle about the hand-off. I looked at him, but he wouldn't make eye contact with me. Instead, he opened the door, which consequently pushed me behind it.

"Hey bro!" Kai said as he walked inside.

"Hey," Briggs replied.

I peeked out from my place in the corner as a very pretty women walked in after Kai. I assumed it was his fiancé, Tori. She looked at me and smiled, reaching her hand out.

"Hi, you must be Charlie—I'm Tori. It's nice to meet you," she said sweetly.

"You too," I replied. I was still trapped behind Briggs, who seemed to be in some sort of trance-like state. He hadn't budged an inch, which made my handshake with Tori quite awkward.

"Briggs? Earth to Briggs?" Tori said, hitting his shoulder while Kai carried the pizzas into the kitchen.

Briggs jerked a bit, eyes finally focusing on her before pulling her in for a hug.

"Sorry, I was just thinking about something," he said quietly.

She furrowed her brows, "Well, don't hurt yourself. Maybe you need to do that in smaller doses."

Yep, I like her already.

Once in the kitchen, I took out the plates and napkins. Tori and I chatted about her job as a trauma nurse, and how long she and Kai had been together. Her wedding was only five weeks away.

Wow…weird to think that I would have already been married.

The thought surprised me. It had only been recently that I had started thinking in terms of a wedding time-line again. The date had only been set for two weeks before Alex had left me. There were no invitations to recall, no caterers to cancel, and no photographers to get deposits back from. The only proof that I had even held the title of *fiancé*, was the ring in my sock drawer, and a digital date on my iPhone calendar. Oh, and those stupid calendar reminders that Sasha had put on my phone from some unknown wedding website.

Those started a week ago—exactly thirty days out.

Briggs

I knew I was scowling, but I couldn't help it.

How can she be so heartless? A secret wedding while her parents are away in Greece?

Not while I'm her manny.

That last thought might have been a bit too much—but still.

This was not going to happen—not on my watch.

There she was, chatting away with Tori as if everything in the world was hunky-dory. As if she was a perfect little angel. Well, she may have been an angel—but not the heavenly kind. I was certain her little red horns probably came out to play as soon as the clock struck midnight.

Wow…she even took her ring off! I knew she was a con.

I could smell it on her.

"Dude…what is the issue, here?" Kai asked me quietly.

"I'm just a little distracted is all," I said, heat fuming into my face.

"Uh, no kidding." Kai looked from me to the she-devil and back again.

"Lover's quarrel so soon? You've known her what—all of 4 days?" Kai asked, still keeping his voice low.

"Oh, there's gonna be a quarrel alright, but not of the lover's variety," I said.

Kai put his hand on my shoulder as if he knew what I was about to do, but I pushed him off.

"Charlotte, I need a word with you…*now*!"

Charlie

I froze.

Everyone froze—except for Briggs who was marching toward the back deck.

I hadn't been called that name since…since a lifetime ago. I was so shocked by his outburst I could do nothing but follow after him.

I felt sick to my stomach as I closed the door behind me, watching him pace like a mad man on the deck—the same deck we had been on only moments ago. *What had happened?*

My mind raced to make sense of what this could be about. Had he heard something from my parents in the last ten minutes? Did he miss a dose of anti-psychotic meds? Fear started to rise inside me, but I reminded myself that I had two witnesses just on the other side of that door.

He turned to me—finally, his face like granite.

"Who *is* he, Charlotte?"

He was seething. I had never seen the living definition of that word until this moment. I opened my mouth, but sound refused to come out. I had no clue what he was asking, or why in the world he was using that name?

"Or maybe, I should start by reminding you to call the Tux shop and confirm the fittings!"

Still I had nothing, confusion holding onto me with a tight grasp.

My heart started to race. *So, this must be what it looks like to watch someone lose his mind.*

"You have nothing to say for yourself?" He threw his arms toward the sky, "Now that's the biggest surprise of the night, right there! I'm onto you now, Charlie. Call it off—call the whole thing off! Ya know, it's one thing to let you go out at night when I'm with you, but I'm not going to let you have some *secret wedding* while your parents are in Greece!"

I felt like someone had just thrown me to the ground and kicked me, repeatedly. I was literally stumbling in shock. I grabbed onto the chair near me and gripped it with every fiber of strength I had.

I took three deep breaths before looking up at him again, "It's already off, you moron."

Silence.

"Come, again?"

"There is no wedding. I. Am. Not. Engaged."

I pushed my left hand out as if the evidence—or lack thereof—could prove my truth. It shook with an unanticipated surge of adrenaline.

His eyes narrowed further as he took several steps closer to me. "I saw it, Charlotte. I *saw* the reminder on your phone…don't lie to me."

That did it.

That stupid name did it. I snapped.

"Don't call me that! Don't you ever call me that!"

I put my hands out in front of me and pushed him—hard.

His body barely budged, as if he had anticipated the force of my shove more than I had. But as he watched me, his face changed—it softened.

"Charlie, I-"

"No! You had your turn, Mr. Drama Queen. It's my turn now. I *was* engaged, okay? Last December—not that it's any of *your* business, but it's over now. All of it. The relationship, the engagement, the wedding! It's all over!"

Tears poured from my eyes faster than I could wipe them away. I was mortified. I hadn't seen this coming—heck, hot lava pouring out of the kitchen faucet would have been less shocking than this conversation had been.

I covered my face with my hands.

Briggs

My bad.

Charlie

My back was turned away from him, but even still, I knew he was there.

A heavy hand pressed down on my shoulder after a few quiet seconds, and I didn't shrug it off. Even though his stupid tirade had brought this on, he was not the reason for my pain; he was not the reason for my tears.

"Shortcake, I'm…I'm so sorry." Though his voice sounded gruff, his words were heartfelt.

I nodded, my face still buried in my hands. I sniffled.

"Hang on-"

He left, coming back a minute later to hand me some Kleenex.

"Thanks," I whispered, lifting my head so I could wipe my eyes and nose.

He moved to stand directly in front of me, looking visibly distressed. Although, I was pretty sure I looked worse in this moment. He raked both hands through his hair, before shoving them deep into his pockets. It was definitely the first time I had seen the all-too-confident Briggs look unsure.

"You were just trying to protect my parents," I said, softly.

"Yeah…but I didn't do a very good job of protecting you in the process."

I looked at him, holding onto his gaze steadily, "I don't need your protection, Manny." The words lacked the sarcasm that I had intended, instead, they sounded painfully fragile.

He nodded. "Well, do you think we can start over? I'd like to be your friend, Charlie." He put his hand over his heart as if he were in a courtroom, "From this day forward, I will do my very best to restrain from all outbursts and accusations unless I have obtained physical proof first." The right side of his mouth lifted in a smile. "Truce?"

He reached out his hand for me to shake. I took it, biting back a smile of my own.

The tiny spark which had started in my palm as our hands met, traveled quickly to my chest, warming it instantly. "Truce. But Briggs, if you ever call me that name again, it will be with your last breath."

Briggs

I believed her.

Not only was I certain that she had told me the truth about her broken engagement, I also knew she would cause me physical harm if I ever called her *Charlotte* again. I don't know where exactly that had come from, but I would banish it from my vocabulary forever.

Don't have to threaten me twice.

"Did I totally ruin the mood for game night?" I asked her.

She laughed—at least a little bit.

"Hell hath no fury like a woman scorned, Manny. You're on."

If she hadn't been smiling when she said it, I would have feared for the evening ahead.

I followed her inside the house. Much to my satisfaction, Kai and Tori played it cool. There was no mention of the drama that had just occurred.

I knew they were my friends for a reason.

"You two ready? I have us all dealt," Kai said.

"Absolutely," Charlie said, pulling out a chair.

I couldn't help but smile at her.

She wasn't anything if not resilient.

Chapter Five

Charlie

Briggs and Tori seemed to have it out for each other during poker. Of the six rounds of Texas Hold'em played, they had each lost as many as they had won. Apparently, Tori's brother-in-law had taught her well, much to the dissatisfaction of Briggs.

When they finally noticed that Kai and I were growing restless with boredom, they agreed to switch gears. We were grateful.

"So, I think Charlie should pick the next game—since she's our guest," Briggs said.

"I don't really think that courtesy applies when you're sitting inside *my* house," I said smiling at him.

"Ooh...touché!" Kai said.

Briggs and Tori laughed.

After a brief mental debate, I chose Uno, but not just regular old Uno—*Spaz-attack Uno*. The game was a chaotic mix of speed and randomness. The quick plays and bogus rules were sure to cause a lot of groaning, especially when the players had to switch hands with the person on their right when a certain sequence was discarded. For the player who had dwindled themselves down to just a few cards, that particular play was brutal. I didn't mind it so much as Briggs was the player to my right.

"I see what you're doing Shortcake."

I laughed as I purposely increased the number of cards in my hand. Tori and Kai busted in hysterics.

"Could it be that Briggs has finally met his match in twisted game plays?" Tori asked.

I looked at Briggs and stuck my tongue out—childish yes, but oh-so-satisfying.

"I should ground you to your room," Briggs said.

"Hmmm…take a number, pal. I can only serve one punishment at a time."

That got a laugh from everyone.

Kai and Briggs declared it was time for a snack break, leaving Tori and I sitting at the card table waiting for their return.

"I'd love to hear more about your music, Charlie," Tori said.

Tori exuded kindness when she spoke. I could see why Kai loved her, aside from the obvious beauty she possessed. It wasn't just that she was nice, it was that she was genuinely interested. There was something about her that put me at ease—made me want to share my every secret with her. I had no doubt that she was an excellent nurse.

"Sure, what would you like to know?" I asked.

"How long you've played the piano—what made you choose it as your major?"

I smiled. "Since I was five. Sometimes I feel as if it chose me, actually. It just fits who I am—the same way nursing fits you, I'm sure. There was never any competition for what I wanted to do with my life. I wanted to write music and share it with whoever would listen. There are not many things in life that can reach a person's soul the way that music can," I said getting lost in my thoughts.

"That's beautiful, Charlie."

I shook my head—slightly embarrassed by my honesty.

"Thanks."

"So, you write music," Tori repeated, looking at a point somewhere beyond me as she spoke.

"Uh-huh."

"Have you ever written music for say…a wedding processional?" Tori asked smiling.

My stomach dipped a bit, but I worked hard not to show it on my face.

I dreamed of writing my own wedding processional once…

"Not really," I said.

"Well, I'd love to hire you, Charlie. I would really like something original for the processional—for my walk down the aisle specifically. Do you think you'd be willing to write something for me?"

How does Kai ever say no to that face?

"Uh sure, I will just need to know a few details—like how long you need it to be and such."

"Oh wow! That's fantastic Charlie, thank you!" Tori squealed.

Briggs

While grabbing the last slice of pizza, Kai leaned back against the counter and crossed his arms over his chest. He was staring at me.

"What?" I asked defensively, my mouth full of pizza.

"Are you seriously asking me that?" His voice was flat as he shook his head like a father does to a child.

"Uh, yeah. What's the issue…Did you want this last piece or something?" I took an exaggerated bite.

"No. Try again, Romeo."

I furrowed my brows at him. *What?*

"You really don't see it?" Kai asked.

"See what?" I asked, gesturing with my arms as three pepperoni circles fell to the floor with a splat.

Kai shook his head again. "Be careful with her, Briggs. She's the Chief's daughter. You don't want to screw that up." Kai's eyes were intense as he spoke.

"Screw *what* up, exactly? I'm just her security guard for the month, Kai. Relax."

"Don't be a moron…you're way more than a security guard to her. Have you ever seen the way a girl looks at a mall cop? It ain't like that," he said pointing to the room where Charlie and Tori sat, "She *likes* you, and I can see that you *like* her—just don't do anything stupid."

Why does everyone keep calling me a moron tonight?

Tori squealed in the other room, breaking up the big brother drill.

I was grateful.

Charlie

"Hey keep it down in there, neighborhood watch is gonna tag us with a noise violation," Briggs said walking back into the room, Kai close on his heels.

"Kai, Charlie just agreed to let me hire her for the wedding! She's gonna write my processional," Tori said as Kai bent over and gave her a kiss on the lips.

"That's awesome, can't wait to hear it, Charlie," Kai said smiling.

Briggs stared at me intently, but I broke its hold and smiled at Kai instead.

"Oh, and Briggs, I finally confirmed everything with Angie," Tori said.

My ears perked up. *Who's Angie?* Briggs nodded knowingly at her.

Kai leaned in then and whispered to me, "His sister Angie is a florist."

I flushed at how easily he must have read my face, and took a long drink of water hoping it would cool my cheeks.

"Cody's agreed to be my ring bearer too, although I think he might actually think he's going to get to be a *bear*...not a bearer," Tori said.

I laughed. Now *that* was funny. "Who's Cody?"

"Just the coolest seven-year-old you'll ever meet—also known as my nephew," Briggs said proudly.

"Ah," I said, nodding.

"Yeah, since my niece Kailynn is only four months-old, I'm gonna have him pull her in a wagon. My sister will just hold her during the ceremony. There was no way around it, Stace was bound and determined for her to wear a flower-girl dress, no matter what."

Kai laughed, "And when Stacie sets her mind to a fashion quest—it happens."

I watched them relate to one another.

I had a lot of friends at school—and at home—yet the interaction between them felt so different to me. I listened to them talk and laugh so easily.

I could see it then, clearly. They all truly loved each other.

I felt Briggs' eyes land on me again as I stood to start the clean-up process. Tori followed my lead.

Briggs

The evening had been fun—even more than I had anticipated it would be. Kai and Tori had left some time after 1:00am.

After taking the pizza boxes out to the recycle bin, I went back inside to grab my jacket. Charlie was shutting-off the lights. Before I headed out the front door, I instructed her to lock it behind me. She rolled her eyes as the corner of her mouth curled into a half-hearted smirk.

Even with Kai's caution fresh on my mind, there was something I just had to say. It had been on the tip of my tongue during the majority of the evening and I needed to get it out. I took two steps onto the porch before turning around to face her. The door was almost closed, but she pulled it back slightly when she saw me.

She yawned.

Holy crap she's beautiful.

No—that's not what I was going to say...

Think.

She leaned her head on the door sleepily.

"Did you forget something?" she asked.

I shook my head. "No. Good night, Shortcake. See ya tomorrow."

Okay, so I'm not always great at follow through—so shoot me.

Chapter Six

Charlie

"How are you, sugar?"

"I'm fine," I said honestly, "Are you and mom having a good time?"

"Yeah, who knew cruise food could be so good?" He laughed.

"Uh, *everybody*, Daddy. That's why people come home to clothes that don't fit!"

He laughed again.

"So…you're really doing okay? Having Briggs at the house—it's been alright?"

I sighed. "Yes, everything is fine around here…you can stop worrying about me."

"I'll be worried about you until the day the good Lord takes me home. You'll always be my baby girl no matter how old you are, Charlie," he paused as if wanting to say more. There was a strain in his voice, which seemed to parallel the one in my heart. "I'm sure mom will email you some pictures in a couple days."

"Sounds good, bye."

Though my dad had emailed a couple times, I was surprised he had waited over ten days to call. I wondered if he had been keeping tabs on me through Briggs without my knowing. It was likely.

Life had fallen into a bit of a new routine over the last week. My house-arrest didn't seem quite so horrid anymore. Briggs and I had been riding to work together each day in his truck and eating dinner together in the evenings. We'd played cards a few times, visited a book store to fulfill my fiction cravings, and tonight we were going to watch the first *Indiana Jones* movie. Briggs about spit his coffee out when I couldn't place some line about a holy grail he'd made reference to.

He said he couldn't allow me to live another week without watching it.

Whatever.

The truth was he made me laugh. I enjoyed being with him—no matter what we were doing. His company was unrivaled by anyone else in my life.

I finished up with yet another stack of files and headed out of the office.

Briggs

Charlie knocked on my door a tad after eight, and for a second, I hesitated.

Is this really a good idea—Charlie and I alone together in my apartment?

I swallowed hard and reassured myself that it was fine. We were *just friends.*

Friends watched movies together all the time, right?

"Hey, Manny." She walked past me, placing a bowl of popcorn on the coffee table. But it wasn't the fragrance of popcorn that overpowered my senses. It was the smell of fresh peaches—coming from her wet hair.

Charlie—recently showered—was clad in flannel pj's and slippers.

Get a grip, Briggs.

Why does she have to look so good in flannel? I mean, who looks that good in flannel?

As my inner-dialogue progressed, I suddenly realized she was talking to me.

"What?" I shook my head slightly.

"I asked if you wanted the recliner?"

"Uh no, go ahead. I'll sit over here," I replied, not-so-smoothly.

"Okay." She shrugged.

Just put the movie on, Briggs.

…although , I doubt even Harrison Ford could smell that good after a shower.

She curled up on the recliner, pulling her legs beneath her like she was some sort of carnival pretzel.

"When was this movie even made?" she asked snottily as I made my way over to the couch.

"I don't know—the 80's I think?"

"Awesome." She rolled her eyes.

I picked up a handful of popcorn and threw it at her. She laughed.

That laugh was my favorite. I had learned that Charlie had many laughs—at least a dozen. Some were soft and airy, some were strong and showy…but this one, this one was completely unabashed. When she laughed like that, her defenses were down. Her pride was gone, and it was just her—raw and open.

I sat on the far end of the couch—the end farthest from the recliner. I grabbed the remote and put my feet up on the table.

I pressed play.

"So where does your sister live?"

I pressed pause.

"About an hour north."

I pressed play.

"Do you get to see her much?"

I pressed pause.

"About once a month, sometimes more."

I pressed play.

"What's your nephew like?"

I pressed pause.

"Charlie…we will be here till three in the morning if you don't shut it," I said.

"Oops, sorry," she shrugged, "I'm not a very good movie watcher."

"Gee, I couldn't tell."

She laughed.

I smiled.

****

For the next two hours Charlie stayed relatively quiet, except for her snarky remarks about fashion or special effects. To which I told her to shove it. To which she would hurl more insults my way. It went on like that till the end credits rolled.

When she stood and stretched, it was difficult to find something equally distracting anywhere else in the room. Her hair was a wild mess of waves as it had dried while being pressed against the back of the recliner. Yet somehow, it still looked amazing.

I swallowed hard.

She walked over to the sink to get a glass of water, stopping in front of the fridge.

"Cute—is this from Cody?" She asked, looking at the picture I had put on the freezer door.

She remembered his name?

It was a drawing of a fireman that he had done last year after I spoke to his class during safety week. It was one of the few things I treasured. I had brought it over with me when I picked up the poker paraphernalia from my apartment last week.

"Well, I can tell it's you," she said, her words dipped in mockery.

"How's that?" I asked, too curious to let it slide.

"Toothy grin, broad shoulders—but what really tipped me off was how he nailed your *big, fat head*." With that, she flashed me a smile and laughed heartily.

I made a beeline for her as she shrieked, running to the other side of the kitchen. She realized a second too late that she had nowhere to go.

She had boxed herself into a corner. I put my hands on either side of her, gripping the counter.

"Take it back," I said.

"Never."

I inhaled. *She smells so good.*

I was so close—closer than I'd ever been to her.

Her laughing eyes changed then, our smiles fading-out at the same time.

I wanted to kiss her. No, I *needed* to kiss her.

But with some supernatural strength unknown to me, I released her, taking several steps back. She seemed just as dazed in that moment. I cleared my throat, turning to walk her to the door. She followed behind me, quietly.

At the bottom of the stairs, I shoved my hands into my pockets and watched her walk toward the house. I wanted to make sure got inside okay, but as she passed, a familiar urge crept up into my throat again, begging to be released.

And this time, I didn't hold the words back.

"Charlie?"

"Yes?" She stopped, turning to stare at me.

"He was a fool."

"Who?" she asked.

"The idiot who left you. He didn't know what he had—if he did, he wouldn't have let you go."

Though it had been dark all around us, the motion light came on in that instant—illuminating her in its spotlight. She stared at me, as if contemplating my words. Finally she spoke, in a volume that was practically soundless, "Thanks."

She disappeared beyond the light a second later.

The instant I was back inside the apartment, I banged my head against the door.

"And I am an even bigger fool for falling for the Chief's daughter."

Charlie

I couldn't sleep.

I tried for hours, but rest never found me. I got out of bed and walked down to my music room. I opened the doors and turned on the single lamp that sat atop my piano. It shone onto the keys, causing a halo effect to surround them. I sat down, closed my eyes and let my fingers explore. My mind was open to the melody that flowed through them. The notes were powerful, depicting images, emotions and words.

They told a story, one that came directly from my soul. There were no two the same.

Melodies were intimate.

The room echoed triumphantly as the aggressive swells filled the air, holding the passion inside it even as the soft, delicate treble notes were played.

This room was made for music; this room had been made me for me.

****

"Charlie, we have one more present for you, sugar," my daddy said.

He led me down the hallway toward my mom's sewing room as he shielded my eyes with his large, rough hands.

I was ten. It was my birthday—or at least the day we celebrated as my birthday.

My mom stood behind me, I could feel her nervous anticipation as she awaited my reaction. I heard the doors open in front of us. My daddy moved to the side before dropping his hands away from my eyes. And when he did, I gasped.

There, in the middle of my mom's old sewing room, was the most beautiful thing I'd ever seen—a black, baby grand piano.

I couldn't move. I just kept looking at it in disbelief, blinking. My heart was pounding so hard that I could hear next to nothing other than it's strong beat inside my ears.

"Go ahead Charlie, go sit down on the bench, sweetie," my mom coaxed.

But I remained frozen—still.

This gift was too big, too nice, too overwhelming for me to understand. This gift was beyond anything I could ever repay—much less deserve. I began to cry, my chest heaving with the heavy burden of what this must have cost them.

My daddy knelt down in front of me, his eyes glistening with tears as he spoke.

"This is a gift, sweetheart. It might seem overwhelming, but our love for you is even bigger than this. You have been our gift, Charlie. Nothing would make us happier than to help you grow in your talent…do you understand that?"

I nodded as they each took one of my hands and led me to the piano.

The moment I sat down and touched the keys, my life had changed yet again.

I was never the same.

****

This room had always been my refuge—my safe haven.

It was the one place I could find answers, even to questions unasked. Its solace had represented hope and peace, no matter what memory waged war in my mind. It not only inspired me to connect with my music, but when I sat here—when I played—it was that same connection which seemed to transcend the confines of my soul.

I was *known* inside this room.

But something was off…

As my fingers slid off the keys, a familiar ache filled my chest. Whatever great connection I had once felt—it seemed a distant memory now.

I wanted to blame it on Alex—on the heartache, on the rejection, on the deception.

Yet, I was just as much to blame as he was. I had done the same thing to the only two people who had ever shown me unconditional love.

I stared at the sheet music again—the piece I just couldn't seem to finish.

I sighed. *Tomorrow I'll start Tori's processional.*

It was almost 4 a.m.

I turned off the light and shuffled to the couch, not having the energy to climb the stairs.

Chapter Seven

Briggs

This new eight-to-five workweek was very odd.

Since becoming Charlie's manny over two weeks ago, this was the schedule we had worked out. Chief had made it clear to me (several times) before he left, that *she* was the priority. There was no reason to make her pull night shifts, so I was simply taken out of the normal rotation so that Charlie could get her office tasks done during the day. It was quite an adjustment from my usual twenty-four on, forty-eight off.

Honestly, I much preferred my old schedule to this one.

It had been said that life as a fireman could be compared with marriage—we ate, slept, worked, cleaned, played and lived at the station together. When Chief Max hired me, I couldn't fully grasp that idea, until I experienced it for myself. Acting as one, working as one, fighting as one for a common purpose had changed the way I saw the world.

We were a family.

Family.

Working for Chief had completely redefined that word for me.

Angie and I had grown up in a family that was nothing short of dysfunctional. It was no wonder why she had chosen Dirk straight out of high school. She had been looking for the same sort of escape I had been—only mine had come in the form of fighting, drinking, and women.

Angie was fifteen months older than me, but I would forever see her as my little sister—no matter what our birth order said. I had always felt responsible to protect her, maybe because no one else had. Our parents were a tangle of co-dependence and self-destruction. They never saw past their own needs or wants. They never *saw* us.

Our home had not been one of violence, but neglect left scars that violence couldn't reach. There was no stability, no consistency, no refuge inside it—we were merely a pit stop in their search for greener grass.

They never did find it.

My mom was a master manipulator, holding an invisible power over us all. She was the kind of crazy that stayed under the radar, too well kept to be noticed, too unhinged to be healthy. My dad was a passive man, letting his work have the best of his time and attention, meanwhile letting his family drown in the chaos.

Their fights would last for hours, some for days. Their verbal battle of insults was enough to drive even the most lucid person toward the brink of insanity.

I was sixteen when they divorced.

Though I'd spent years craving peace—the way one craved water in a desert—it was my endless hours of training that had filled the deep void inside me. But that irony only served as a reminder to my own dysfunction, which in turn caused me to push harder and train more.

Fighting quickly became my whole existence.

When I moved Angie to Dallas, I started at the station soon after, working as a volunteer. I was desperate to find work that could support my sister and soon-to-be nephew, outside of my winnings on the weekends. Though I had saved every penny that I could, the day I was hired into a permanent position was a huge sigh of relief. Kai had been the one to convince Chief to hire me, ultimately securing my loyalty and respect.

Kai never sought praise or affirmation; he was humble, kind, and *good*—likely the best man I would ever know.

I loved him like a brother.

He had been there for me during the darkest time of my life—the night I almost lost my sister.

When Tori crashed into his life unexpectedly, I was none-too-pleased. I was leery of her—suspicious. Kai wasn't weak, but he trusted people to a degree I couldn't understand. I felt it my place to reveal her blind spots to him—to clue him in on the tragic mess that love really was…only that wasn't what happened.

Instead, I watched them battle through hardship, hurt, and heartache. I watched them fight for each other—loving each other with an intensity that I couldn't ignore, no matter how hard I tried to.

And what I had seen, what I had witnessed, had slowly and painfully peeled back the calloused layers of my heart.

The life I had chosen had always *felt* right, until it didn't anymore. Until no amount of drinking, fighting, or sex could *fix* me, or the destruction I had caused.

I had never loved any of the warm bodies that had filled my bed. I didn't know their likes, or their dreams, and I certainly never knew their laughs. Women had only been a means to meet a need, one that only pacified itself for so long before the emptiness found its way back in.

When it finally caught up to me: the past I couldn't escape, the shame I couldn't hide, the truth I had to accept, I was done living for the empty.

****

I'd been sitting in my truck for nearly ten minutes waiting for her to come out. I kept thinking that any second I would see her open the front door with her greek yogurt in hand, but the only thing I saw was the minutes ticking by.

Did she feel awkward about what happened between us last night?

Is she avoiding me?

I drummed my fingers on the steering wheel. That moment had felt…intense, but I couldn't even begin to analyze Charlie. Who knew what she thought? I sure didn't.

I watched the clock for another five minutes after shooting her a text.

No response.

Do I go in?

Do I leave her and go without her?

Why are women so dang complicated?

I turned off the engine, and knocked on the front door. When there wasn't an answer, I started to get a little bit freaked—or a lot bit freaked. I snatched the key from my glove box that Chief had given me, and walked inside a second later.

Why do I feel like I am in a constant state of deja vu with this girl? What is this—my third time breaking and entering since I met her?

Just as I opened my mouth to call her name, I stopped short. There she was—asleep in her flannel pjs, on the couch.

Why is she sleeping on the couch?

I wasn't sure what to do at first; this was a new conundrum for me. Finally, I did the only thing I could; I left, shutting the door behind me quietly.

And then I rang the doorbell.

Several times.

In a row.

To the beat of *Jingle Bells.*

Charlie

Something hideous was clanging inside my brain.

My eyes snapped open as I covered my ears in a panic, trying to understand what was happening.

Jingle Bells?

I stumbled off the couch toward the door, seeing a familiar silhouette beyond the fogged-glass. There was only one person I knew who could match that level of annoying. I marched to the door and jerked it open.

"Oh hello, Shortcake! Welcome to the land of the living."

"Did you get dropped on your head as a kid? Or does *this*," I pointed to the doorbell, "just come natural to you?"

"Someone needs her coffee today," he mumbled, pushing past me to walk inside.

"Oh—well, please come on in." Though my voice was no better than a croak, I hoped it still held the necessary dramatic inflations.

"Thanks, don't mind if I do." He looked at the couch and then back at me, "Why were you sleeping down here?"

"Wow, nosy *and* annoying...your list of qualities just keeps growing by the minute."

He grinned as if I had just complimented him, "Aw, stop…you'll make me blush."

Rolling my eyes, I decided to let that one go as I saw what time it was. "Can you give me twenty minutes, or should I just drive myself?"

"I'll wait," he said simply, walking into the kitchen.

****

Though my sleep had been short, my hot shower had revived me.

It felt a little odd knowing that Briggs was downstairs waiting—but strangely comforting at the same time.

Last night had been…*what had it been?*

For a moment I had been nearly certain that he was going to kiss me, but instead he practically ran from me.

Had I wanted him to kiss me? I flushed.

No, I didn't *want* to kiss Briggs.

What I *wanted* was for my life to feel normal again. I *wanted* the pain to stop haunting me. I *wanted* to erase Alex Monroe from my life—forever.

Yet, oddly enough, I didn't notice the pain when I was with Briggs. He, himself, *was* a pain, but that was entirely different. I rolled my eyes as I thought again about his *Jingle Bells* debut.

As I got dressed, I smelled a whiff of something… scrumptious. My mouth watered instantly as my stomach growled in anticipation. Was Briggs…*cooking*? I put on some lip-gloss and zipped up my black boots over my leggings before heading downstairs.

As I hit the last step, I saw the source of that delightful aroma.

There, on the breakfast bar, were two plates. Each held a steaming omelet—one had a greek yogurt sitting next to it.

He made me breakfast?

His back was to me as he poured a glass of orange juice. A buzz of anticipation filled my whole being—and it had nothing to do with my growling, hungry stomach.

Briggs

I *felt* her.

I could feel her warmth in the room before I even turned around, and as it turns out, it was a good thing I had waited to face her. The orange juice in my hand would not have made it to the counter if I had seen her a second earlier.

Oh, heck no.

No. No. No.

She can't be serious.

I took a deep breath. I knew if I commented on her outfit *before* breakfast, these omelets would have ended up cold and uneaten. That much I had learned about Charlie. My normal aggressive approach to life didn't work so well on her.

"Good morning, Shortcake."

"Well, who knew! You've been holding out on me—a chef, huh?" she asked, tilting her head as she smiled.

My stomach dropped. I looked away, clearing my throat.

"Well, not exactly. I just do breakfast." I pulled out her chair, seeing the surprise in her eyes, as if the gesture was foreign to her.

Geesh…who was this punk she had dated?

No, I didn't *want* to know the answer to that.

She thanked me quietly.

I watched her take the first bite. It was a far cry from watching the guys eat my omelets, that was for sure. Theirs were gone in roughly five large hand-to-mouth motions, but that wasn't the case with Charlie. She ate like the food had feelings, like it was labeled *fragile.*

Something ached inside my chest as I pulled my eyes away again, hoping to clear my head.

"So, got plans this weekend?" I asked her, smiling.

She looked at me, "Is that a trick question?"

I laughed—hard. She was figuring me out.

I looked at her then, calculating my next words. I needed to address her attire. I had to. It was now or never, and there was no way I was letting her go to a fire station full of men, dressed like that. As she put her fork down, even though a good twenty percent of her meal lay uneaten on her plate, I knew it was time.

"So, those are sure some nice boots ya got there."

She looked down. "Uh, thanks," she said, standing up to take our plates to the sink.

"Don't you think though…that maybe they would look better with pants?"

She spun around.

Here it comes-

"What do you mean? These *are* pants," she shot back, defensively.

"Okay…I suppose *your* definition of pants might be a tad different than mine," I held out my hands, as if taming a hungry lion, "Let me explain. *I* think pants should be thicker than a tissue, they should also serve to protect the skin from the elements, as well as from the eyes of peeping men," I said.

Her mouth hung open.

I was right to make her eat first.

"Oh, so what…you think I dress like a-"

"I'm not saying that Charlie, but I do think there are plenty of…more appropriate outfits you could wear to a fire station—other than a nylon."

Okay…probably could have left that last part out.

She crossed her arms over her chest. “Sorry, but I’m pretty sure your job description didn’t include wardrobe Nazi, Briggs.”

I swallowed hard.

She was right. I had no authority to tell her to change, however, I knew the Chief would have been none-too-happy to see his daughter parading through the station in a piece of black saran-wrap and hooker boots. Okay—maybe it wasn’t quite that bad, but still.

My mind raced ahead, searching for a compromise. The one I landed on may have been a bit of stretch, but I knew she would take the bait.

“I’ll tell you what, if you would be so kind as to put on a pair of pants—*my* definition of course, then I’ll take you to a party tomorrow evening,” I said carefully.

She eyed me suspiciously, placing a hand on her hip.

“What kind of party?”

“It’s an annual celebration of sorts. It’s a bit of a drive, but I’ve been going for years. You’ll have fun, I promise. Plus, it will get you out of this house.” I raised my eyebrows at her, waiting.

She was considering it—considering me.

“Will there be dancing at this *party*?”

Does the hokey-pokey count?

Yeah, it does.

“Yep.” I nodded, “There will be dancing.”

“Fine, but don’t think this means you have any control in what I wear in the future,” she said, stomping back up the stairs.

“I wouldn’t dream of it, Shortcake,” I laughed.

Or at least, I would try not to.

Chapter Eight

Charlie

I stared at the first few measures of Tori's processional, trying to will my mind to focus. I suppose it was focused, just on something other than music. Every time I shut my eyes to envision the melody, I saw Briggs, standing in my kitchen the way he had been only yesterday morning. The omelets, the pants debate, the compromise…it all ran through my mind like a movie.

Why had he cared so much about what I wore? And what had he cared about exactly—my virtue?

That concept was about as unfamiliar to me as the inner workings of a microchip. Of course my father had been protective, but I had been out of his house for nearly three years. A lot had happened in three years.

Alex had never asked me to change—at least, not *out of something sexy*. He'd only ever encouraged me to wear clothing that showed my body off, clothing that showed him off when we were out together. I never did live up to his expectations in regard to my attire, but his *approval*, when I had, made me feel good. I wasn't exactly daring in the way I dressed, but I was no longer shy about the attention I received either.

There was no mystery left to uncover.

Alex had seen to that.

Just as I rested my hands on the keys in an effort to ignore the wanderings in my head, my phone buzzed. I jumped, the vibration on the piano reverberating through the room.

I laughed as the text surfaced—the name Briggs gave himself the night he stole my phone, displaying proudly.

The hottie who lives above your garage: Can you be ready by 3? Something came up and I need to leave earlier. WEAR NORMAL CLOTHES!

Me: What kind of party starts before 9? NORMAL? I'm confused:)

The hottie who lives above your garage: The kind that I take you to. Do I seriously need to come in and pick something out for you? Don't put it past me, Shortcake.

I smiled.

Me: You are such a pain!

The hottie who lives above your garage: And yet…you love me for it.

My stomach flipped; my breathing faltered.

I replied, ignoring it all.

Me: 3 is fine.

And that was the end of that.

Briggs

Oh to have seen her face when I had sent that last text. I'm sure it was priceless.

Shock value still had its place in this world—I made sure of it.

Angie had texted me earlier to ask if I could take a look at her car, it was acting up again. I figured it was probably due for a tune-up, her next oil change wasn't too far off either. I could do both before the party started. Luckily, I already had my tools here at the house. I had started to put them in the back of my truck when I noticed the weather.

It was nice out—convertible nice.

Charlie would probably be a tad less furious with me for taking her to Cody's seventh birthday party if we rode in her convertible. She came outside a minute later as I laid my tools down near her car.

"What are you doing?" she asked.

To my very sweet surprise, she was in jeans—high heels—but in jeans nonetheless.

I decided not to mention the shoes.

"Thought we could take your car today since it's so nice out," I said.

She looked at me like an assassin who had found her mark, then crossed her arms in front of her before staring down at my tools.

"I am not going anywhere until you tell me what this whole charade is about. What do you need those tools for? Unless they are required to attend the *awesome party* you told me about," she mocked.

I smiled, shoving my hands in my pockets.

She's a smart little cookie—this one, although I had tipped her off.

"Tonight is Cody's birthday party," I said, preparing for a volcanic eruption.

She stared at me.

I waited.

She kept staring.

I kept waiting.

Finally, she said, "Maybe this will come as a shock to you, but I actually *like* birthday parties. You don't have to trick me into going to one."

She turned sharply and stalked back toward the house.

I watched her, speechless.

What is she saying?

That she would have wanted to come with me?

"Wait—where are you going?" I yelled after her.

"I'm getting my keys!"

I smiled. *Unbelievable.*

****

"I don't think so, Shortcake." I shook my head.

"But it's *my* car," she whined.

I was starting to break down. I could feel it with each pout and whine of her voice.

Call me whatever name that fit the bill, but I *always* drove. The only exception to that rule—meaning, the only people who *drove me*—were the ones who had committed to risk their lives for me.

"Rock-paper-scissors?" I asked.

I knew she would choose rock. She was a crusher of men—it was her *tell.*

She smiled. So did I.

I was right.

"You cheated!" she yelled.

"How can you cheat at rock-paper-scissors, Charlie?"

"I…I dunno! But you did!"

I laughed as she threw her keys at me before walking to the passenger side door.

"Tell ya what, there's a nice long stretch of country road where we're headed. You can drive then, okay?"

That seemed to satisfy her—temporarily anyway.

Charlie:

"So, when does the party start?"

"Think his friends are coming around six, but I need to work on my sister's car for a bit before that," he said.

"Well, I'll need to run into a store before we get there."

"What for?" he asked, puzzled.

"For a birthday present," I said, laying my head back against the seat and closing my eyes. The sun felt so nice beating down on my face, even if the breeze was still a bit chilly. I had thrown a sweatshirt and a blanket in the back just in case it got too cold for comfort.

"Nah, you don't need to do that, Shortcake."

My head snapped up in attention. "I *am* getting him a present, Briggs. I refuse to go without one," I said firmly.

Calm down…he's only trying to be nice.

"Whoa…easy there, if you really want to get him something I'll take you to a store. Please just put the gun down and back away," he said, but there was little teasing to be found in his tone.

I felt the tension in my body relax after he complied, and again, I closed my eyes.

Okay, so maybe that was a bit of an over-reaction, but I wasn't going to be the one without something to give—especially to a child in a single-parent home. That just hit a little too close to home for me.

I could reason that Angie was certainly not like my mama had been, but still…raising a son on her own had to be hard.

"Will you tell me about your move to Dallas?" I asked quietly.

I heard him take a deep breath—even over the noise of the road.

Briggs

A driving distraction?

Yeah, that didn't even begin to sum it up.

Driving Charlie in her convertible was a new sort of torture. We had been talking for the last thirty minutes, nothing too deep, but the conversation certainly hadn't lacked for content. She asked a lot of questions regarding Angie and Cody, a subject I tended to tread lightly through. As I opened my mouth with a question of my own, I stopped short as I saw her.

I tried to pull my eyes away from her face, away from the stray hairs blowing around it, but the sun was a temptress, illuminating her beauty in its concentrated rays.

And I was a sucker for Charlie's beauty.

Her reaction to my gift comment had felt off—defensive even, but she had melted into the sunlight before I'd had a chance to press her on it.

There would be plenty of moments to debate with Charlie, but how many moments would be equal to this?

Charlie

After stopping at the store and standing in the toy aisle for nearly ten minutes, I made my final selections. Being an only child—and a girl—I hardly felt qualified to be choosing a birthday present for a seven year-old boy, but I did it. I had assured Briggs that he should just wait in the car, and I was very glad that he had.

"I'll only be a minute," I had told him.

I didn't need him rushing me.

As I headed back to the car, I couldn't help but notice the disapproval on his face when he saw me.

"Please tell me that's not all for Cody," he said.

"Uh…it's not all for Cody," I repeated, smiling.

He furrowed his brows at me.

"What? There's a pack of gum for me somewhere in here," I said, pointing to the bags in my hand.

"You are unbelievable," he laughed.

"So I've been told."

He handed me the keys as it was apparently my turn to drive. After putting on my seatbelt and sunglasses, I re-tuned the radio. I could feel his eyes on me—just as I had felt them on me earlier, but I didn't turn my head.

The country road that Briggs had mentioned earlier was a twelve-mile stretch of nothingness. It was just a two-lane highway with open fields on either side. It was a perfect road for driving—especially perfect for driving a convertible. I could feel my hair slipping from the clip that secured it, but I didn't care. I loved the freedom that came with the wind—even if it meant tangled hair.

I turned the music up louder, mouthing the words to my favorite song as I drove. Briggs laughed and shook his head. As it ended, I looked over at him and turned it down again.

"What, you don't like my taste in music or something?" I asked.

"It's not that, but no, I don't," he laughed.

"What's so funny, then?"

"You don't do anything halfway, do you? You're-all-or-nothing."

I scrunched my face up as I pondered his remark. I had never thought of myself like that, but it seemed pretty accurate.

"Ten points to you, Manny."

"Ooh observation points, huh? Well, I've got more where that came from."

"Oh, do you? Well I've got a few about you, too," I said, without thinking.

"Well, by all means, lay 'em out, Shortcake."

My stomach twisted with nerves.

What am I doing?

"Uh…" I began, going nowhere fast.

"You got nothing."

As if hearing a challenge in those three simple words, I blurted out my unfiltered thoughts.

"You're a poser," I said.

"A…*poser*? How so?" he asked, a hint of mock defensiveness in his tone.

I swallowed hard.

"You let the guys at the station think that you're some kind of playboy—some kind of carefree joker, but that's not who you are. You *care* about people: Kai, Tori, Angie, Cody. You're better than you let people believe you are."

I did not look at him as I said it. I was exposing too much to risk getting trapped inside those deep brown eyes of his.

He was quiet for longer than felt comfortable, and then I felt a touch on my arm.

"Pull over," he said softly.

I did, no questions asked.

Briggs

As she pulled over, I could feel the truth of her words driving into my heart like a knife. I *did* care about people, but that didn't mean that I was a *good* man.

Kai was a good man.

She opened her door and looked nervous as she stepped out, like she was thinking about apologizing for her statement. I narrowed the gap between us, giving her my best attempt at a smile.

"You're right, Charlie. I am a poser, but you've got it reversed. I'm not a guy who's posing to appear bad…I'm just a guy who's trying for the first time in his life to do better—to be better."

That was just the simple truth; my past was not nearly that simple.

Charlie pressed the keys into my hand lightly and looked up at my face. "But it's not the bad guys who care enough to try."

As we got into the car, the playful mood from minutes earlier had vanished.

Though I knew my future would be different because of the changes I'd made, my past would always be my past. And just like a nail could be pulled out of a two by four, there would always be a hole left in its place.

I had many, many holes.

Chapter Nine

Charlie

Angie's house was quaint, but it was brimming with life.

There was no question that a seven year-old boy inhabited the residence, and we hadn't even made it to the front door yet. A bike and scooter lay in the front yard, along with several transformers on the walkway outside. I smiled; I was looking forward to meeting Briggs' family.

It doesn't mean anything.

The woman that opened the door was striking. She had long, shiny blonde hair, brown eyes, and was nearly as tall as Briggs. She could be his twin. I was more than just a little surprised by their resemblance to each other. He had said she was only a year older than he was, but still, it was amazing.

"Hello, Charlie! I'm so glad my brother invited you—thanks for coming. I was starting to think that Briggs only chose friends who smelled of smoke and rubber," Angie said reaching out to shake my hand.

Okay, I like her.

"Well, don't spill the beans just yet," I leaned-in, whispering loud enough for Briggs to hear, "but I'm still on the fence about the whole *friend* thing."

She laughed. It was the same laugh that Briggs had when he was taken off guard—which was rare, but fabulous when it happened.

Briggs pulled her in for a hug. Within their embrace I could see the love they had for one another—it was obvious they were family. A pang shot through my chest as I watched them. *Would I ever mean that much to someone?*

My attention was immediately diverted when a young boy came running into the room, holding his arms out like an airplane, yelling loudly.

"Uncle B!" the handsome blond boy called out mid-way through the air.

"Code-man!" Briggs picked him up, spinning him in circles. Cody's arms were tight around his uncle's neck as he squealed from the speed.

"Okay, okay, don't make him puke on his birthday, Briggs!" Angie scolded.

Briggs put him down and Cody wobbled through the room as if he had a bad case of vertigo—which he probably did.

"Hey dude, come back here and let me introduce you to a really cool lady," Briggs said squatting down to put his arm around Cody's waist.

Cody held out his hand to me politely as Briggs conducted a proper introduction between us. Cody was delightful—full of energy and spunk. I wondered if Briggs was like Cody when he was a boy. I smiled at the thought.

"Did you come for my party?" Cody asked me, tilting his head.

"I sure did, is that alright?"

He looked at me curiously and then back to Briggs, "Does she know your rules?"

Briggs laughed, "Buddy, this one writes her own rules—although it would be nothing short of a miracle to see her actually follow some of mine."

I punched Briggs in the shoulder and he laughed even harder.

Angie filled me in on what Cody was talking about, as I didn't have a clue. Apparently, there was some water balloon fight, which of course,

Briggs had made up. After seeing how he played poker, I was plenty skeptical of his ability to lead a small group of children in a *safe* water balloon war. He seemed to have misplaced the "plays well with others" skill when it came to games.

While Briggs and Cody went outside to look at Angie's car, I stayed to help her prepare for the big taco feast. She was expecting about ten boys as well as a handful of parents.

She was a brave woman.

Briggs:

"So how's first grade treatin' ya, bud?" I asked Cody.

"It's good. I like recess."

I smiled. *Kid after my own heart.*

"Cool. Can you hand me that wrench?"

"Yeah."

Cody was a good kid—with an even better heart.

He had more energy than most people should be allowed, but in my opinion, too much was better than not enough. After Angie enrolled him in soccer though, he had settled down quite a bit. Even his focus during school hours seemed to be better. All he needed was a good outlet, something to hone some of that extra drive of his.

He was like looking in a mirror.

"Okay bud, do you think you could be my tool man once I go under the car? I'll need you to hand me a few things while I'm down there."

The old Honda Civic had seen better days, but it was still chuggin' along. Angie was in no shape to buy another vehicle, so the longer we could make this one last, the better. She had been stripped bare financially after her divorce and medical bills, and was finally starting to get back on her feet. So far, she had been doing well since she moved north with Cody; her boss loved her, and the pay was decent.

"Sure! Can I go under there too, Uncle B?"

"Not this time Code, but soon…okay?"

"Okay," he said, disappointedly.

As I pulled out the old filter and changed out the oil, Cody never left my side. He watched my every move, and I let him help with anything that his small hands could turn or lift. He loved it.

And I loved that he loved it.

"How's your mom?" I asked.

I talked to Angie a couple of times a week, but Cody's perspective was always insightful. I asked him about her every time we were alone.

"Fine…I guess."

I was bent over the engine working on some fried spark plugs, when I heard the change in his tone. I knew there was something he wasn't saying.

"What's up, dude? You can tell me," I said, wiping the sweat from my eyes with my sleeve so I could see him clearer.

"It's just that…I don't get to play soccer anymore. Mom said I won't be able to start in the spring with my friends," he said, kicking some rocks toward the lawn.

Now *that* got my attention. *Why hadn't Angie mentioned that?*

"Do you know why?" I asked.

He shook his head, "No, but I don't think I was supposed to tell you."

"Why not?" I asked, having a pretty good idea without him even having to say another word.

"Cause she said that we need to be a *team*—since it's just me and her now, and that sometimes teams have to…have to give stuff up so they can stay together."

My jaw clinched tight as I processed his words for a second more.

"Okay, well don't worry about it Code. I'll talk with her."

I sure will.

"Alright. Can I start filling the water balloons up now? Mom said I had to wait for you to get here first."

"Sure, I can be out there in about thirty minutes. I just need to wrap this up and then wash my hands," I said, holding them up to his face, eliciting a big laugh from him, "Thanks for your help handy-man."

He smiled, running up the driveway to the side yard.

I took a deep breath before leaning over the engine once more.

And thanks for the info.

Charlie

I had tears streaming down my face, and it wasn't just from cutting the onions. For the last hour and a half Angie had given me the reality TV version of what life with Briggs had been like growing up. I was bursting with laughter. My mind was on overdrive trying to recall all these new fun facts and details so I could use them later.

Even through all of our laughter though, there was one thought I kept coming back to: She had never mentioned their parents. I realized then that Briggs had never spoken of them either. I logged this detail away in the back of my mind; maybe I would ask him about it, someday.

"He was a handful back then—still is," she said, while sweeping her hair up into a ponytail.

"That he is," I replied softly.

I felt her eyes on me as I scooped the remaining onions from the cutting board into a serving bowl.

"Ya know, he's talked about you quite a bit to me, Charlie. You've made a pretty big impression, I'd say," she said in a tone that seemed to be leading somewhere…somewhere I wasn't sure I wanted to be led.

I felt my cheeks grow warm.

"Oh…well, his life's been kinda thrown for a loop these last couple of weeks, ya know, with moving above our garage and all, " I said carefully.

"I don't think that's what's thrown him for a loop," she teased.

I blushed again under her scrutiny. Her smile was sweet, yet her words held a boldness that surprised me.

"I've wondered for a long time if Briggs would ever stop long enough to…" She paused as if reflecting on some personal revelation. I stayed quiet, uncertain if I should even be in this conversation at all, "let himself be known."

When she turned toward the stove to stir the meat, my curiosity won out.

"What did he need to stop?" I asked quietly.

"Lying to himself."

I heard a door slam shut and I jumped, nearly knocking the bowl of lettuce off the counter in the process.

Briggs

"Ang…can I have a word with you, please? Outside."

"The kids are going to be here in twenty minutes Briggs… can it wait?"

"No," I said firmly.

She handed the wooden spoon to Charlie and followed me out the door. Charlie had a strange look on her face when I came in, but I didn't have enough focus to decipher it. I needed to get to the bottom of what was going on with Angie.

She put her hand on her hip.

"You know, it's poor manners to leave your guest alone-" Angie started.

"Nope, that's not gonna work. You can't make this about me, Ang." I crossed my arms over my chest. "Why are you telling my nephew that there are only *two players on your team*? And why isn't he going to play soccer in the spring?" I asked her—compassion temporarily lacking from my tone.

She threw her head back in frustration.

So, it's money.

The only time I ever saw that face, money was involved—or the lack thereof.

"My hours got cut—it's not forever, but business has been slow lately. It should pick up again around Mother's day, but since Valentines it's just been…dead."

She didn't look at me, instead she stared at the tree just beyond me.

"Ang…why didn't you tell me?" I touched her shoulder, forcing her see me.

"You've given up so much for us B, and I'm just so *tired* of being needy. Can't you understand that?" she asked softly.

I was really trying to, but when it came to them…

I shook my head.

"No, I can't," I said, "Because I am a part of this team too, Angie. You don't get to shut me out when you're in need. I make enough to help you and Cody, and there's no other place I'd rather invest than in the two of you. Please don't do this again. I don't like having to hear it from a seven year-old boy."

She nodded, though I could tell she didn't like what I had said. I didn't care; she would have to deal with it. There was a time and place for independence, but this wasn't that time—not when I was more than capable of helping them.

"I'm paying for his soccer, and I want to contribute more each month—at least for groceries and gas," I said firmly.

She started to protest, but this time I found that quiet compassion that lived somewhere deep inside me. I pulled her in for a hug.

"*We* are still a team Angie...it will always be us against the world."

Charlie

I wasn't trying to eavesdrop.

In fact, I had tried to drown their voices out by humming to myself, but neither of them were soft-spoken—especially the male one. The door had been left open, leaving their voices to carry inside—inside to where I stood, trying to stir the ground beef back to life.

I was certain I had probably ruined it by now, but I had to calm my nerves somehow.

At first I was worried that Briggs had heard us talking about him (yes, I was aware of the irony), but their tones had indicated otherwise. Though the story of Briggs wearing a cowboy hat to bed for nearly a year was funny, there was nothing amusing about the conversation he was currently having with his sister.

My heart skipped a beat when she admitted that her hours had been cut, I hated to hear anyone was struggling—but this felt especially personal to me. I felt hot tears spring to my eyes as Briggs offered his help and support. Although his reaction to the news was noble—his words didn't shock me.

This was Briggs.

Whatever reason he saw himself as something other than a good man boggled my mind, because *this man,* the one I had practically lived with for the last couple of weeks, had not been made overnight. There were people who worked their whole lives to make small improvements to their character, but Briggs was not a new transformation. He was practiced in loyalty, and it showed.

What would it have been like to have brother like that?

To have been part of a team?

****

I never knew the word for lonely, before I came to live with the Lexingtons.

Lonely had been my only existence.

It knew me. It called to me. It was me.

There was no one who came in the night if I was scared of the dark, or of the shadows, or of the noises. There was no one to hear me cry, or help me if I was sick. There was no one to hug me or kiss me, or tell me they loved me.

It was just me and lonely.

One and the same.

Briggs

"Charlie?"

She jumped, the wooden spoon slipping from her hand, clanging against the tile floor.

"Oh, hi. Sorry," she said bending to retrieve the spoon and wash it off in the sink, "I didn't hear you come in."

I studied her. The look on her face before I had said her name was the one I had seen only a handful of times. It was the one that seemed to be marinated in sad, the one that felt like a blow to my chest.

She smiled, turning to me with her laughing eyes, causing me to forget my every thought.

"Did you need me?" she asked.

More than you know.

I shook my head and stared at the floor. "Uh, I just wanted you to know that I'll be outside with Cody filling up water balloons…you're welcome to join us."

"Oh, okay…sure," she said looking at the stovetop and wiping her hands on a kitchen towel, "I think I've probably done more to detract from his meal than anything else…"

You and detract could never be in the same sentence.

"Well, if kids can eat jelly beans called *booger* and *vomit*…then I'm pretty sure they can handle eating your taco meat."

She laughed and walked passed me, heading out to the backyard.

****

One would have thought Angie was hosting the team from *Friday Night Lights* in her backyard, by the noise alone. These kids were crazy.

Using two fingers, I whistled, the sound piercing through the yard like a rocket launch.

The boys quieted immediately, freezing in their tracks.

"Alright, listen up!"

Hey, that was kind of awesome.

If only I could get Charlie to listen to me like that.

I smiled at the thought.

"In two minutes we will head across the street together toward the field. You *will* walk in a single-file line. You will *not* push, fight, hit, wrestle, or give wedgies without my permission to do so," I paused for dramatic effect. Some kids chuckled. "Just like the year before, there are new rules, so listen up. Each of you will work with a partner. There are six teams represented here. Each team has a color—which matches the color of balloon you will go for. The object is to get as many of your team's balloons off of the giant tarp and into your team's bucket. Does everyone understand so far?"

The kids cheered wildly.

"What's the catch?" Angie yelled from the patio.

I smiled wickedly.

"There can only be *one* team member on the tarp at any given time. The other one should be guarding the bucket. Whatever team has the most balloons in the end—of their color—will be the winners. You may pop any color balloon you see that is not your team's color."

"Can we steal balloons from inside the buckets, Uncle B?" Cody asked.

"Good question, Cody…yes, you can."

Excited energy sizzled throughout the young crowd.

"Line up!"

My eyes roamed the yard as each kid ran to join the line. It was then that I saw Charlie roll up her jeans and kick off her heels. The flip-flops she was sliding her feet into looked a couple sizes too big for her. *They're probably Angie's.*

When she joined the line, I couldn't help but laugh.

She was barely a head taller than Cody's birthday buddies.

This is gonna be good.

Charlie

Thankfully, Angie had loaned me a pair of flip-flops so that I could participate in the annual game of water wars. I was grateful for them. She had decided to stay back with some of the other parents so that she could frost the cake, but as I joined the group, she patted me on the shoulder and wished me luck. I hoped I had only imagined the forewarning in her voice.

My partner, a kid named Kevin, had already deemed me "bucket guard". I was bummed at first, but quickly reminded myself that I was twenty-one; he was eight.

Our color was red.

The tarp that lay in the center of the field was huge and scattered with at least three hundred water balloons. Apparently several parents had contributed to the small supply, which I had helped fill up. They had also squirted the tarp with dish soap. I had laughed several times during the game explanation, thinking that Briggs had taken his dramatics a little too far, but now I found myself nervous. These boys—though young—looked ruthless, as did Briggs.

He had teamed up with the birthday boy, and lucky for me he was several buckets away from team red. I didn't want to be anywhere near the crossfire of Briggs. It wouldn't end well for me, I was certain of that.

My strategy was a simple one: Guard and block. But somewhere in my head was a voice that yelled, *"Don't draw attention to yourself, Charlie."* I vowed to listen to that voice.

As Briggs whistled, indicating war to commence, I took my battle stance. Nothing and no one was going to steal our balloons. It was Kevin and I all the way.

"Red rules!" I yelled, feeling a bubble of adrenaline squeeze at my insides.

Okay, so much for not drawing attention to myself...

Poor Kevin was slipping and sliding all over the slick tarp. With six kids going after their color at one time, while simultaneously trying to fend off attacks, the sight was pure chaos. Briggs was guarding his blue bucket and laughing hysterically as the scene in front of us played out. When he caught my eye, I looked away quickly. I did not want him concocting any evil plans where I was concerned—especially not while I was surrounded by all this ammo.

Kevin finally staggered off the tarp carrying four red balloons in his arms. He hurried over to me so he could drop them into our bucket. After a slap on his back to show my team spirit, I pushed him to retrieve more. He did.

Only once did someone try a sneak-attack on my bucket, but I was too quick for him—or perhaps, in reality, they were not-so-sneaky. All that mattered was my job as *bucket guard* remained in good standing.

Our bucket had nearly twenty red balloons inside it when the insanity really started. The ground around us had quickly turned into a giant pool of mud. The water that had been poured onto the tarp to make it slick, had seeped into the already wet ground causing it to resemble more of a sink hole than a soccer field. The bursting water balloons that flew all around me only added to this thick sludge.

Just as I let my mind wander to how I could help Angie with mud-cleanup once back at her house...I was hit from behind. I straightened immediately, stunned by the slap of water that soaked my back. Blue balloon pieces fell to the ground near my feet. It was that moment that I decided to un-man my station for the first time—to retaliate.

After plunging my hands into my bucket, I ran after Briggs.

I realized way too late, however, that I should have heeded my earlier intuition. I was no match for Briggs. He was the expert hunter, and I was Bambi's mother after the shots were fired.

He hit his target every single time he threw a balloon at me, while I made *maybe* three. Soon I was just running with no balloons in hand at all.

And where was my faithful partner, now? The one I had cheered for and encouraged while he had been dying a slow death on the slippery tarp? He was rooting for Briggs, in fact, all the kids were. And helping him, too!

If I hadn't been so panicked I would've been livid at their disloyalty.

I trudged and splashed through the muddy-muck that was to be my final demise, and with one last scream, the world went upside down.

Chapter Ten

Briggs

Okay, so maybe I had started it, but in my defense it was one balloon.

One.

How was I to know that it would wake her inner-Rambo?

Unfortunately for her, she had the aim of a windsock in a tornado. When she had started running toward the mud pit, I knew it wouldn't end well—at least not for her. I had just halted my launches, yelling for her to steer clear of it, when her feet were no longer on the ground. She hit the mud with a smack, sliding on her back.

I felt sick as I ran to her.

"Shortcake…are you okay? Does anything hurt?" I leaned over her.

She was splattered with mud—and that was just the part I could see. I was certain that her backside was completely caked with it. She looked up at me, blinking. Her eyes resembled that of a hurt puppy. She reached her muddy hand up to me as I hunched over her. I took it without hesitation.

This is when Charlie went from hurt puppy to perturbed Pit Bull.

With one, hard, unsuspecting yank, I fell face first into the mud. Her laugh was the cackle of an evil villain.

I wiped the mud from my face as I surfaced, "Well played, Shortcake."

I helped her up—our bodies resembling swamp monsters.

"Will I still get retaliation points even though my team lost?" she asked, hand on her hip.

Without thinking, I pulled her to me and wrapped my arms around her as I laughed. And even through several inches of caked-on mud and grass, I could only think of one thing:

Charlie Lexington is hugging me back.

Charlie

Clean-up was a bit of a nightmare.

The taco feed was moved to the backyard as muddy pants and shoes were the common denominator amongst the group. Briggs and I were the exception, however. The mud we wore covered the majority of our bodies.

Angie laid a pair of sweats and a t-shirt on her bathroom counter for me to change into after my shower. When she first saw us walking toward the house, she laughed for a good five minutes straight. I now knew why she had stayed behind to frost the cake.

As I stripped off my mud-covered clothing, my wrist began to throb, a feeling like pins and needles shooting through it from every angle. I had felt an initial stab of pain when I had landed on it, but when Briggs had come to check on me, I was much more focused on his demise than my discomfort.

I stepped into the shower, watching as the water uncovered my pink skin once again. I stood, letting the heat thaw me as I closed my eyes.

Briggs had hugged me.

A rush of nervous, swirling energy filled the base of my belly.

I didn't understand it—this connection I felt to him. Wasn't it just last week that I had been crying over my broken heart and now I was swooning over a fireman—one who was sent to babysit me?

Maybe men had it right: Women were crazy.

Washing the mud out of my hair, while using only one hand, took an eternity. Once I was out, I picked up the pile of mud-free clothes from Angie. I rolled the sweat pants down a few times on the waist, and tightened the drawstring as much as I could. They still hung low on my hips, but at least the t-shirt was long enough to cover the waistband. I dried my hair and looked in the mirror at my clean, make-up free face. It was ironic how only earlier today I had hoped to be going to a glamorous party tonight, and here I was now, *au natural.*

And celebrating a seven year-olds birthday.

I walked into the hallway, just as Briggs stepped inside the house from the backyard. I couldn't help but smile at the sight of his ruggedly, handsome face—dried dirt and all.

Briggs

"Hey," I said, not trusting myself to say anything more. She may have been drowning in my sister's clothes, but even still, she was breathtaking.

"It's all yours," she said nodding toward Angie's room. I was grateful that I hadn't had time to change earlier after working on the Honda. A hot shower and clean clothes was the perfect way to remedy the Loch Ness monster look I was currently sporting.

I peeled my eyes from Charlie's face and looked down at her arm. It was bent at the elbow and was pressed against her body stiffly. It was an unnatural pose for her.

Is she hurt?

"What's going on with your arm?" I asked.

She instantly moved it down to her side, but not before I saw the painful grimace on her face. She was hurt.

"Let me see it," I said, reaching out.

She shook her head, "It's nothing—really, my wrist is just a little stiff from how I landed."

I continued to hold out my hand, giving her a look that said, "*You're full of it*".

She slowly lifted her arm again, biting her lip as she did. Even in the dim light of the hallway, I could tell it was swollen. As I rotated it, she winced again, proving my quick diagnosis.

"It's sprained, Charlie."

"Really?" she asked. Her voice held more disappointment in it than surprise.

"Yes, it's probably minor, but we'll need to ice it and wrap it regardless. Come over here and sit down, hold it up like this while I get you some ice," I instructed, watching as she elevated it above her heart.

"Can't we deal with this a little later—Cody's about to open his gifts."

She must have picked up on my look a lot quicker this time, because she sat down without saying another word. I laid the ice pack in a towel and gently wrapped it around her wrist, giving her a dose of ibuprofen as well.

"We'll ice it like this for about twenty minutes to reduce some of that swelling, and then I'll wrap it for you. Let me go ask Angie where the first aid kit is."

"Thank you, Briggs, but since I'm just sitting here ice-ing, you should go take your shower. I'm fine to wait," she said, flashing me a weak smile.

I looked at her, contemplating her request.

"Please…I don't want you to miss any more of this party over my stupidity," she said, trying to make a joke.

My hand reached out then, insubordinate to the commands my mind had given it. Since the first day I met Charlie, I had wondered about the feel of her hair—that hair that smelled like an orchard of peaches in springtime. As I touched it, the damp, ginger waves slipped through my fingers like silk, leaving me breathless as it fell against her face once more.

"There's nothing stupid about you, Charlie," I said quietly, retrieving my duffle bag from the corner before walking down the hall to Angie's bathroom.

Maybe a shower would be the best thing for me right now.

Charlie

He *touched* my hair.

No one had ever done that before—not like that.

My face burned, my pulse raced, and my thoughts were on a man who was not Alex Monroe.

Briggs

After a quick shower, I found Angie's first-aid kit on the floor of her garage. I took out the ace bandage. While still kneeling on the cold cement floor, I squeezed it in my palm, taking in a deep breath. In a minute I would be close to Charlie again—*touching* her again. I exhaled hard and rubbed my forehead with my fisted hands.

How is it possible that a girl I haven't even known for three weeks could make me feel this way?

The door opened behind me. I jumped to my feet, brushing a hand through my hair.

"Oh—good, you found it," Angie asked letting the door swing closed behind her, "Did you want me to save you some cake?"

"Sure, that would be fine…" I said, staring down at the bandage in my hand.

"Is everything okay?" Angie asked crossing her arms in front of her.

I looked up briefly, before making a move to walk past her, "Yep."

She blocked the doorway, scrutinizing me.

"You're freaking out."

"I am not—now please move, Angie. I've gotta go wrap a wrist."

"Oh, just *a wrist*, huh?" she challenged.

"We all got 'em," I mocked.

"Yeah, but not all wrists are created equal."

"Your point?" I asked, meeting her eyes for the first time.

"My point is, I like her, Briggs. And yeah before you say it…I get that she's *very likable*, but that's not what I mean. I like her for *you.* She has something…something you need, and I'd be willing to bet that you've got something she needs, too."

I shook my head, "It's not like that, Angie. Charlie doesn't see me that way—besides, she was engaged five months ago."

Angie smiled, "*Was* being the key word. And if he was stupid enough to lose her, then he didn't deserve her."

My thoughts exactly.

"And what makes you think *I could* deserve her?"

She laughed softly, and shook her head. "Because the men who don't would never ask that question."

****

"Okay, let's get this wrapped, Shortcake, and then we should probably get on the road. Angie's making you a to-go bag of ice for the car."

I sat down next to her on the couch, carefully taking the icepack off her wrist. The swelling had gone down, but she would be sore for a while. Some bruising had already surfaced on her pale skin.

"We may need to get you some stronger meds tonight so you can sleep. I'm guessing this is gonna take about a week or two to heal."

"A week? How am I supposed to play the piano?"

"You're not, Shortcake. It needs to rest, the ligaments are strained and they have to heal," I said apologetically.

She sighed as I started to wrap.

"Spread your fingers as wide as you can so I can get the tension right. I know it hurts, but the pressure of the bandage will help a lot." I smoothed the tail of the bandage out and clipped it into place.

Feeling her hand in mine was the reminder of everything I hoped to be, along with the reality of everything I was not: A man good enough for Charlie.

Chapter Eleven

Charlie

Angie and Cody walked us to my car to say goodbye.

The sun had set a couple of hours ago, and the partygoers had all gone home. Cody was more than thrilled with his birthday loot and had thanked me profusely for the gifts I had given him. Briggs rolled his eyes at me, but I was grateful we had stayed through the present opening.

"Bye, Uncle B, and thanks for the tickets!"

I looked at Briggs for clarification, but Cody answered instead.

"He's taking me and my friend Dillon to opening day at Six Flags! It's only two weeks away—Mom, lets mark it on the calendar!" Cody said looking at Angie.

"Okay, sweetheart. We can mark it," she laughed before leaning in to hug Briggs, "Thank you both for coming tonight. Sorry about your wrist, Charlie, I hope it won't keep you from coming again. Running in the mud is not the norm around here—despite what Briggs may tell you."

"I'm very glad I came—sorry to have caused the medical drama of the party…but someone's got to do it, eh?" I laughed.

Angie hugged me as Briggs opened my door to help me inside. He was extra careful to keep my arm from bumping into anything as he pulled my seatbelt across my lap. I felt a zing of electricity shoot through me as his hand pressed against my hip to secure it. When he pushed himself upright, the warmth I had felt went with him.

"Let's leave the top down on our drive back," I said to Briggs.

"Charlie, it's barely fifty degrees out right now, you'll freeze."

I watched him give one final hug to Cody before he ran to catch up with Angie at the front door. Briggs turned back to me.

"No, I won't, I promise…it will be so fun, *please*. I have a blanket in the trunk and we can blast the heat and turn on the seat warmers," I begged.

He shook his head as he reached into the backseat. I could see that half smile of his start to take over his face.

I win.

I wished I had put my sweatshirt on before my wrist had really started to hurt. The once dull ache had turned into a constant throb like a child beating on a drum. The idea of putting anything over my head that would require arm coordination was completely out of the question.

A blanket would work just fine.

Briggs went to the trunk and unfolded a large fleece blanket. He laid it over me, tucking in the excess underneath me like I was one of my Aunt Carol's hot tamales.

It was nice.

He was nice.

As we pulled out of the driveway, I looked at him.

And then, despite the pain of my wrist, I started to giggle.

Briggs

"Have you been drinking? Is that what you were *really* doing when I thought you were ice-ing?" I looked at her, surprised by her sudden bout of hysterics. She was an explosion of sounds and snorts. Every time she opened her mouth to speak, she would launch into yet another round.

"Nnnoo….I ssswear. Angie…told me…something ffunnnny!"

Oh great, about me no less.

Finally, she took a deep breath, securing her bad wrist closer to body. I felt a tightening in my chest as I looked at it. The idea of Charlie being in any sort of pain was not one I wanted to dwell on for long.

"What did she tell you?" I asked.

Out of the corner of my eye, I saw her lift her head off the seat and look at me, "The story of the pickle juice ice cubes!"

Ah yes, now that was a good one.

"Hey, those kids had it coming. How were we supposed to know Mrs. Brown would be there, too?"

She laughed again, and I joined in, remembering.

Angie and I were in the third and fourth grade when we had decided to start selling lemonade at the sports field near our house. We had each saved some of our lunch money so we could buy the supplies we needed. We were determined to get a pool for the summer, one that didn't take our parents to set up. We had started selling in April, and were hopeful that by the end of school we would have the funds we needed.

Sales were going great, as both parents and kids would pass us each time they came on and off the field—that was, until Jimmy Han started coming around. At first he seemed to be complementing our efforts by bringing us customers with his verbal advertisements, but that quickly changed.

One Saturday, Jimmy beat us to the field and took our set-up spot. He and his big fifth grade buddies were not only selling lemonade, but cookies too.

We had been nice about it at first, telling him we could all work as a team and share our profits, but Jimmy was not the negotiating type. It was almost funny now to think back on a time when I resolved conflict without the need for physical blows, but I wasn't a match for size then.

I was however, a match in wit.

Angie and I went back to the house and I thought up a plan: Pickle Juice Ice Cubes.

By the next weekend, we had stocked up at least a dozen ice cube trays filled with frozen pickle juice. We poured them all into a large bucket and walked over to Jimmy and his gang of idiots, pulling our special bucket and supplies in a wagon. It was then, that Angie put on the show of her life.

"Well I guess you boys win, it's fair and square since you got here before us. I just don't know what we should do with all these extra supplies? I mean, we just filled this bucket up with ice," she'd whined to Jimmy.

I smiled as he took the bait—and our ice.

I helped Angie pour it into his giant industrial-size drink cooler, hopeful the smell of pickles wouldn't be too obvious. After we screwed the lid back on for him, we ran all the way back home, laughing till we cried.

Unfortunately for us, our principal was also at the field that day for a tournament, and she had been especially thirsty for some lemonade. When Jimmy investigated the sour taste that people were complaining of, they were able to pin-point the source, easily. Mrs. Brown did not find our little prank funny, earning Angie and I her *special attention* for the rest of the school year.

Ultimately though, it had been worth it.

"That was a great day," I said.

"I can just imagine that taste…how awful!" Charlie cried.

I watched as Charlie awkwardly inched the blanket higher onto her chest with one arm. The wind was chilly, but the heater and seat warmers had made it bearable—she had been right about that. I reached over and lifted the top of the blanket up to tuck it behind her shoulder.

"How's your wrist, Shortcake?"

"About the same. I don't feel it as much when it stays stationary like this. I think the ibuprofen really helped."

"Are you just saying that so I don't take you in for a stronger prescription? Or is that really the truth?" I challenged.

Her brows furrowed into the sassy look that I had come to expect from Charlie.

"I have never been dishonest with you, if anything *you're* the liar here."

"Whoa…those are some big words for a munchkin. When have *I lied* to you?"

"Uh, hello! Although I had a great time tonight, coming to this party was not the result of your stellar honesty," she said, "and…you did tell me there would be dancing."

"Hmm…the party was a bit of stretch, but I did fess up to it before you got in the car. The dancing? Well, we'll have to remedy that when you're not sportin' a broken wing."

She turned her face to me and smiled, the wind whipping her ponytail to the side.

"Is that a promise, Briggs—or should I say…*Calvin*?"

I grimaced.

Angie better be very glad she lives an hour away.

Charlie

Oh, that was even more satisfying than I had imagined.

I have Angie to thank for that.

I had wondered about his name—I mean, who named their son Briggs? But the answer had been simple enough. It was the first half of his hyphenated last name, *Briggs-Morrison.* It had started out as a sports nickname in middle school, but by the time he was in high school, it had replaced his given name—*Calvin*, entirely. According to Angie, no one knew him by anything other than Briggs.

I smiled; it was unique, just like he was.

He parked the car and was at my door before I could even unbuckle my seatbelt. He opened it, focusing his eyes on mine.

"Okay, so I'm going to help you out, and then I'm going to help you get settled-in for the night, Shortcake."

What? No.

"Um, that's okay, Briggs. I'm sure I can manage-"

"No."

"But it's just my-"

"No."

I huffed in exasperation. The look on his face wasn't likely to fade—I knew it well.

"Is there anything I can say to-"

"No."

"Alright then, sounds like a plan," I said, rolling my eyes.

An insane fluttering started deep within my core as he leaned over me. I wanted to laugh from the anxiety welling up inside me, but thankfully, I didn't. The meds I had taken hours earlier had all but worn off, and I was definitely feeling the pain now, yet his close proximity dulled it tremendously.

"Don't try to help, Shortcake, just relax—otherwise you'll strain your wrist, and it will hurt."

I raised my arm as Briggs un-tucked the blanket from my body, an immediate shiver running down my spine like a pulled zipper. My seatbelt was off a second later. He carefully scooped his arm behind my back as I kept my arm pinned to my abdomen, and slid me out of the seat to stand on the pavement. I felt my face flush with heat as our bodies touched, deciding then to keep my eyes away from his, which took every ounce of will power I had. I focused instead on my wrapped wrist, as if my gaze alone could heal it.

He followed me inside the house.

As we neared the top of the stairs, I realized he had never been up there before. I told myself it was stupid to feel so nervous—he was a paramedic—wasn't he put in awkward situations like this on a daily basis? I was just another patient, some injured girl with a hurt wrist that he was providing care for.

He stopped in the doorway of my bedroom as I went to sit on my bed. I kicked off my heels—which felt completely ridiculous since I was still wearing Angie's sweats pants—but they were the only shoes I had with me since I had destroyed her flip-flops in the mud pit. As they thumped on the floor I looked up at him, his face curious and conflicted.

"What do you need, Charlie?"

The question caused my chest to constrict like a rubber band—proving my answer was far from simple.

I needed to figure out what on earth was going on with me.

I needed to understand how Briggs could be undoing the damage in my heart, with just a look.

I needed…

I just *needed.*

Briggs

I needed to move.

I needed to do something other than stand in the doorway of her bedroom.

"What do you need, Charlie?" I had asked.

She didn't respond at first, she just kept staring at me as if I was wearing the answer on my forehead.

I asked again.

"Charlie, what can I get for you? Want me to find you a pain reliever that can help you sleep? You should also ice it again," I looked around her room, "Maybe I can find something to prop your arm up-"

"Briggs…" She took a deep breath.

I waited, watching an inner-battle take place inside her. I was certain a big part of her wanted to tell me to leave—tell me that she was fine—not that I would have listened. I knew she wasn't fine, and as I searched her face again, I had a feeling it was for reasons beyond the pain in her wrist.

"Sure—thank you. The meds are downstairs and there's some extras pillows in the hall closet to the right," she said.

I found the extra pillows easily, and then searched the medicine cabinet downstairs in the kitchen. It was not only stocked, but well organized (thanks to Mrs. Julie). I carried a glass of water, along with the pain pills, into Charlie's bedroom. She hadn't moved an inch.

"Here you go. These should knock you out. I also brought you some extra ibuprofen so you can take it first thing in the morning. You may even want to set your alarm—it's better to stay ahead of the pain," I said.

She nodded absently; putting the pills in her mouth before washing them back with the water I brought her. She worked to scoot herself back with her good hand, but bumped her bad arm in the process, wincing in pain.

"Charlie, stop. Let me help you," I said.

I pulled back her blankets, helping her lay down before propping her arm up on the extra pillows. If I had ever thought Charlie smelled good before, her bedding was the embodiment of that blessed scent. She flinched as I pulled the blankets up to her waist.

"Did I bump it?" I asked, concerned.

"No, it just hurts all on its own," she said, trying to smile.

"I'm sorry, Shortcake—I'm sorry for chasing you through the mud, too."

I smiled back at her as she laughed softly.

"Will you…" she began.

"What?"

"Will you…stay? Just until I fall asleep, I mean?"

The vulnerability in her face matched the softness of her voice. I swallowed hard.

This was dangerous for me; *she* was dangerous for me.

This kind of proximity to a woman had only ever ended one way. Charlie wasn't just *any woman* to me, though. She wasn't a part of my past, and I would never allow her to be.

I took a step back from the bed—my eyes landing on a temporary solution:

A chair.

Chapter Twelve

Charlie

I had been nervous to ask him.

But the fear was already starting to creep in, like an old bad habit. I knew if I didn't change its course and distract from it soon, the nightmares would claim me again tonight. They would deprive me of sleep by robbing every droplet of peace that I had accumulated over the last seventeen years.

When Alex left, it triggered something inside me—uprooting memories I had long ago buried. I didn't want to spend my time and energy trying to figure out why they were back again, my mama had stolen enough of that already.

Briggs walked across my room to my desk chair, turning it around, but not moving it an inch closer before he sat in it.

I felt a pinched of hurt, wondering why he would choose to sit so far from me, but his distance didn't lessen my need for a distraction.

"Will you tell me about your parents?" I asked, feeling my eyelids grow heavy.

He slid his elbows down his thighs, stopping to rest them on his knees, and took a deep breath.

Briggs

I was surprised at her question, but I was even more surprised that I was willing to answer it.

Where do I start?

It was like trying to direct someone out of a traffic jam—unless they were familiar with the side streets, it was a wasted effort.

"Angie and I were born in Boulder, Colorado. My mom was an attorney and my dad was the VP for a local bank. From the outside we were a perfect family. Nice house, nice cars, two nice kids and a nice golden retriever. But it was far from nice."

I looked up and she nodded for me to continue.

"It's hard to describe the chaos, Charlie, but that's what it was…chaos. No structure, no discipline, no care. Angie and I were our own family unit from as far back as I can remember. They would fight, scream, cry, yell for days on end, and some days they wouldn't come home at all. They worked all the time, but they played too—without us. They gave us money, of course—there was *always* enough money, but that's about all there was. Our material needs were met, but not much else. They were so absorbed in chasing after their dreams, that they didn't even notice when we stopped following."

"Where are they now?"

"Divorced. Mom's in Colorado, and last I heard, Dad was somewhere back East."

"You don't talk to them?" she asked with quiet wonder.

I smiled sadly, keeping my voice soft as I saw her eyes blink with sleepiness. "No Charlie, we don't talk. It's better that way. There's not much left that hasn't already been said, and I'm happy with the family I do have…even though most of them aren't blood relatives."

Her eyes closed then, and her breathing slowed with a heavy calm. I stood to make my exit. The meds had obviously done their job. As I neared the doorframe, I paused, watching her. She looked so peaceful.

Despite myself I quietly walked over to her bedside and pushed back the hair resting on her face. I leaned down then and brushed my lips against her forehead.

With that one simple act, my heart was gone, my fate sealed.

No other woman would ever compare to Charlie Lexington.

She was the only one I wanted.

Charlie

As it turned out, I didn't need an alarm.

My wrist woke me up about thirty minutes before I could take my next dose of pain medication. I dragged my stiff body to the restroom—which proved to be interesting. Managing menial tasks while one-handed was quite a talent.

How is it possible that my wrist feels worse today?

As I finished up, I stood in front of the mirror, gasping at the frightening reflection that stared back at me. At least it was consistent with how I felt. I looked down at my wrist, which was throbbing with a whole new level of intensity.

This better not really take a week to heal! I have stuff to do…how will I get dressed, or compose Tori's processional, or work at the office?

I wanted to scream in frustration, but it was too early for that. Instead, I cried. And it wasn't a trivial cry, it was my *ugly cry*—the one that spurt big, fat, pitiful tears while contorting my face like a fun-house mirror. I didn't care, though. It had been a long time since I had let myself cry like this—and with no one home, I could be as dramatic as I wanted. Living in such close quarters at school had left little room for an anti-humiliation tear-fest.

This ugly cry was long overdue.

I remembered when my mom had first talked to me about hormones. She had put her hand on my shoulder, "Charlie, some days a woman just needs to cry—even if there doesn't seem to be a good reason for it."

There were times my tears had started for one reason, but by the time I was finished crying, I had convinced myself that they were a result of something entirely different. I wiped at my face, clearing my dripping nose and wet cheeks with the sleeve of Angie's t-shirt.

There was a knock at the bathroom door. I jumped, wincing as my wrist jerked away from my body in surprise.

"Charlie…are you okay in there?"

Oh my—no way! This isn't happening!

Silence.

Could someone just shoot me, please? I cannot answer him! Not after…

"Charlie?"

"I'm okay," I croaked out.

Except for the fact that I look like an idiot sobbing in my bathroom. Wait—why is he even in my house?

Suddenly, my mortification made a U-turn, heading toward anger instead.

"Why are you even here, Briggs?"

"I…I stayed downstairs. I didn't want you to…be alone if you needed something in the middle of the night and couldn't get to it."

Urgh! Why does he have to be so nice to me?

"Oh." *Way to sound grateful, Charlie.*

"Are you gonna come out of there?" he asked weakly.

"It depends."

"On?" he asked

"How long you've been standing there."

Silence.

Silence.

Silence.

"Wow…*lying* would've been so much better, Briggs."

He laughed, "Open the door, Shortcake."

I did.

Briggs

I woke up to the sound of a door closing somewhere upstairs.

It took me a second to remember where I was and why I was there, but then my mind drifted to Charlie.

Lately, almost all my thoughts had to do with Charlie.

As I started up the stairs I was about to call her name so she'd know I was there, but then I heard her crying.

Angie used to cry like that.

When she thought I couldn't hear her, or when she thought I was asleep, she would cry. I dealt with the rejection from our parents in other ways, but crying was how she coped. I knew now that if she hadn't, it would have changed her—hardened her. But though I could reason through Angie's tears, Charlie's were different. Knowing that she was just on the other side of that door was like smelling the smoke without being able to extinguish the flames.

I hated it.

I also hated feeling like a stalker.

My relief was instant when she opened the door to face me.

She stood there with her bedhead hair and red-rimmed eyes, Angie's clothes still hanging on her loosely, yet she had never looked more beautiful to me.

"Hi."

"Hi," she said, staring at the floor.

The urge to reach out to her and pull her into my arms, was almost unbearable. I clinched my fists closed to keep from doing it. Her vulnerability was too high and my uncertainty of being able to let her go was far too low.

"Can I make you some coffee, or were you planning on going back to bed? It's just after six."

"Coffee."

Good, at least she isn't going to hide from me. That's something.

"Okay—is there anything you need help with before I go downstairs?"

She looked up at me, her cheeks flushing pink.

I cleared my throat.

I'm sure that getting dressed with a sprained wrist would be tricky, and if it had been the apocalypse and not a just typical Sunday morning in Dallas, I would have stepped up to the task. Somehow though, even with years of experience as a paramedic, conducting myself with Charlie in a professional manner, didn't feel possible. To date, she had been the only woman to cause my heart to race when wrapping her injured wrist.

"Do you have a girlfriend you could call if…?"

Her blush deepened.

Geesh…0 for 2.

"I've got it. Thanks."

I nodded, turning away quickly. "Sounds good."

Charlie

Did he actually think I was going to ask him to help me get dressed? I could have died right there in the hallway—again! His question had only made me evaluate the chores of my day—the ones I was going to have to manage one-handed.

I could ask Jackie?

She wasn't the best choice in friends, but she was probably my only choice. Everyone else was still away at school. Jackie went to community college part-time and lived close by, plus it was Sunday. More than likely she was home—nursing a hangover.

Maybe having a friend over would be nice today, and maybe an extra hand—*literally*—would prove helpful?

I walked downstairs after him and watched him pull out a chair for me to sit down at the breakfast bar. Alex had never done that. Charm he had, but proper etiquette between males and females wasn't his thing. His charm was purely selfish.

"I was thinking I'd make you some peanut butter pancakes, they are sell-your-soul good," he said grinning.

Not peanut butter.

"Uh…I'm allergic," I lied.

He spun around. "You're allergic to peanut butter? How did I not know that? That's pretty serious…" he said, looking miffed.

"Uh…it's actually fairly mild, but yeah…can't eat it." I shrugged.

He looked at me, nodding with brows drawn in. "I make a great strawberry crepe?"

"Now that sounds perfect." I smiled.

****

Breakfast with Briggs was wonderful, even if I did have to eat it with my left hand.

"Okay, so…*why*, with all these mad breakfast and care-taking skills of yours, don't you have a girlfriend?" I conveniently stared down at my last few bites of crepe while I asked, but I had been dying to know. Had he just been in a long-term relationship? Was he only a casual dater?

"Don't forget my creepy stand-outside-the-bathroom-door skill," he said wiggling his eyebrows up and down. I laughed hard.

"Yes, that's a skill I'd rather you'd not cash in on again," I said. I shrunk down in embarrassment.

His hand gripped my upper arm lightly, "I'm sorry if I made you uncomfortable, Charlie. I was just worried about you, but you don't need to feel embarrassed. I understand that tears are needed sometimes…and I'm here too if you need someone to listen."

Though I liked the warmth of his touch, I was grateful when he dropped his hand. No man had ever said that to me before. I hated being seen as an overly sensitive, overly emotional drama queen—Alex saw me that way, although he never cared enough to ask me what was wrong. Not once. He claimed my tears were my personal business, not his.

How had I been so blinded to his faults?

Or was the contrast of Briggs the only reason I can see them now?

I smiled at him, "Are you deflecting my question?"

He laughed, "No."

"No? That's not an answer. My question started with a *why*." I laughed.

"No I'm not deflecting, and… because I just don't."

I stared at him incredulously. For being so full of quick wit and easy responses, he was being awfully cryptic now. "I feel like you living here, while playing the roles of guardian, security and medic, should constitute more of an answer than that, Manny."

His smile reached his eyes as he leaned on the counter, bracing himself with his elbows. He took a deep breath and rubbed his face. A cold chill ran through me as I remembered my conversation with Angie in the kitchen yesterday.

"I've wondered for a long time if Briggs would ever stop long enough to let himself be known."

"What did he need to stop?"

"Lying to himself."

Maybe I'd made a mistake by asking him—crossed some imaginary boundary line between us.

I was about to say so, when he answered.

Briggs

"My life used to look very different." I took her plate and laid it next to the sink before coming back to the counter. "I made a lot of stupid choices—living for escape, living to mask my pain, living to avoid the truth in the mirror." I paused, glancing at her briefly. "What I told you before was true, I wasn't a good man. I hid behind the honor of my job. When people view you as a hero, they usually don't imagine that you're throwing your life away when you're off duty, but I was. I hurt a lot of people, was careless and reckless—especially with women. I didn't believe in relationships, I thought they were too much work. I only wanted uncomplicated and easy…but there are consequences to that kind of thinking."

I felt the guilt start to pull at me the way it did whenever I opened up the box of my past. She stared at me, unblinking, as if waiting for me to continue.

"I don't want to be that man again." I stared at my hands. "I take one day at a time now, Charlie. Dating hasn't really been a priority for me, yet. Changing one bad habit takes self-control, but changing a way of life takes nothing short of a miracle."

After several seconds of silence, Charlie finally spoke. "It's hard for me to imagine you that way—the way you described."

I dropped my head, nodding. *It's even harder to know I was that way.*

That's when she hit me with, "But the only way to overcome our past, is to deny its power over our future."

I shot my eyes back to her.

"*Our* past?" I asked.

She picked up her phone and scooted off the stool carefully, bracing her arm. "My past has won more times than I care to count." She walked upstairs with the phone to her ear without saying another word.

Everything in me wanted to ask her what she meant—why had her past won? What was in her past? But I could not ask of her what I was unwilling to share myself. I glanced at the clock, I only had thirty minutes before I had to meet Kai, and I still needed to shower.

I wrote a note to Charlie and left it on the counter, placing the dishes in the sink before heading up to my apartment.

Chapter Thirteen

Charlie

Briggs left a note for me, telling me that he'd be out for a few hours. Apparently he'd gone to church with Kai.

Church wasn't a foreign concept to me; I'd grown up attending church every Sunday. And even though I hadn't graced the inside of one in quite some time, I couldn't help but feel a bit miffed that he hadn't thought to invite me. *Does he think I don't believe in God?*

Thinking back over the last couple of weeks I guess I hadn't given him much reason to assume otherwise, nor had I asked that question of him; religion wasn't something I threw into casual conversations.

Yet the way he had talked to me this morning…

My phone buzzed.

Jackie: Leaving in 20. I'll bring a movie.

Me: Great. Thx. Let yourself in. I'll be in the bath downstairs.

Jackie: You're not expecting my help with that, right?

Me: No, I can manage.

Jackie: Good.

I made my way to my parent's bedroom down the hall. My mom had recently won the battle of which room in the house to remodel first: their bathroom, which now included a giant soaker tub. Today I was very happy for her victory. Dad had wanted to change the guest room into a home gym, but he caved in the end. There was never any question that he would, of course, but he put up a pretty decent fight. The truth was that he would do anything for my mom.

After doing a one-handed jig to get undressed, I slid down deep into the tub, keeping my wrist elevated out of the water. It was still wrapped, yet the throbbing had gone down with the meds I had taken with breakfast.

If I could only choose two hobbies in all the world, they would include: playing the piano, and soaking in a bathtub full of bubbles. Dorm-life hadn't quite provided me that luxury. I would have to get my fill for the year while I was home.

I leaned my head back against the cold porcelain and closed my eyes. A minute later my mind found its way to Briggs. I thought again about what he had said earlier in the kitchen about his past. I wanted to ask him more questions, but how could I do that when I had never shared the secrets that lurked in my own. What I did know, though, was that whoever he used to be, whatever former life he had lived before, didn't match the definition of the man I had come to know. I hoped he could see that.

It had taken nearly ten years of intermittent therapy for me to recognize the difference between the girl who had been born into hardship, versus the girl who had been rescued from it. Those lines were easily blurred—feelings, memories and physical reminders, seemed to pull me back every chance they could.

It's a common misconception when adopting a young child from a hard circumstance, that life will resume back to normal fairly quickly. But to a child that has never known *normal…* life starts over. Day one starts the re-birthing process. Trauma doesn't extend extra grace to children—it only changes the symptoms.

Though I was fortunate to gain a family in the Lexington's, the road had not been easy.

****

A lady that smelled like wild flowers drove me to what she called, "my new home."

I didn't talk. I was afraid of talking. The last time I had, mama died.

We drove for a while. The flower lady turned on the radio when I wouldn't answer her questions. I liked the music. We parked in front of a big white house with more grass than I'd ever seen. She said this was it.

Mr. and Mrs. Lexington stood on the porch watching us as we walked up to the house. I had no bags, no things to carry—except for one ratty blue blanket.

It was mine.

They spoke softly to me, their words kind and thoughtful. I climbed the stairs with them as they opened a door to a lavender bedroom with a white princess bed against one wall, and a play kitchen on the other.

They said it was for me.

I blinked.

I didn't know if this was just another story in my head…or if it was real.

After taking the first warm bath I could remember, they told me it was time to sleep. But that bed wasn't my bed. Once they left and closed the door, I pushed back the unknown blankets of the unknown bed. I crawled down onto the floor and slid underneath its metal frame, pulling with me a single, blue blanket.

I slept that way for two years.

****

A knock at the bathroom door brought me back to reality.

"Charlie, I'm here."

"Hey Jackie…I'll be out in a minute, just need to rinse my hair."

"Alright. I'll be downstairs—hey, is hottie home?"

"No."

And he's not your hottie.

****

I gave up on any article of clothing that had required a hook, clasp or button, and finally settled for yoga pants, a sports bra (which took some creativity to get into) and a t-shirt. I met Jackie downstairs a few minutes later. She was already lounging on the couch, looking like a Greek goddess. It was sickening the natural beauty that some people were allowed to flaunt to the rest of the average world.

Jackie had brought over the latest Pride and Prejudice remake, as well as several others. Apparently, she was planning on staying for a while. I found myself growing anxious as the hours passed, thinking about when Briggs would arrive. I reminded myself to be grateful for Jackie's willingness to help me…even if all she had done was watch TV, even while I had loaded the dishwasher.

I had to *keep* reminding myself.

I smiled as my phone buzzed.

The hottie who lives above your garage: What can I bring you home for lunch?

I wasn't sure if I was happier that he had thought about bringing me lunch, or that he referred to my house as "home".

I smiled and lifted my phone. Texting with my non-dominant hand suddenly didn't feel so difficult.

Me: Oh um…let me think, thank you! Jackie is here btw.

The hottie who lives above your garage: Jackie from the club? Interesting choice, Shortcake.

Me: Hey, beggars can't be choosers. Didn't you just leave church? Isn't judging looked down upon…?

The hottie who lives above your garage: Yes, but God gave me eyes, ears and a brain to use them. I call it like I see it. Okay, so is fast food out?

Me: Was it ever in? Yuck.

The hottie who lives above your garage: Fine. I'll pick up some sandwich makings, then. You make things SO difficult.

Me: And that's why you love me :-)

A full minute went by and I started to feel nervous about my lame joke—maybe I should have included a row of *hahahahaha* after it?

The hottie that lives above your garage: That's just one reason.

I stared at the text like it held the answer to all life's mysteries. My stomach dropped to the floor. *I just might save this text forever.*

"Why ya smiling so big over there? Is that *lover* boy?" Jackie cooed, as she crossed her ankles on the coffee table.

"Not lover boy, *just* Briggs."

I put my phone down, not wanting to draw any more of her attention to it—or to him.

"Hmm…okay."

She smiled and flipped her hair over her shoulder, combing through it with her fingers.

Did I just give her more ammo or less by my reply? I couldn't tell.

I pushed the thought out of my mind and decided that I was being *way* too paranoid and jealous over someone that wasn't even mine.

But I wish he was…

The rebellious thought shocked me.

Sure, I thought Briggs was good looking—okay, I thought he was very good looking. I also thought he was nice, funny, caring, kind, strong, and loyal, but did that mean-

Do I want Briggs?

My stomach flipped again, as if answering my question.

Is this what being on the rebound feels like?

Am I not broken over Alex anymore?

I didn't know the answers to those, but I *did* know that I thoroughly enjoyed our friendship. And if I wanted to keep that, then I needed to stop thinking like a typical girl. Besides, dating wasn't a priority for Briggs, he had made that perfectly clear this morning.

Friends, that's all we are.

Briggs

"How's my little Captain Hook doing?" I called out as I walked through the front door. I laid the grocery bags on the counter and looked around for Charlie.

Barbie jumped up instead.

"Oh, hi Briggs! Aren't you *so sweet* for bringing us lunch?"

It wasn't meant for you…but whatever.

"Its just sandwiches, no biggie. Where's Charlie?" I asked flatly.

"Think she's in the laundry room," Jackie said, shrugging.

I narrowed my eyes at her, "Doing what?"

"Um…laundry I guess?" She shrugged as I felt a blaze of frustration burn in my veins. She took the bread from my hands as I set the bag on the counter, deciding to check on Charlie (or scold her for doing laundry with a sprained wrist), yet before I could, I was distracted by what felt like a trailing of a finger on my back.

Jackie's hand gripped my shoulder, and a second later, her breath was hot in my ear, "How can I help you?"

There was so much more than a friendly offer to make sandwiches within her tone. It made my skin crawl. I brushed her hand off, reaching into the bag to grab the brick of cheese.

"Nothing. I can manage."

She hopped up onto the counter, her rear about six inches from where I was laying out the plates. She crossed her legs toward me.

Wow…she sure is determined.

"Ya know, my girlfriend Francesca dates a fireman," Jackie began.

"Hmm…that so."

I started slicing the cheese, hoping that my obvious disdain for her would speak for itself.

No such luck.

"Yeah, she has plenty to say about it, too," she cooed.

Within a second, her foot that was nearest to me was on my hip…and traveling quickly.

That's when I was done playing nice. I set the knife down and grabbed her foot—hard. She seemed stunned by the change of events.

I looked at her square in the face. "Jackie, you seem like a smart girl, and I appreciate whatever help you might have offered Charlie today, but *this*," I said gesturing from her to me, "is *never* going to happen. And when I say never, I mean the kind of *never* that parallels a snowstorm in August, or the end of Elvis impersonators in Vegas. Is that clear enough for you?"

I let go of her foot as she stared at me, opened-mouthed. *Had no one ever told the girl no before?*

There was a first time for everything.

"Fine," she hopped off the counter and grabbed her purse, "You can tell Charlie she can have you. I don't do leftovers, anyway."

I would bet otherwise.

I heard the front door slam about five seconds after she passed me—her last sentiment was a gesture that she showcased on her hand for me, quite dramatically I might add.

Hope the door doesn't hit ya on the way out—

My attention was immediately diverted when I looked up again. Charlie was standing in the hallway, only a few feet away.

Suddenly, I was nervous.

Chapter Fourteen

Charlie

I blinked a thousand times, trying to decipher what I had just witnessed.

What did I just witness?

In the course of what was likely no more than ninety seconds, I had experienced a flip-book of human emotions: jealously, anger, fear, anxiety, insecurity…betrayal. But as I started to step out of the shadows to unleash my Hulk-rage on them both, I heard Briggs turn her down.

He turned her down.

Jackie.

That's when a giant wave of guilt came crashing over me, pulling me under its tide and washing my every assumption away with it. Our eyes locked onto each other. We both turned our heads toward the driveway a second later—the sound of squealing tires peeling down the street, likely alerting the neighborhood to the estrogen rampage that was occurring.

"I'm sorry." We said in unison.

We found each other's eyes again.

"Why are *you* sorry?" Again, we spoke at the same time.

He laughed nervously.

I walked over to the counter where he stood.

"After everything you told me this morning, I can't believe I was so stupid to invite her here—not when I know what she's like. I feel horrible-"

"Stop, Charlie…none of *that* was your fault." He nodded toward the front door where Jackie had exited. He stepped closer to me. My heart hammered inside my chest.

"At first I thought—I was afraid that you would..." I let my eyes fall away from his face, but the gentle touch on my chin guided them back to his.

"Afraid that what?"

"Afraid that you would...*want* her."

As if completely caught off guard by my reply, he started laughing—bellowing actually—like I had just told the world's best joke. I could not find the humor in it though. I put my good hand on my hip, waiting impatiently for him to finish. He calmed himself quickly once he realized I wasn't going to join in.

An intense look blazed in his eyes; all amusement drained from his face.

"You're serious?" he asked.

"Yes I'm serious! It's *Jackie*...she's a living, breathing Barbie doll! What man *wouldn't* want her?"

"Me. I don't want her, Charlie," His tone was deep, almost dangerous sounding, "She's not my type."

I swallowed hard as I stared into his eyes, pushing the vulnerability bubble that was building inside me away, running instead toward the emotion I was far more comfortable with: Anger. I had all but forgotten my feelings of guilt, which had started this whole conversation in the first place.

"She's *every* man's type—even men on the reform, like you. So don't patronize me, Briggs. *Beautiful* is every man's type!"

He flinched at my words, but held his ground all the same, a new expression taking over his face.

"Where's this insecurity coming from, Charlie?"

Of all the things he could have said, really? What is wrong with him?

"Don't try and make this about me!"

"I think it has more to do with that loser you dated, actually." He crossed his arms over his chest.

My mouth hung open. *How had this conversation spiraled down so quickly?*

"Let me tell you how I see it, Shortcake. That jerk you dated must have sold you some pretty pricey lies if you honestly believe that a girl like Jackie is *more desirable* to a man than you."

I blinked rapidly, trying to keep up with the direction of this conversation while the truth stabbed at my heart like a dull knife. *I'm not that different from her.*

"You don't even know what kind of girl *I am*, Briggs! Despite what you think, I'm not some innocent little flower, so you can take whatever virtue and purity notions you've concocted about me and squash 'em. I'm a lot closer to *a Jackie* than you might want to believe. Alex didn't sell me anything that I didn't willingly offer to him first…"

I was shocked by the bitter honesty of my words. I'd given Alex all of me within days of meeting him. I felt sick under that looming haze of regret.

I couldn't stand there for one more second. I was so tired of pretending to be someone I wasn't anymore, and I didn't need to see another disappointed face staring back at me. I saw that face everyday in the mirror.

My resolve to wait for love, prior to meeting Alex, had failed to match the intensity of my need to be desired, wanted, and cherished. Yet in the end, that one decision only compounded the emptiness I had longed to fill.

Briggs

A single tear rolled down her cheek as she turned from me. I struggled between comforting her and thinking of the ways I could dismember *Alex*.

Her tear won me over.

"Don't turn away from me, Charlie, *please*."

Slowly, she faced me again. I took a step closer, resting my hands on her shoulders. The pain in her eyes ripped something open in my chest.

"Can I ask you something?"

She nodded.

"If you knew then what you know now…that he would leave you, would you have been so willing?"

"No," she said without a second's hesitation.

"*That's* how you're not the same, Charlie. Sex wasn't a sport for you. I can point those girls out of a crowd easily—most guys can—but those girls aren't you," I paused, moving my hands to cradle her face. "But you were sold a lie, sweetheart, and for that I'm very sorry."

She questioned me with her eyes.

"You believed it could be bought," I said, wiping a rogue tear from her cheek.

Her voice was a shaky whisper, "That *what* could be bought?"

"Love."

I pulled her into my chest and wrapped my arms around her, kissing the top of her head.

There was a very real possibility that I'd never let her go.

Charlie

Infinity times infinity, that's how long I hoped his hug would last.

Time wouldn't need to exist, the future didn't have to make sense, and my past wasn't even a blip on the radar.

"Charlie, I want to-"

My pocket was vibrating.

Who would have the audacity to be calling right now—in the middle of my infinity moment?

Briggs dropped his arms and I was overcome with a chill that started at my scalp and worked its way down to my toes. I struggled to grab a hold of the phone, as the corner of it was stuck on a seam in my pocket, but Briggs plucked it out for me in one fluid motion.

My knees felt like Jell-O.

"Hello," I croaked out.

Get a grip Charlie!

"Sugar! It's so nice to hear your voice. How are you?"

Dad, of course. Captain of the Worst Timing Ever Club.

"Doing great, Dad. Just about to have some lunch."

"Oh good. Has Briggs been around much? Or does he keep to himself in that apartment? I'm sure he's been enjoying that extra cable package I got for him." He laughed.

I'd say he's been around…yep.

"Uh, yeah we've hung out a few times." I see Briggs smile at me from the corner of my eye as I grab my plate from the counter with my good hand, forcing the phone to stay between my head and shoulder as I walked to the couch. Briggs stayed in the kitchen—*to give me privacy*?

"Good. Well, I hope it's hasn't been too bad for you, sugar. We miss you…and we're excited to be home next week so we can spend some time with you before your summer classes start. Charlie…I…"

"Yeah?" I felt my throat thicken with emotion for the hundredth time that day.

"I just want you to know how much I love you. I know you think my rules are a bit crazy, and maybe I am over-protective, but everything I do…everything I want for you… is because I love you. I hope you know that—even if you're still angry with me."

I put my plate down on the table in front of me. I had heard those words countless times before, and I did believe him…but they meant something more today.

"I know, Dad. I love you too…and I'm sorry." I couldn't finish my statement. But he knew.

"I am too baby, and I'm sorry he broke your heart."

I swallowed hard, "And I'm sorry I didn't listen."

Silence.

"I love you, sugar. We'll fix this when we get home. I'm glad you've had this time to think, and take a break from school. Your mom just sent you another email with pictures. She picked you up a little something today at an outdoor market, too. We'll see you next week. Take care of yourself, and tell Briggs we say hello, ok?"

"Okay. Tell mom I love her, too."

"Will do. Bye, Charlie."

"Bye, Dad."

I laid the phone onto the sofa next to me, pulling my plate onto my lap.

"They're doing well?" Briggs asked.

"Yeah…he sounds really happy. I'm glad they went," I said, still deep in thought.

"They miss you." It wasn't a question.

"I miss them, too. I just wish…" I shook my head.

"What?" he asked.

I looked up at him, sitting across from me on the loveseat.

I smiled, "Ya know, what? I think we've met our quota on heavy conversations today…don't you?"

He stared at me as if deciding if he would let it go, ultimately he did.

"Well, then, what do you have in mind for today, Uno?" he asked.

Uno?

I laughed as he pointed to my arm.

"Nice," I laughed, "Maybe something that doesn't take a lot of skill or energy—or two hands."

We each took some bites of our sandwiches, thinking.

"Well, since you already did laundry," he baited, scowling at me with mock-frustration, "I think that just leaves lazy activities: TV, reading, one-handed charades?"

I laughed. "Perfect."

"Sounds like an excellent Sunday afternoon to me, too."

Chapter Fifteen

Briggs

I'd never put a lot of stock into the word *happy,* until recently.

It had seemed so fleeting, so temporary, so overused.

But this week had changed that; this week had given me a regard for all things *happy*.

Happy was in every minute I spent with Charlie, no matter if we were driving to work, laughing over Chinese food, or telling scary stories by the fire pit in her back yard. *Happy* was in her looks, in her texts, in her voice and in her laugh.

Happy, I discovered, was simply doing life with Charlie.

By Friday afternoon, my thoughts were consumed with telling her how I felt. With this being my last weekend staying at her house, I knew I couldn't wait one more day. By next week things would be different. There would be distractions, schedule changes, responsibilities, but I hoped none of those things would change *us* once she knew how I felt about her.

"Dude…you know you're walking around here like a smitten puppy, right?" Kai asked, dragging a soapy sponge across the front of the fire engine.

I shrugged and smiled. Denial was pointless.

"So what's your plan?" he asked.

"What do you mean?"

"What are you going to do about it?"

I looked at him, "You mean like…how am I going to tell her?"

He stopped washing and stood upright.

"No, not how you're going to tell *her*…how are you going to tell *him*? What's your plan with Chief?"

It wasn't like I had forgotten about that tiny detail exactly, but Charlie's dad had not been at the forefront of my mind as of late. He was not present in my head for the conversation that had been on repeat since being struck with Cupid's arrow.

Kai's question had just thrown cold water in my face.

I frowned, "I suppose you have a thought or two about it."

"Listen, I can tell you really like her—I like her, too. She seems really great Briggs, and I've never known you to…feel this way about any woman-"

"'Cause she's not just *any* woman, Kai…" I snapped.

He smiled, putting his hand on my shoulder. "Hey, I know that, and I also know you, remember? I get what it means for you to want to take this next step."

I felt the tension in my shoulders relax. Kai moved to stand directly in front of me.

"I think that you need to sit down with Chief and talk to him first, before you make any commitments to Charlie."

"Kai…it's not like I'm going to propose to her tonight!" I said louder than I needed to. I looked over my shoulder to make sure no one had overheard me—particularly a strawberry-blonde who was just on the other side of the wall we stood in front of.

"No, but if you want to pursue something with her…you better feel pretty darn sure that's where it's headed. Chief's not going to let his only daughter get hurt again by any man—not even you."

I stared at Kai. He had a point.

"How did you know…about Alex?" I hated that he had a name. I hoped I'd never have to see the face that went with it. *He'd hate it even more though if I did.*

"Mrs. Julie talked to Tori about it a couple of months ago."

"Oh." I nodded.

"So, you're suggesting I ask him if I can date her?" I clarified.

"I'm suggesting you tell him how you feel about her and make your intentions clear to him," Kai said.

I felt sick.

In just a matter of seconds, my excitement about asking Charlie to dinner so I could tell her how I felt had just become much more complicated. The chief knew me—he'd seen the changes in my life as much as Kai had over this last year, but Charlie was *his* daughter, *his* only child.

"When is he back again?" Kai asked.

"Tuesday."

Kai nodded, going back to the sudsy bucket of water.

"Tuesday it is then," he said.

I swallowed hard, "Tuesday it is."

****

At five, I met Charlie in Chief's office. She had just finished the last of the filing. I looked around the room, it was impressive what she had accomplished. We always worked to keep the station clean, but there was something extra that Charlie had brought to this space. Besides her fruity candles and her disposable coffee cups (I didn't understand why she was so set on those), she just made the place…better.

Just like she makes me.

I smiled as I watched her turn and grab her purse.

"How's day two of no ace wrap?" I asked.

"Fantastic! That thing was really getting hard to accessorize. Not much goes with stretchy brown bandage material—who knew?" She bent her wrist back and forth slowly.

I reached out and took it in my hand.

It's so teeny.

Charlie was petite, no doubt. But the fragility of her wrist in my hand sent a shiver down my spine. I rubbed my thumb over the bone lightly, assessing it. An unexpected thought flashed through my mind then.

I couldn't live with myself if I ever hurt this woman.

She was talking, but I didn't catch it.

"What?"

She gently pulled her arm back, "I said I'm excited to play the piano later today. I can't believe it's been a week. A whole week! The longest I've ever gone without playing was three days, and that was because I had to get my appendix out."

We walked out to my truck together, passing several guys in the dining hall.

"Do you two want to stay for the Thai food delivery? It should be here in about ten minutes!" Andy called out to us.

I glanced at Charlie, she shook her head.

"Nah, we're good. Thanks!" I yelled back.

With that, we were on our way.

The anticipation of an evening spent with Charlie grew rapidly with each second that passed. I thought about my conversation with Kai again on the drive home. Though he was most likely right about how I should handle it with Chief, I would still say *something* to her tonight. I wouldn't make any promises or commitments yet, but one thing was for certain: This night would not pass without Charlie hearing what she meant to me.

Charlie

Something felt different on the ride home. I couldn't put my finger on it, but Briggs seemed lost in space. We had talked and joked like normal, but there was no fluidity to our conversation.

Did something happen at work?

He didn't seem upset, just a little out of sorts—like he was deep in thought. I decided to leave it alone. If he wanted to talk, he would. Briggs didn't keep stuff to himself for long, I'd learned that about him over the last month. Whatever he thought, he said.

I took comfort in that.

He wasn't the strong silent type that I used to find so appealing. I had actually come to understand that there was more strength to a man who could verbalize what he wanted, needed, and expected. True, that sometimes it meant an all-out-verbal-war on the back patio fighting about a secret wedding that wasn't actually in the works, but the air was always cleared faster having someone like Briggs around, without a doubt.

My wedding.

I pushed the thought from my mind. I wasn't ready to think about that.

I didn't *want* to think about that.

Briggs parked his truck in the driveway.

"So-," we both began.

"You go," I said.

"No, you go," he said.

We both laughed.

"I was just going to tell you that I need at least an hour of good practice time. I have a lot to do for Tori's processional still and it's only two weeks out. I'm meeting her next week to show her what I have, and since this happened," I said raising my right arm in the air, "I don't have much to show her."

He nodded. I started to open the door and slide out of the seat when I felt his hand on mine. It rested on top of my left hand, engulfing it completely. The warmth sent an army of goose- bumps marching up my neck and into my scalp. I searched his face, my stomach flipping instantly when I saw his expression.

Despite the rapid increase of my heartbeat, my breathing slowed dramatically. I waited for him to speak.

"Can I take you out to dinner tonight, Charlie?"

Random, incomplete fragments of thought floated in my head.

I tried to tell myself that this dinner was just the same as *every* dinner we'd shared together over the last four weeks. That it was probably just some new place he wanted to try, or maybe he was tired of the same old take-out we had been getting. I tried to tell myself that his deep, husky voice was in relation to the allergens in the air.

That the intense look of longing on his face had nothing at all to do with me…

But lying to myself never seemed to pay off in the end. And even more than that, I wanted it to be true—I wanted it to mean something new, something *more*.

Afraid to speak, I simply nodded at him.

"Okay, well…why don't you go in and spend some time being Beethoven, and I'll come find you around seven. That work?"

I nodded again before getting out of the truck, forcing myself to walk away with steps I hoped were regarded as normal.

Inside though, I was skipping.

****

I sat down at the piano and rotated my wrist for the hundredth time that day. Though it was still fairly stiff, the constant ache was gone. It was nice to not be in pain anymore. The ice, the anti-inflammatory meds and even the stupid wrap had made all the difference, and of course *time* had also played a key role in my healing as well.

A week…I had actually gone an entire week without piano. Unbelievable.

I laid my hands on the keys and closed my eyes thinking of the melody I had heard in my heart for Tori.

Without more than a second's hesitation, the notes came out fluidly. I could picture the walk of her bridesmaids, the stroll of the ring-bearer pulling the wagon with her niece on board, and I could visualize the start of Tori's walk. I paused the higher notes for dramatic effect as I repeated the bass line, preparing for what would be her grand entrance.

Then, the melody came again, like a soft, delicate whisper.

The next two times through, I wrote out the music as I played. Though my strength was to play by ear, the university had pushed me to hone my music theory and composition skills to a new level. Writing music was now like brushing my teeth. Not much thought was involved; it was second nature.

I laid the sheet music out before me and played it through again—although I closed my eyes halfway through. I hoped Tori would be pleased with it. Even though I hadn't known her long, I felt this composition was tailored for her. We had spent a few evenings together now, and within that time, I had learned that she was truly someone very unique. I wanted that quality to shine through this piece.

I wanted *her* to shine through this piece.

Briggs

After showering, I studied my face in the mirror, rehearsing in my head the words that were written in my heart, the words that Charlie had written on my heart.

I can do this.

I'd seen the way she looked at me when I asked her to dinner. She knew something was different about tonight. Much to the delight of my nerves, she hadn't looked worried. *She'd looked…surprised?*

It was hard to know for sure, but her eyes had been *happy*. That, I knew.

I left the apartment and headed down the stairs, my phone buzzing in my pocket.

The station.

"Briggs here."

"Hey man, it's Thomas. I think you're gonna have to come in tonight."

"What's going on?" I asked.

"Five guys just left here…all with what I think is food poisoning."

"What? No way…was it the Thai food?" I asked.

"Yeah…uh, dude I need to go…I'm not feeling so hot myself, but we are way understaffed now."

"I'll head in. I can be there in thirty minutes."

I threw my head back in frustration as I entered the house.

So much for a nice, quiet night alone with Charlie.

I thought of the chief's words to me, about her being the *priority*. But this was an emergency and Charlie hadn't even tried to break the rules since that first weekend I was here. As much as I hated to leave her, it was the right thing to do.

At most, it would be forty-eight hours until the new rotation was back on, but I couldn't leave them high and dry. I wouldn't.

Urgh. Responsibility sucks sometimes.

I sounded like Cody.

****

I didn't know how I got to the French doors of the music room. I had no memory of it. I didn't know how long I stood watching her—studying her, as she played with her eyes closed. I didn't even know *what* she was playing. That didn't matter.

What I did know was that I had never experienced anything like it before.

When Charlie played, nothing short of transformation took place in everything and everyone who was nearby. I was certain that she didn't just play a melody, she *played* her soul. It was the kind of awakening that separated life from death, or light from darkness.

I was completely mesmerized.

If I had thought Charlie beautiful before this moment—and I certainly had—this undoubtedly trumped any of my previous assessments of her. How could one appreciate the full potential of beauty until it was seen in its truest form? It would be like looking at a caterpillar before it metamorphosed into a butterfly, or a seed before it had grown into a flower.

But *this,* this was Charlie's truest form of beauty.

She *was* her music, and everything about it was breathtaking.

As her last note resonated in the room, I clapped. She jumped of course, and then a slow, shy grin appeared on her face.

"I thought you weren't going to use your creepy-stalker-skill for a while?"

"Technically, I was standing in the open. You were the one with your eyes closed."

She smiled wider. I walked to the bench where she sat.

"You were—that was—I honestly don't even have the words for it, Charlie." I said, getting lost in the aqua of her eyes.

Her cheeks blushed pink and she looked away, briefly.

"Do you play an instrument?" she asked.

That's not what you just did.

"Not anywhere close to that level," I laughed.

"But you do play something…I bet I can guess which one, too." She pursed her lips, thinking. "Guitar."

"How did you guess that?"

"You're too cool to play a horn, too punctual to be a drummer, but you're just the right amount of cocky for a guitarist."

"You do know me well, Shortcake." I laughed.

My smile dipped as the words soured in my mouth. *Yet there are still some things you don't know about me.* I scooted her over with my knee and sat down next to her on the bench. Her bare arm brushed against mine, and I fought the urge to reach for her hand.

"So, was that the song for Tori's wedding?" I asked.

"Yes, but be honest, do you think she'll like it?"

Her brows wrinkled with the question, and I wanted to kiss them both—reassure her that she and it were perfect, but I didn't.

"She will love it, I have no doubt."

"Are you in it—the wedding, I mean?"

"Yeah. Crazy, huh? Kai entrusting me to be his best man." I nudged her with my elbow.

"Oh, I don't know…it's the crazy ones who make life more fun."

And that was it. My willpower was gone.

I took her hand in mine, and slowly laced my fingers through hers. I heard a faint gasp come from her mouth, but she didn't pull away.

"Charlie, let me take you to the wedding—as my date?" I asked, looking into her eyes.

An eternity passed before she spoke, but her eyes never left my face. We were so close. I could feel her breath, I could see her neck pulse, I could count her eyelashes.

"That's ten points to you, Briggs."

I smiled. "That's an affirmative?"

"Yes."

Chapter Sixteen

Charlie

The angle was too awkward for kissing, but that didn't make me want it any less.

Our eyes held for a second more while my insides turned into a hot liquid that bubbled inside me with each breath I took. The touch of his hand on mine had started this molten reaction.

He broke our gaze, looking down at our united hands.

"I have some unfortunate news…"

"What?" I asked, startled back into reality.

"Food poising has hit the firehouse. Bad Thai, I guess. Good thing you weren't feeling it tonight…'cause we would have really been feeling it later if we'd stayed," he said.

I chuckled a bit before disappointment overtook me. "So, you'll be gone tonight through when? Sunday?"

"Most likely. I'm sorry, Shortcake. This isn't how I wanted our night to go."

I felt another bubbling sensation in my belly as tingles shot up my arm from where he rubbed his thumb over my knuckles.

Our last weekend together…gone.

"How many guys are out?" I asked.

"The count was five as of twenty minutes ago, but I'm sure it's more now. Usually we all share one large order," he said shaking his head.

"So you have to leave, now?"

"Yeah. I probably should have left already, but I couldn't miss the performance of a prodigy."

I smiled at that. "Okay," I said.

He slowly withdrew his hand from mine, wrapping his arm around my shoulders instead. I leaned closer to him, resting my head on his chest as I did.

"I'll make it up to you, Charlie—soon." With my ear against him, his soft words resonated as if his heart was the one who had spoken them to me.

I nodded, not trusting myself enough to speak.

"You gonna be alright here, Shortcake? You'll call me if you need anything, right?"

I lifted my head and smiled, "Yes, Manny. I'll be just fine. You should probably get going though."

And unfortunately, that is exactly what he did.

****

With Briggs gone, a vortex of emptiness seemed to surround the house. I worked on Tori's composition for a few hours more, perfecting it as much as I could. I ate cold cereal for dinner. I watched the Late Show. And then I stared at my cell phone as if willing it to ring.

It didn't.

Overall, the night was a bust.

Around two in the morning I climbed the stairs to my bedroom, hoping I had tired my mind out enough for sleep. But my hope was in vain. I stared at the ceiling fan directly above my bed, wondering if the rhythm could hypnotize me.

I closed my eyes, but never found rest.

****

For as long as I could remember, the man had come.

I never knew when or why, but he always came. He knew my mama, though I didn't know how. He would bring one brown bag of food every time, and every time the contents were the same: peanut butter, cheese-its and bread. The food never outlasted the hunger, but I was grateful for that bag, and for the man who brought it. He would talk to mama for a while, and then he would leave until the next time I saw him.

One day after watching Cinderella—the video he had put on for me during a visit—I asked him if he was like the man on the screen.

"What do you mean, Charlotte?" he asked me.

"Are you like the prince?" I asked again, while trying to untangle my hair with my fingers, which was an impossible task.

"No, Charlotte. I'm afraid there are only princes in fairytales. Life doesn't work like that," he crouched down before me, and it was the first time I saw him so close.

He had black and silver eyebrows and a big nose, and his eyes were very sad.

"I want to live in a fairytale," I said quietly, careful not to speak too loudly inside the apartment.

He put his hand on my head. "I wish things were that easy. I wish your mama's life had turned out differently, but life's cruel, and we usually get the opposite of what we wish for."

"What does…op-po-site mean?" I asked, repeating each syllable.

"It means your mama never wanted this life. She never wanted to be sick, or poor, or a mother. You see, fairytales just aren't real, Charlotte. It's best you know that now." He turned and ejected the video from the VCR.

As I watched him leave and walk down the stairs to the parking lot, I saw him throw it into the dumpster on the way out. He never brought another one. I stared at the blank screen in front of me for a long time that day, tears rolling down my cheeks as I heard his word again, "…your mama never wanted to be sick, or poor, or a mother…"

Maybe I was the reason that fairytales didn't come true.

****

I jolted awake, gasping for air, my cheeks damp with tears. I was glad to see that it was after nine—at least I had managed to get a few consecutive hours of sleep. I picked up my phone. Briggs had texted, but before I could respond to it, another text caught my eye—no, not a text, a *reminder*.

Today is my wedding day!

I threw my head back on the bed and covered my face with a pillow.

The man was right: Life was cruel.

Briggs

There were several calls during the night, but nothing of great significance. I found myself awake and meandering toward the station's gym around the midnight hour. The punching bag that was isolated in the back corner called to me, the way it always did when I was anxious. Chief had purchased it for me a couple years ago. Though I no longer fought for sport or money, there was no better way for me to condition my body or deal with my frustrations.

After a hard workout I showered and fell into a restless sleep.

I had texted Charlie first thing in the morning, but she hadn't responded yet. I hoped she was able to sleep in, but as noon rolled by, I had grown increasingly concerned. It wasn't like her to not reply; the girl's phone was practically sewed into her hand. I tried again.

Me: If you don't respond to this, I'm sending over fifteen pizzas…and they will be staggered on the hour. You have five minutes. Starting now.

This time she responded. Charlie wasn't an abbreviated texter. She was funny, witty, and full of spunk. That usually translated into long-winded texting rants, but not today.

I stared at my screen, tensing with uneasiness.

Miss Strawberry Shortcake: I'm fine.

Those two words were as startling as a punch to the jaw. I looked at them over and over for the next four hours. She texted nothing more.

Maybe she was tired?

Maybe she was busy at the piano?

Maybe she was-

"Girl troubles?" Evan asked, slumping down by me at the table. We each held a sandwich that looked like it could be on *Man Verses Food.*

"Nah," I said, shaking my head, not wanting to talk about Charlie at the station—except with Kai, but he was off today.

"Well, you've been staring at that same screen for hours now—what gives?"

Evan was a nice guy—a bit of a geek, but genuine. Chief had pushed him on me when he first started at the station, telling me I needed more *good influences* in my life. Naturally, that had been my reason to stay away from him at first. Kai was enough of a good influence on me. I didn't need more than that. I couldn't handle more than that.

But as my friendship with Kai grew, Evan had somehow managed to work himself into the mix. He was alright—a friend.

"It's nothing, just…trying to figure something out." I mumbled to myself.

"Well…let me know if you do. I'm still waiting on an app to come out that will tell me how to talk to a woman, much less figure her out," he laughed.

"I'll be sure to let you know, Evan."

****

As the sun set, I started to pace.

Around dinnertime I had thrown in the old pride towel and called her. She didn't answer. Something was wrong. Something was *very* wrong. Three more men had joined the crew for the evening as I walked down the hallway.

I couldn't stay another night here—not without knowing what was up with Charlie. I felt like I was starting to go crazy. As I passed the bulletin board on my right there were all sorts of brightly colored flyers tacked to it. During my shift I had passed it at least a dozen times, but this time…this time I saw something that made my blood turn cold.

Saturday, April 28th!

Join us for a Fun Run…

I let the words at the bottom blur. I didn't care about the details. But that date…that date, was today. And today was the day that Charlie would have married that pathetic loser.

I walked back down the hall, grabbing my duffle bag and keys from my locker.

"Evan, I have to leave. Can you take care of things? Call Smith or Matty?" I asked him, borderline frantic.

"Yeah, sure—you figured it out?" he called after me as I ran through the parking lot.

I didn't reply because I hoped I hadn't. And more than that, I hoped I wasn't too late.

****

The black storm clouds overhead blocked the moonlight, as the drizzle of rain from minutes earlier turned into an all-out monsoon. I pulled into Charlie's driveway, banging the heel of my hand against the steering wheel. Her car was gone.

How could she do this? How could she leave and not tell me?

A nauseating feeling of dread washed over me as I thought about her out at some stupid club numbing her pain, while falling prey to a thousand other kinds of horrors at the same time. Fear, anger, rage—those feelings I could deal with, but this feeling?

This feeling was the worst one of all: Helplessness.

Charlie

It crinkled between my fingers—the one thing I had kept besides the ring.

Sasha had made me burn the pictures, except for the one I had destroyed on our dorm room wall a month ago. Any memorabilia from the concerts, clubs, and museums we'd gone to had long ago turned to ash, but I couldn't part with the note.

It outlined my reality; it outlined my greatest fear.

Charlie-

In music, there are many instruments that serve just one purpose: to complement.

They work to enrich the sound of another, to blend, and to harmonize—adding to the collective whole of a melody line. But there are other instruments, which were only ever meant to stand alone, to solo. We, unfortunately, both fall into that latter category, Charlie. And two solo instruments should never share the stage.

We want different things, have different goals, and in the end I know we would both find ourselves as unhappy as I am now. The idea of faithfulness to one woman for the rest of my life is one that suffocates me. I told you that from the start…you were the one who pushed for something more, something I didn't want.

Goodbye Charlie,

Alex

Even in his goodbye note he hadn't said the words.

I, of course, had told him I loved him early on. But his response was always the same, a kiss, as if to shut me up so I wouldn't say more. When he finally did say it, I knew now that he had only wanted to keep the peace.

Our engagement was a final arm-twist—a last desperate attempt instigated by me. I needed something tangible to prove that I hadn't made a huge mistake in choosing Alex over my family, or my friends, or my faith. I needed to know that I hadn't thrown them away for no reason at all.

I believed marriage would prove his love.

I believed marriage would make him faithful.

I believed marriage would right the wrongs.

But a marriage to Alex wasn't the miracle I had been looking for.

I could finally see that now, but knowing truth and feeling truth were very different things. I stared into the ominous night as the rain pelted down around me. I wished it could wash away the past. I wished it could wash me whole. If only it had that kind of power.

A blinding light interrupted my wishing.

Briggs

Maybe she left a note? Maybe she didn't want to text, but had written it down somewhere inside?

I knew I wasn't being rational, but trying to rationalize how you're not being rational in the middle of a crisis, just doesn't work. I grabbed the key to the house out of my glove box and threw open my door, leaving the ignition running.

I ran through the rain to the front door. As I shoved the key into the cold metal lock, I startled back at the sound of a voice.

"I thought you weren't coming back until tomorrow."

I threw my head to the left, but couldn't see her. The glaring light from my headlights was pointed in the opposite direction, leaving nothing but shadows on the porch. I fought the impulse to yell…to rant…to roar at her in frustration, but the tenderness in her voice had melted all those reactions away.

I moved closer to the direction her voice had come from, straining to see her silhouette in the darkness. About two feet away, my eyes finally adjusted enough to see the outline of her body. She was sitting on the porch swing, but there was no movement to it. Her knees were drawn-in, her arms wrapped around herself.

I knelt down in front of her, a few inches away.

"Charlie, sweetie…are you hurt? Did something happen tonight? Where's your car?" The gentleness in my voice was surprising, even to me.

She lifted her head from her knees and seemed to look at me, or at least look toward me—I couldn't see her eyes.

"In the garage. I parked it inside before the rain started."

She doesn't sound drunk.

I took a deep breath. "Charlie, I'm gonna go shut off my truck. I'll be right back."

"Fine."

There was that unnerving word again. I turned off my truck and in the process, the motion detector light came on. I could see Charlie now, fully illuminated.

"Can I sit next to you?"

"If you want to."

"I do."

"I haven't been drinking if that's what you're worried about."

She turned her face toward me, laying her head down on top of her knees while keeping eye contact.

"I can see that," I said, pushing the swing to rock back a bit, "I'm sorry I wasn't here today, Charlie. I forgot. I know it must have been a hard day to spend alone. Were you...out here thinking about *Alex*?"

It was like swallowing a live roach to even say his name, but to my surprise she shook her head *no.* I waited, giving her time, but what came next was a statement I couldn't have prepared for.

"My mama killed herself when I was five."

Chapter Seventeen

Charlie

I hadn't planned on telling him. I had never told before.

Not to Sasha, or Jackie, or even to Alex.

Simple was easy for people to understand, *complicated* meant even more complicated relationships. I didn't want it following me, or the word I couldn't bring myself to say aloud: Suicide. It was bad enough that I had to tell my grade school friends I was in an "art club" on Tuesday afternoons—a club they could never join, primarily because it didn't exist. Therapy wasn't a world most kids were familiar with. I wasn't about to isolate myself even more by becoming the foster kid who had lived in a glorified hole for the first five years of her life and who had consequently found her mother dead next to several empty pill bottles.

That truth was hard to swallow.

Briggs stared at me. Even as the motion light clicked off, I could feel his gaze like a warm touch on my face. I knew he was confused. I lifted my head up again, shifting my gaze back to the inky sky. The rain had picked up in intensity, as had the wind. I shivered involuntarily. Briggs quietly took off his jacket and put it over my shoulders.

"Max and Julie—my mom and dad—adopted me. I was born to Abigail Dawson, she was my mama. My life was…*difficult*, although it took me years to understand just how bad it really was. I had a very skewed definition of normal. She wasn't mentally stable, and rarely got out of bed, leaving me to fend for myself. I was always worried about her. I wanted to fix her, and make her better. But one day, when I got back from another unsupervised wandering…she was dead. I found her that way. It was two days before anyone came for me. I went to live with the Lexington's after that."

"Charlie, I…I-"

"I know. It's ugly—there's no other way to say it." I exhaled, "Today was just a big, fat reminder of it all."

He seemed to contemplate this as his hand moved to the top of my head. With slow, steady movements he stroked my hair. I closed my eyes, letting the rhythm calm me. It reminded me of something my mom—Julie Lexington—used to do for me when I had had a bad dream. She would come into my room and sit on my bed and stroke my hair. Sometimes we would get up together and she would make me apple cinnamon tea, my favorite. She never made me go back to sleep right away. It was as if she knew what was waiting for me there—or who was waiting for me: *Mama.*

In my relaxed state I felt the piece of paper slip through my fingers and flutter down in front of us. The sound was barely that of a whisper as it hit, but Briggs heard it, and reached for it a second later.

"What's this, Charlie?"

I swallowed, the burning hole in my gut still raw, still open.

But again, I surprised myself.

"It's the note, the one Alex left for me. The one where he tells me that I'm only good as a solo instrument," I laughed, but there's no humor it in.

I felt Briggs tense beside me. He stared at it, "And he…he reminds you of your mom?"

"Not my mom…my mama. And yes, now he does."

"How?" he asked. It was a curious question, but there was something deeper it in that I couldn't quite identify without being able to see him clearly.

"Because in one way they're the same," I sighed, "Neither of them *wanted* me in the end."

Briggs

I stopped touching her hair.

Her words were a rare form of suffocation, like breathing through a wet washcloth.

"Charlie…you believe that?" I asked, my voice cracked with emotion.

"He never loved me, Briggs. And neither did she. I offered myself to them both, gave them everything—was willing to be anyone, do anything to make them happy. But in the end, they let me go." Her voice changed to a whisper, "Like I meant nothing to them at all."

There were no tears, but every word she said was marinated in a thick sadness, the kind that had taken years to flavor.

I gritted my teeth against the anger that welled in me—particularly toward Alex. I wanted to hurt him—to hurt anyone who had hurt Charlie. I couldn't understand why or how someone could do that to her, but I felt confident that no one ever would again.

Not if I had something to say about it.

"You are *not* nothing to me."

She looked up at me. I reached for her face, cupping her cheek as she relaxed into it. That one movement lit my veins on fire.

"I've never told anyone that…before now."

"And I've never wanted to kiss you more…than I do right now."

My words came out choppy, breathless, but I couldn't contain them anymore. She made no sound, but I could sense her approval as she leaned toward me. With my right hand still firm on her face, I pushed it back to grip the nape of her neck. My other hand was anchored on top of the porch swing. I leaned in slowly, letting the heat from her breath guide me. And the instant my lips brushed against hers, I was overcome with a feeling I had never known.

Her lips were softer than I had imagined them—sweeter, yet the seconds ticked by unbearably fast. I craved more, but I wouldn't take advantage of this moment, this rare vulnerability she had shown me. I broke away, planting my lips firmly against her forehead instead. I let my heart rate level out again before I spoke the words that rang in my head like an anthem.

"*I want you*, Charlie."

Chapter Eighteen

Charlie

Disoriented, I flailed my arm onto my nightstand, whacking my phone to the floor with a bang.

What day is it? What time is it?

I reached for my phone; my alarm playing some annoying country song that Briggs must have set last night. *Had it really only been six hours ago that we had been sitting on the porch swing together?*

I smiled then, remembering our kiss.

And what a kiss it had been.

I bit my lip in silent appreciation. I hadn't expected anything like that to happen last night: Briggs leaving the station early, the conversation about mama, the kiss—all of it seemed like a distant dream.

But it hadn't been a dream.

The kiss had been far too short, but wonderfulness can happen in less than ten seconds—this I knew firsthand. He had been so gentle, so tender, so kind. Just thinking about it made the butterflies take flight in the base of my belly again.

And then I remembered something else.

The words. *His* words.

"I want you, Charlie."

We had sat in silence for several minutes as I let his statement soak into my bones. There was so much I wanted to say to him—yet the emotional toll of my day had left me utterly spent. Briggs must have felt my exhaustion because without another word, he pulled me to him, putting his arm around my shoulders while he rocked us both on the swing.

Yes, there was more to be said, but midnight on the day of my would-be-wedding, was probably not the best timing for that conversation. It was simply enough to know that there was more, that possibly *we* were more.

I climbed into the shower, the steam and heat easing my tired muscles. I closed my eyes as I stood underneath the hard stream hitting my shoulders, neck and scalp. I reached for my body wash. I laughed as I squeezed the peach creamy-substance into my hand, remembering something Briggs had said before I turned in for the night.

He had sighed deeply, leaving me to believe that something profound would follow such a pensive act, but instead he asked why I always smelled like peaches. I, of course, told him that it was my natural scent, and that he shouldn't be jealous that he wasn't born with one. He had laughed, even though it was a blatant lie on my part. The truth was, that Briggs smelled like the log cabin my parents owned on Lake Owens. He smelled like natural comfort.

In the early hours of the morning, Briggs had talked a lot about Cody, what it had been like to watch Angie raise him from a newborn in the home they had shared for the first few years of his life. He told stories of him as a toddler and of the funny things he had said as a child. But what struck me the most was the undercurrent of what he didn't say. There was no question how much Briggs loved the boy, but I sensed there was something deeper than the typical bond shared between uncle and nephew. And then I knew.

Cody represented hope.

My heart had tugged at that revelation.

We had both lived in homes where hope did not exist, where love did not abound. I knew without asking that he wanted Cody to have the life that he didn't. I would want the same if he were my nephew.

Tori had invited Briggs and I out to her parent's house for Sunday brunch today—which in Texas, ultimately meant attending a church service together first, but after Briggs was called into work Friday night, I assumed the plans were off. Kai had assumed otherwise.

Kai texted late last night letting us know we were both still welcome and that he hoped to see us in the morning. I had to admit, it did sound fun, but going anywhere with Briggs sounded fun to me. I wore my sleeveless, blue wrap dress, which tied at my hip and slipped on my wedged heels. I left my hair down, letting the waves dry naturally as I applied my makeup.

As I walked down the stairs I could hear him in the house, smelling the brewed coffee.

“Hey there, good morning,” I said, as I rounded the corner from the stairs into the hall.

His back was to me as he poured a cup of coffee, glancing over his shoulder to smile at me. My stomach dropped.

That smile should be illegal.

“Good morning to you, Shortcake. Ready to go?”

“Yes, I’m ready.”

Chapter Nineteen

Briggs

Tuesday. Tuesday. Tuesday.

My heart seemed to pulse the word over and over on repeat, bringing a new round of torture as I counted the minutes. I had to tell her soon. My every thought was one I wanted to say aloud, but more than ever I wanted to do it right—for Charlie's sake. If that meant waiting a couple more days so I could talk to Chief, I would do that.

I could live for days on the memory of that kiss alone.

As I watched her sip her coffee with those same sweet lips I had felt against mine last night, I hoped they would be the only lips I would ever kiss.

Did I really just think that?

And yet I knew what the answer was without a second thought. Imagining any other woman in my future made my heart recoil. Charlie was my one in six billion.

On the other hand, picturing *her* with anyone else would make waterboarding seem like a pleasant way to spend my eternity.

Just two more days.

I had pulled grown men from burning buildings, rescued children from twisted metal prisons after car-accidents, and defended Angie from her abuser. I could wait until Tuesday.

"So since I finished up at the office last week, I'm gonna stay home tomorrow so I can clean and grocery shop before my folks get back. They fly in late afternoon I think, so I want everything to be ready for them."

"Oh, okay…that's a good plan," I said, thinking it would also give me one less day to screw up before I talked with Chief, "I start on rotation again tomorrow."

"Oh, okay," she said.

We both took a deep breath.

"Yeah," I added absently.

It was weird to think about not working at the station with Charlie anymore, or going days at a time where I wouldn't get to see her, or nights that I wouldn't get to watch her walk inside her house, or mornings that I wouldn't get to make her coffee.

The *new* normal we had created was coming to an end—correction, it already had. Tomorrow would solidify that truth even more.

"So when do you think you'll move back…to your old place?" she asked, pulling me from my thoughts.

"I should probably do that later this evening since I'll be at the station till Wednesday night. Good thing I really only have a couple of duffle bags to pack."

She sat quietly, as if lost in a thought land far away—maybe it was the same land I had just visited.

"Hey," I said, reaching across the seat for her hand. She looked over at me, "Nothing's going to change but our schedules, Charlie. We're friends. You can't get rid of me that easily."

The word betrayed me as I spoke it, but I couldn't say more—not yet. She nodded and smiled at me briefly, but there was something in her eyes that told me she wasn't exactly satisfied by my declaration.

I took another deep breath.

Tuesday. Tuesday. Tuesday.

Charlie

Kai and Tori saved us seats at church, and next to them were a row of people who seemed just as excited to see us, though I had no idea who they were. Tori introduced them as her family members. Her parents, her sister, her brother in-law and then the cutest baby girl I had ever laid eyes on.

"Oh my gosh, she is adorable! Tori, is this Kailynn—your flower girl?" I asked, letting the little princess grab my finger and shake it over and over.

"Yes, isn't she sweet?" Tori asked, kissing her on the head as she held her.

"That doesn't even begin to describe her…wow. I will have to become best friends with your sister so I might get a chance to get on the babysitting list," I said.

Stacie laughed and reached around Tori to touch my shoulder as she spoke.

"Charlie, you're welcome to hang out with Kailynn and I anytime…we usually start our day together around four a.m., so believe me, when I say anytime, I really mean it," Stacie said dramatically.

I laughed hard as Tori rolled her eyes. I was gonna enjoy getting to know her family. It was hard to believe that in just two weeks I would be with them all again on Tori's big day.

We slipped into our seats. Briggs was at the end of the row while I sat in between him and Tori. I looked down at our aisle and my heart warmed. *Is this what it feels like to have a big family?*

The band that played was awesome. I was easily distracted by how in-sync they were, watching each other's movements, following and transitioning flawlessly to each new song. It was impressive. As my emotions started to rise to the surface, a rogue thought forced its way in.

"But there are other instruments, which were only ever meant to stand alone, to solo. We, unfortunately, both fall into that latter category, Charlie. And two solo instruments should never share the stage."

I hated that statement.

I hated even more that I had memorized it. That it haunted me the same way mama did—lurking in some dark corner of my mind. I didn't want to be a solo instrument for the rest of my life. I didn't want to be alone.

I wanted *this.*

I looked down the aisle again at the row of family and friends, and then to my right at Briggs. *How does Briggs see me? Like a shiny, solo instrument, or as one that could compliment?*

Our uncomfortable conversation in the truck came back to my mind then as the congregation continued to sing. He was moving out…tonight. I knew it was coming, obviously. But deep in my core was the building of a feeling that I wasn't going to be able to shake off anytime soon. Yes, I wanted to let things progress naturally, I had made a commitment to myself to never again force my hand in a relationship, but what if…what if natural only turned out to be *friends*?

He had called us that just this morning.

But he had kissed me—told me that he wanted me just last night.

That lone argument quickly became too weak to combat the doubts that started rolling in faster than I could push them away. The over-thinking, over-analyzing female in me started to question—everything. He had kissed me on what could have been my most vulnerable moment to-date, on a very vulnerable night. What if it wasn't meant to be romantic at all? What if the real reason he didn't say more last night after our kiss was because he didn't have anything more to say?

Maybe he was only trying to comfort me, show me compassion after I had just revealed the ugly truth about my mama and Alex.

Another thought hit me then, plunging my new conclusions ever deeper into the well of assumption.

I could not recall even one time when Briggs had complimented my appearance. Other than his abrasive comments about my leggings, I had no memory to prove he was even remotely attracted to me. He had never used words like beautiful or pretty with me—he hadn't even said the one that I considered to be the most pitiful of them all: *Cute.*

There was nothing to recall—that cold revelation was like a slap to the face.

He didn't see me that way. He didn't see me the way I saw him.

Oh gosh. I've been such an idiot.

The surge of insecurity pumping through my body had raised my sensitivity meter to an all-time high. *How could I have thought there was something more between us? I hadn't been paying attention…I had only been thinking of my feelings for him—not the other way around.*

I jumped at the sound of Brigg's voice in my ear. "You alright?"

I nodded absently, smiling. He did not look convinced, but re-directed his focus once again to the front. I did the same.

Briggs

"I hope you'll join us today," Mrs. Sales—Tori's mother said after the service.

"Well, let me double check with my Activities Director, but I think that is still the plan. She seems to be ogling your grandbaby at the moment," I said.

She looked toward where Charlie was standing, "Tori tells me how talented your girlfriend is at the piano, she was just overjoyed when Charlie agreed to compose her processional," Mrs. Sales said.

At the word *girlfriend* my mind sharpened instantly.

Tuesday. Tuesday. Tuesday.

"Oh…we're not…uh, it's not that way with us. We're friends," I smiled awkwardly, but knew if I didn't address her error now it would likely come up at lunch in front of the entire family later.

The attractive older woman in front of me raised her eyebrows and lowered her voice as she said, "Well, you could have fooled me."

You and me both lady—especially on nights when I'm kissing her!

I smiled and told her I would confirm lunch with Charlie before exiting the conversation. I turned to where Charlie was standing in a group with Stacie and Tori—talking baby lingo. She was currently kissing the chubby cheeks of the four-month-old.

I am not jealous of that baby.

I am not jealous of that baby.

I am not jealous of that baby.

"Hey," I said, breaking my mental rant as I approached them.

"Hey yourself," Charlie replied, never diverting her gaze from the baby.

"Are you still good with going to lunch at the Sales-," I started.

"Ha! We were just talking about that. I figured since she said yes, you were likely on board too—like a package deal, right?" Stacie asked, her voice surprisingly loud for indoors.

I laughed. "Who wouldn't want to be shrink-wrapped next to this cute little pixie?" I said, nudging Charlie who was now standing at full attention, her face turning a shade of dark pink.

Huh? What did I say?

Both Stacie and Tori laughed, but Charlie's face stayed frozen—mortified at something. Her pink cheeks grew darker.

Recover!

"Uh, yes, I'm game if you are, Charlie," I said.

She nodded, while averting her gaze back to the baby.

I looked back to Tori, "We'll meet you there."

"Sounds great," Tori and Stacie said in unison as they broke away from the pod we'd formed in the lobby.

I couldn't get a read on Charlie's face before she had turned and walked toward the parking lot.

Urgh...Women!

****

A full five minutes had ticked by without any talking as we drove.

This was not the usual comfortable silence we shared; this was like breathing in paint fumes—pretty noticeable.

"So," I began, "Correct me if I'm wrong here, but am I getting the silent treatment right now?"

"You don't ask someone who's giving the silent treatment if they're giving the silent treatment. That's like asking an opera singer if they are going to use vibrato," she said flatly.

"Oh…well, I guess you're talking *now*, so let's hear it. Why are you ticked at me? Why did you turn all shades of red back there?"

She turned toward the window, staring out. I thought I was going to have to come up with another way to crack her, when she finally opened her mouth and spoke.

"I was embarrassed, Briggs," she said softly.

"I gathered that much…but why? I don't understand. Did I say something wrong? You reacted like I called you an ugly green ogre or something."

She sat quietly, something I wasn't used to from her.

I searched the files of my socially-lacking man brain, desperate for some clues to tell me what I was missing. *Blank*. That's what beamed back at me when I double-checked the folder labeled *Women*.

"Charlie…help me out here, *please*," I said, trying to control the frustration that was leaking into my voice.

"Your joke, Briggs—it just made me feel...young."

What? Okay, I understand women so much less than I thought I did.

My mouth hung open. I had no words—like nothing. I blinked several times trying to form a cognitive thought so I could rebut her statement. It was then I remembered debate class—one of the only classes I didn't fail in high school. We would start by reiterating the other team's argument. That was the best plan I had—or really the only plan I had.

"Charlie, you're saying that my joke about shrink-wrapping you made you feel…*young*?" I asked, testing the waters cautiously even though everything in me wanted to laugh at the ridiculous question I had just asked.

"No."

I took a deep breath, replaying her previous words in my head again.

"Um…that I agreed we were a packaged deal?" I tried again.

"No!" she said, looking at me like I was the crazy one.

But that's when a light bulb went off. What had I called her—*a cute little pixie*?

"I embarrassed you by calling you a cute little pixie?" I asked, watching her shoulder drop in confirmation. "Charlie, I didn't mean anything by it. You know I don't actually think you're a pixie, right?"

She turned her head sharply, "I couldn't care less if you thought I was a pixie or a sprite or even a zombie, but I don't want to be *cute*, Briggs. I'm a grown woman—I may be shorter than most sixth grade boys, but I don't want to be cute. That term is reserved for children with pigtails and missing front teeth." She said pointed to her mouth.

That's what she thinks? That I see her as cute?

I turned off the two-lane highway that led to Middleton, pulling onto the shoulder. She jumped in her seat, looking at me like I was some kind of crazy ax-murder. I wasn't. I was just a man on a mission.

"Get out, please," I said.

"What? What are you doing, Briggs?" she asked folding her arms over her chest.

"Get out, *please*," I said, again.

She huffed, stepping out of the vehicle. I came around to her side as she tried to find her footing in the gravel, which proved difficult in those tall cork-like heels she had on.

I stood in front of her.

"Have I ever told you a lie?" I asked her.

She looked up at me, startled. Her arms gesturing to the sky as she answered.

"How would I know the answer to that?"

"Do you *think* I have ever lied to you, Charlie?"

"No," she said, taking a deep breath, "I don't think you've ever lied to me."

"I can promise you that I have never told you a lie—other than my slight misleading about Cody's birthday party," I said firmly.

"Okay?" Her eyes were narrowed, waiting with confused concentration.

I took one step toward her.

"You are, without a doubt, the most beautiful woman I have ever known—outside, inside, every side. You're beautiful when you laugh, when you cry, when you rage, and when you sleep. You're beautiful from sunrise to sunset, and each moment in between," I said, taking a step closer to her as she leaned against my truck door, "When I watched you play the piano, I couldn't even *define* that kind of beauty, and it was right in front of me. I have said it a thousand times in my head Charlie, but I could say it all day long and it still wouldn't make it any less true. *You* are beautiful."

TUESDAY!

TUESDAY!

TUESDAY!

Charlie

I leaned against the cool metal of the door behind me as if willing it to help me stand—or keep me standing. I wasn't sure which. I swallowed hard, searching his face, his eyes, his mouth. I could feel the heat flash up through my chest and into my cheeks again, but embarrassment was no longer at the cause.

Briggs was.

He stood only inches away from me now, but we both seemed frozen.

"Do you believe me?" His voice was husky yet soft, breaking the spell between us.

I nodded.

"Good," he looked down at his feet, "I think we should probably get up to the house before they send out a search party."

I nodded again.

It was the first time in the month I had known Briggs that he didn't open my door for me. Instead, he took a step back, waiting for me to climb in. *Was he afraid to get close to me?* He walked around the back of his truck, taking his time before joining me again in the cab.

Am I still breathing?

I honestly wasn't sure.

Chapter Twenty

Briggs

"This can't be just one house, can it?" Charlie asked, walking up the driveway.

"Well, I guess that's completely relative to how one defines *house.* To the Prince of Persia, this is a house…yes," I said, watching Charlie's eyes grow wide as she took it all in.

The Sales Estate was massive. They had something like twenty-plus acres, a driving range, a pool, a spa, and patios on every side. This was a house built for entertainment, and that was what the Sales did best: Entertain. I had been to Kai and Tori's engagement party here, as well as a fundraising event for some charity or another. Both those events had been first class—no doubt about it. Before we made it to the front door, Stacie was there, ushering us in with exuberance.

"Hey ya'll! Come on in—Briggs, the guys are out back. Charlie you can come with me to the kitchen, we're just going over some last minute details for the wedding before we serve lunch," Stacie said, pulling on Charlie's arm.

I felt like we had just been ambushed by the paparazzi—only it was just Stacie. Not a single camera to be found. I was certain now that this woman did not have an *inside* voice. Instinctively, I pulled back on Charlie's arm, caught off guard by our forced and immediate separation. Charlie looked at me, shrugging her shoulders and giving me her most endearing smile.

Reluctantly, I let her go.

"Relax, Briggs, you'll get her back," Stacie said, looking over her shoulder at me. Her arm was already looped through Charlie's as they headed to some unknown location, away from where I stood.

"Okay…" I mumbled to myself, before tuning into my testosterone radar and seeking out the man-hideaway location.

****

The three men: Tori's Dad—Richard, Tori's brother-in-law—Jack, and Kai, were all outside, standing around a large stainless steel grill. The outdoor kitchen was massive and I was sure that the grill could easily handle several hundred pounds of steak at one time. It was impressive.

"Hey there, Briggs, glad you could join us today," Richard said, giving me a hard pat on the arm as I approached them.

"Thanks for the invite. I never pass up a good steak," I said.

"You never pass up free food *period*," Kai laughed.

I shrugged. It was true.

"So, is everything confirmed for the bachelor party this weekend?" Jack asked me.

"Yep, and I have a few more things up my sleeve, too." I said, smiling.

"Good…we'll have to connect on those later," Jack said.

Kai was totally in the dark when it came to the upcoming weekend, which was exactly how I wanted it.

"Why do I have the feeling that I'm going to regret asking either of you to be in my wedding after this weekend?" Kai asked, looking at each of us with raised eyebrows.

"Brother, you can *regret* all you want, it won't change a thing I have planned, though!" I laughed.

Richard laughed as he poked at the sizzling meat and Kai smiled, shaking his head as he turned toward the grill.

I could hear the cackling of a sinister villain inside my head.

Next weekend will be memorable—no doubt about it.

Charlie

"Do you want to hold her?" Stacie asked as she took Kailynn out of the travel crib she had been sleeping in.

"Yes, please!" I said, holding out my arms to take her from Stacie. "I don't think I'll want to give her back though."

"Oh you will, believe me. That girl has a hunger-awareness cry like no baby I've ever heard. She'll let everyone in a three-block radius know when it's time to eat," Stacie laughed.

I followed her into the kitchen and snuggled Kailynn closer to me, wrapping her soft pink blanket around her little bare legs. Stacie must have taken off her pink tights, but she was still in her Sunday dress. I smiled at her as she reached her hand toward my mouth, trying to curl her fingers around my bottom lip. I could have melted right then. I laughed, kissing her tiny fingers.

The women were on some tangent about the food tent rental, but I was in my own world swinging my hips from side to side, bouncing slightly to keep the giggles from Kailynn coming. She obviously loved movement. Every once and a while, Tori's mom, Lucina, would glance over at me and ask my thoughts on the matter, but I never offered an opinion. If I said anything, I would simply reiterate what Tori had already expressed. I knew better than to go against the bride.

Regardless, Lucina was likely to get her way in the end. Tori looked up at me, diverting from the tent conversation entirely.

"So Charlie, Tori told me that you're finished with the processional piece, is that correct, darling?" Lucina asked me.

"Yes, I just finished it a few days ago," I said smiling.

"Oh, that's fantastic! I hope you'll do us the honor today and play it for us? We have a piano in the den just off the dining room."

I froze, I hadn't prepared for that—I hadn't even played it for Tori yet. But again, Lucina's face suggested that *no* wasn't really an option.

"I um, I was hoping I could get Tori's feedback first before I played it for anyone else," I said politely, switching Kailynn to rest on my other arm.

"Tori you don't mind, do you dear?"

Tori searched my face as if gauging my response.

"I would love to hear it today, Charlie, but if you're uncomfortable with that then we can wait and do it privately later this week like we had planned," Tori suggested.

I smiled at her thoughtfulness, but I could see the excitement on her face.

"Okay, should I play it after lunch?" I asked the group.

"Yes, please!" Lucina said, offering me a shoulder squeeze and a kiss on the cheek.

I flushed at the sudden attention shift. Though I had performed for hundreds of people, it was the small, intimate gatherings that sent my anxiety soaring.

****

Lunch was served outside under a canopy on one of the many decks that wrapped around the house. I offered to hold Kailynn so that Stacie and Jack could enjoy their meal. I would rather hold a baby than eat any day of the week. She had fallen asleep in my arms and Stacie told me that I was quickly making my way to the top of the babysitter list. I smiled.

I sat next to Briggs as I continued to slowly rock the baby in my arms. He kept adding things to my plate even after I had scolded him to stop. He paid no attention to my pleas, however. As the meal came to an end, Stacie started to reminisce about some wedding tablecloth fiasco at her and Jack's wedding. The table roared with laughter at her dramatics. She had quite a way of telling stories. Apparently, a few wrongly marked receipts had nearly meant her island themed wedding reception would have sported Beeswax yellow tablecloths instead of the Bahaman Blue she had ordered.

I was so caught up listening to Stacie that I didn't notice Briggs at my ear until he spoke, goose bumps pricking my arms immediately.

"You need to eat, Shortcake."

I looked at him, scrunching up my face in rebellion. He raised his eyebrows in a silent challenge. Before I knew it, his arms came underneath mine, scooping Kailynn onto his chest in one smooth movement. I bit back a smile at the sight.

"Baby thief," I whispered.

He winked at me, gesturing toward my plate again with a nod of his head. I picked up my fork and knife, mumbling just loud enough for him to hear, "And a food pusher, too."

The quiet rumble of his laugh shot flames through my chest, and I could not hold back my smile any longer.

Briggs

After clean up—which I was excused from on account of the sleeping baby in my arms—Lucina directed everyone to the music den. Stacie took Kailynn from me, claiming she would be screaming in a matter of minutes, demanding to be fed.

I saw Charlie trailing behind the group at a very slow pace. She had smoothed out the front of her wrinkle-free dress a dozen times in the last thirty seconds. I reached for her arm and pulled her back a bit, out of earshot.

"Hey…you alright?" I asked, keeping my voice low.

"Yeah, it's just nerves, I guess."

As dense as it might be, I was stunned by her answer. I said as much.

"Nerves? You're kidding me, right?"

She rolled her eyes and huffed, trying to break away from my grasp. I didn't budge.

"You wouldn't understand—just let me go."

Nice one, Briggs. Way to show your support.

"Hey, that's not what I meant. I'm sorry. It's just surprising to me that someone with you kind of talent would still get nervous. You're brilliant, Charlie; don't let yourself think any differently, okay?" I said.

"My nerves are worse when I play for smaller crowds. It just feels a lot more exposing to me than when I play at larger venues."

I realized then that I didn't even know half of what Charlie had done with her talent. We had talked quite a bit about her schooling and scholarship details, but I knew very little about her future dreams and goals regarding piano.

Why hadn't we talked about that? I made a mental note to ask her—soon.

I hugged her tight, pulling away to rest my hand on her shoulder a few seconds later, "Whether you notice it or not, it's that exposure that draws us in when you play, Shortcake. It's captivating."

Her eyes smiled at me as she bit her bottom lip. *How can I not kiss her when she looks at me like that?*

As I leaned close, drawn in by some unforeseen force, I heard the loud clearing of a throat behind me.

Kai.

"Sorry…but the natives are getting restless in here," Kai asked, avoiding my eyes, "We still on for the mini concert, Charlie?"

"Yes, absolutely," Charlie answered, slipping out from under my arm.

I leaned my forehead against wall with a thump, rededicating myself again to my previous resolve.

"Tuesday?" Kai asked, empathetically.

"Yeah…Tuesday," I grumbled.

Kai chuckled and together we walked into the music den.

Charlie

My palms were clammy as I rested them on top of the cool keys.

This piano was a dream. It was a full grand—ivory in color. It was unparalleled to any I had played before, including those at the finest auditoriums and concert halls I had preformed in. This was a rare gift—to play an instrument of this caliber. I took in a deep breath as I saw Briggs walk into the room. My heart was instantly torn between elation and calm at the sight of him. I mouthed the words *thank you*, as our eyes met.

What he told me in the hallway I wouldn't soon forget.

I began.

The deep notes of the baseline announced that something significant was about to commence, followed by the smooth careful wanderings of the treble soon after. Then it was time for the unique melody that would accompany the bride's walk. I closed my eyes, focusing all my passion, all my joy, all my heart into those last few measures. I could feel the intensity of the room's gaze on me, yet my nerves had all but disappeared. As the last note resonated off the walls, I lifted my head and drew back my foot from the sustain pedal. Richard stood from his seat on the sofa and started to clap.

Within seconds, everyone was on their feet, clapping. My face flushed at the response, but I couldn't help but glance at Tori. She was the opinion I valued most at the moment. From her eyes streamed tears that she didn't try to wipe away. Her smile was beautiful. Before I could get up from the bench, she sat down next to me and put her arms around my shoulders, hugging me tight.

"Thank you, Charlie. That was beyond anything I could have hoped for."

I felt my eyes grow damp at the joy in her voice.

That was the only form of payment I would ever need from my music: *Happiness*.

****

After desert was served, the men went out to the driving range while the women sat outside, soaking in the sunshine. I was grateful for my short dress as I stretched my legs out, exposing them to the glorious rays—it was heavenly.

Tori put a ban on all "wedding talk" for the rest of the afternoon. Lucina and Stacie seemed at a loss for words at first, but Tori kept right on talking as if it didn't faze her in the slightest. The more time I spent with her, the more I liked her.

"So, when are you planning to go back to Austin?" Tori asked, adjusting her sunglasses while leaning back onto the lounge chair.

"I am not exactly sure. The term ends in a couple of weeks and I was originally thinking of doing some make-up work over the summer—taking a few classes at least, but I'm not sure now."

The truth was I didn't want to go back early anymore. I didn't know what was going to happen with Briggs and I, but I wasn't looking forward to leaving him. He had quickly become my closest friend.

"Hmm...*that* wouldn't have anything to do with a certain fireman would it? Because if so, you should know that he's currently making his way over here," Stacie cooed.

My head shot up with a snap. The movement startled Tori and she did the same. We both looked at each other and started laughing. Tori shook her head at Stacie, as if to silence her. It worked. *Thank goodness.*

"Hey there, did you know it's after five already?" Briggs asked me.

No way! Had we really been here all day?

"Oh my gosh! I had no idea it was so late. I hope we haven't overstayed-"

"Are you kidding? You're a hoot, Charlie. Please come back soon!" Stacie said.

"Yes, absolutely. I can't tell you how much we've enjoyed your company today, and also your talent," Lucina said before turning to Briggs, "And it's always a pleasure when you're around, Briggs."

"You don't know him that well then, Mom," Tori said, throwing her arms out instantly as if to block Brigg's retaliation. She slapped his hands away from her as he laughed.

Tori stood up from her chair a second later as Kai walked over. He wrapped his arms around her waist from behind, resting his head on her shoulder. "You gals enjoying yourselves out here?"

"Yes, it's been a great day," I answered, as Briggs held his hand out to me, pulling me up from my comfortable sunbaked coma.

"Please thank your husband again for the excellent steaks, and thank you for your hospitality today Mrs. Sales," Briggs said to Lucina.

After our goodbyes were said, Tori walked with me to the driveway, holding me back slightly as Briggs kept on toward the truck.

"Charlie, I know I've said thank you a hundred times today for the song, but truly I'm so touched that you wrote that for me, and so is Kai. I also wanted to tell you," she paused, as if hesitant to continue, "if you ever find yourself in need of a friend—for however long you're here in Dallas, or even after you move back to Austin, I'd love the chance to get to know you better."

Her smile was so sincere, I felt as if I might cry for the second time today because of her words to me. I knew she meant them.

"Thank you, I'd love to get to know you better, too. I could use a girlfriend," I said.

"Good…then it's settled. I'll give you a call this week. I'm sure I'll need to escape the wedding planner twins in there."

I laughed, I'm sure she was right.

Briggs pulled his truck up. With one last hug, I said goodbye to Tori. I could hardly remember a time my heart had felt so full.

Briggs

"Do you need any help getting your things out of the apartment?" Charlie asked.

"No, I can handle it."

The last thing I needed was to be alone with Charlie in that apartment.

I'm losing my ever-loving mind and we're inside a three-thousand square foot house!

"Oh okay, well if you're sure," she said, shrugging her shoulders.

"Yep, I'm good. Thanks."

Her hair was up in some top-knot looking thing, and she was in yet another pair of flannel pants again—those *irresistible* flannel pants. Charlie was working on a list of what she needed to get from the store before her parents arrived home tomorrow. She was expecting them around four in the afternoon, coming directly from the airport. She opened and closed the fridge door multiple times, comparing items on her list with those that were still in stock. Each time she matched an item to her list, she made a clucking sound with her tongue, before sliding back across the tile floor in her socks.

It was adorable.

Did I seriously just think the word adorable?

Someone needs to knock me out.

"Okay, Charlie. I should probably start packing."

"You're not up for one more season of *The Office*?" she asked glancing up from her list, smiling at me like some sort of she-devil.

"A *season*?" I laughed, apologetically. "No, Shortcake. I can't tonight. I need to go in early before my shift starts tomorrow, I'm sure there are a lot of things that need to be done before your dad gets back. Plus, I have a mound of laundry waiting for me at my place."

She stuck out her bottom lip and sighed.

You're killing me, Charlie.

"Alright…who knew you were such a domestic bore?"

She couldn't even get the phrase out without busting-a-gut laughing.

"Didn't anyone ever tell you that laughing at your *own joke* makes it way less funny?" I asked, smirking at her.

"Didn't anyone ever tell *you* that it's a sour sport who can't take a joke?"

I laughed and headed toward the front door.

"I'll be back in a minute smarty pants. I'm gonna go pack…*alone*!"

"As you wish Sour-Sport-Sam!" she yelled.

I could still hear her laughing as I closed the front door and headed up to my apartment.

No, not my apartment anymore.

Charlie

I told myself I was fine—everything was fine.

Briggs was only going to be a few miles away. We were still going to see each other. We were friends—no matter what did or did not develop between us, he had said so himself.

But I wasn't fine.

I thought again about his declaration today in the middle of farm town USA as we stood on the side of a highway. *Who said that kind of thing?* Wasn't that only supposed to happen in romantic comedies and chick-flicks?

I flushed again as I thought about his words, *"I have said it a thousand times in my head Charlie, but I could say it all day long and it wouldn't make it any less true. You are beautiful."*

Not only did he say that I was beautiful, but that he had thought about me—a lot. My stomach fluttered as that realization sunk in. My mind and heart were so divided lately. I wanted to make sense of our relationship so I could justify the feelings that were quickly overtaking me, but I didn't know how to do that.

What I did know was simple, Briggs was everything Alex was not, which I was learning, was everything I truly wanted.

When I heard the slam of a truck door, a panic ripped through me, shocking me into action from the pensive stupor I was in. I had no thought; I just started moving—sliding actually—down the hall toward the front door, in my socks. I threw it open, barreling into the driveway, straight into the blackness of the night. My eyes had not fully adjusted to the dark when I hit something hard, briefly knocking me back.

"Dear Lord, Charlie. What on earth are you doing?" Briggs asked as he tried to steady us both. Apparently, I had collided smack into the center of his chest. He pulled his arms away after a second, breathing heavily from the impact.

I was breathing heavily too, but not from that.

"I thought…I thought you were leaving," I said sheepishly as I looked at the closed tailgate on his truck—the one we were standing right next to. *Oh, that's embarrassing.* His bags were inside, already loaded. I guess I hadn't heard the driver's side door after all, but it didn't make the sight any easier to take in.

He chuckled softly, yet there was no humor in it to detect. "And what? Not tell you I was going—really?"

I felt stupid. "My mistake?" I looked up at his face in the moonlight.

Wow, what a face it was, too.

We both fell silent as several seconds ticked by.

"So…" I began.

"So…" he repeated.

I didn't know why I did it exactly, but I regretted it instantly. My hand shot out in front of me, as if to *shake* goodbye. He looked down, staring at it like I had rabies. I pulled it back to my side again, awkwardly.

"It's been a good month, Manny. Thanks for everything." I was careful not to make eye contact. My throat felt tight as the burning sensation behind my eyes increased, I did my best to ignore them both.

Do not cry. Do not cry. Do not cry.

I'm being stupid!

I could feel his eyes on me, their intensity unrelenting. I bit the insides of my cheeks. Only once did I peek up at his face, and my suspicion was confirmed: I couldn't handle it.

Don't look.

"Shortcake, this *isn't* goodbye."

He made no move to touch me, yet I could feel the warmth radiating off of his body. It was as if his very nearness could smite any chill that tried to come for me. I needed that warmth; I needed him.

"Then, why does it feel like the family dog just died?" I asked.

He laughed, this time finding me funny. I knew the difference.

"Nothing has died, I can promise you that."

I smiled as I looked up at him again, internally scolding myself the instant our gazes locked, but this time I didn't pull my eyes away. This time, I was fairly sure it was physically impossible to do so.

Stupid. Stupid. Stupid.

"Maybe I can come by the station this week—bring you lunch sometime?"

"I'd like that," he said, "I always like to see you, Charlie."

My stomach was going insane, the dips and dives and flips and flops. It didn't even feel attached to my body anymore. It was its own entity now.

I took a deep breath. I had to get the words out quickly, or else the tears would come and I would never be able to say them. I had missed out on too many important goodbyes in my life, and I wasn't going to let this one slip through my fingers as well. So, I just began talking—quickly.

"Thank you for everything, Briggs, I mean it. You've been such a good friend to me and I didn't even know how much I needed that—a true friend, I mean. After Alex, I didn't think I'd ever be able to stop hurting, much less trust someone again. But you..."

I couldn't finish. The swollen lump in my throat inhibited the words that were trapped somewhere behind it. I swallowed again, trying to push the tightness away.

"Charlie...breathe. I'm not exiting your life, I'm just moving to the other side of Lincoln street...this is *not* goodbye. There are no last words you need to say tonight."

His hand gripped my arm lightly and I wanted to lean into it—to lean into him, but I didn't.

“Okay,” I said.

“Okay.”

“Can I…can I give you a hug as long as I don’t say goodbye?”

He laughed and pulled me into his body, which turned everything inside me to mush. But in a moment that came much too soon, he pushed me back gently. Surprisingly, my bones and muscles could still support the weight of my body. His hands found my face as he leaned in to press his lips to my forehead, lingering there for only a couple of heartbeats.

As he backed away toward the driver’s door, a look crossed his face that I hadn’t seen before.

“Charlie…it would be best if you never tell me Alex’s last name.”

A nervous bubble of laughter escaped my throat, but his look did not change.

“Oh. You’re serious.”

“As a heart attack.”

“Right, got it.”

“Good, now go inside and lock the door behind you, please. I’ll text you in a bit to say goodnight, but please promise me you’ll call if you need anything.”

I smiled, crossing my heart with my finger. “I promise.”

He nodded in silent approval before I turned and walked back inside the house, fighting the urge to chase after his truck when I saw his taillights reflecting in the windows.

Instead, I watched him drive away, a tortured smile planted on my face as I saw him turn off my street.

This isn’t goodbye.

Chapter Twenty-One

Briggs

My mental countdown was in full swing before my eyes had even cracked open, but luckily, the day proved busy. I had never been more grateful for *busy*.

There was not a surface that wasn't scrubbed, shined or polished—even the gym had been thoroughly cleaned by late afternoon on Monday. Though I had my own motivations for Chief's homecoming, we were all looking forward to his arrival at the station. He had been at this station for over twenty years, and acting as chief for twelve of that. Sure he was twice my age, but there was nothing *old* about the man. On several occasions he had proved his endurance was greater than any of the "young pups" he had hired. Nearly two years ago he had stood in a frigid lake with Kai, myself, and five other guys to see who could be the last one standing. The catch was we were only allowed to stand on one leg, while holding an America flag.

Chief won.

The rest of us had to do several laps in our boxers at midnight. Not the best time of my life, but a memorable one for sure.

The calls today had been non-stop. One middle school nearby had evacuated at lunch due to a pizza catching on fire in the school's old industrial oven. No one had been hurt, but the kitchen had extensive damage. I had also been called to a scene involving a motorcycle and telephone pole. I hated those calls. I had owned a motorcycle at one time, but I sold it within a few months of starting at the station.

Those are images that don't erase easily.

My phone buzzed.

Miss Strawberry Shortcake: Folks just got in. Kinda weird you're not here to hang out with us…but I'm sure you'll get your fill of my dad soon enough☺. Hope you're having a good day, and remember you promised to make those crepes again sometime for my family. My mom will freak out. Okay…babbling, I know. But is it really even called babbling if it's on a text? A question for heaven I suppose…five points to you though if you know the answer.

Me: Hmm…I feel honored you think me wise enough to contend with a question as significant as that one. I think the short answer is no, although my calculations are rocky at best. Day is simply going…wish I was there to hang out too, but alas, some of us must work for a living. I bet ten points that you just rolled your eyes at that? Am I right? Don't lie. Texting is like being under oath. Yes, I will make crepes again, but only if you promise to freak out over them again as well.

Miss Strawberry Shortcake: I feel it might be safer for me to believe it IS babbling, that way I have some sort of mental filter telling me to stop typing. Otherwise, these already ridiculously long texts could end up as a novella someday. And fine, I'll admit--ten points to you, but don't gloat. Gloaters are ugly. Lastly, if the term "under oath" is just a new way for you to play truth or dare…please note I will always choose dare.

Me: That, Shortcake, might just be the best information you've ever divulged about yourself.

Miss Strawberry Shortcake: Great :-) Folks want to chat. Ttyl…

Me: Count on it.

My day had just improved exponentially.

Charlie

As I sat outside on the patio with my parents, I felt an odd sense of relief. We hadn't parted ways on the best of terms, but that seemed a lifetime ago now. My dad's rough tan hand laid over mine as he smiled at me. I smiled back, genuinely.

"It's good to see you, sugar."

"It's good to see you too, Dad," I said before turning to look at my mother, "Mom, I've never seen you so tan before. You look beautiful."

My mom laughed softly, and shook her head at me. "Thank you." She studied me for a second, "You look different too, Charlie—you look…*happy*."

Her eyes glossed over with tears and she pursed her lips together.

"I feel happy, Mom." And it was the truth. I hadn't felt this happy in a very long time.

"So the month has been good to you?" my father asked.

"Yes...the month was very good to me."

And so was a certain hottie who lived above the garage.

We talked for hours, eating the ready-bake lasagna I had made for us. I looked at their pictures and heard some wonderful stories about their time in the Greek isles. Every once in awhile my mind would wander back to Briggs, but I tried to keep my focus on them. We had spent too much time *not* being a family over the last year, and I was ready for that to change.

They went to bed fairly early as their internal time clock was off, but I didn't mind. I texted with Briggs well into the night, my phone still in hand when my body finally surrendered itself to sleep.

Briggs

Chief had been in his office returning phone calls and emails for three hours and forty-seven minutes. Not that I was keeping track or anything.

Though guys had been popping in and out of there all morning, I waited for my turn—for the right moment.

When the door to his office opened around noon, I thought I was hearing things when my name reverberated off of the cement walls. Kai confirmed it wasn't my imagination though when he shot me a look that said *now's your time buddy*. I stood.

"Briggs? A word in my office, please," Chief said as I made my way to him.

My nerves were wreaking havoc on my insides.

"Have a seat," Chief said, sitting across from me at his desk. A large smile played on his face. I couldn't help but reciprocate it, even though I had no idea of his reason for it. I hadn't even told him I wanted to speak with him yet.

"Julie and I want to thank you Briggs, for staying at the house. We feel very grateful to you for paying us that favor. We wanted to give you this," Chief said, pushing a sealed envelope toward me. I looked at it and swallowed, my mind racing with ways to break into this conversation as smoothly as possible. "I also wanted to thank you for whatever you did to help Charlie."

At this I startled a bit. *Was it really going to be this easy?*

"Help her, sir?"

"Yes, she seems…very happy. We haven't seen her like that in quite a while. She said you've become good friends."

He smiled at me again. His words seemed genuine—honest. *Friendship* was what he thought had taken place over the last month, and to a large extent that was true, but there was definitely more to it than that. I took a deep breath, realizing that this was the moment to elaborate on what exactly that *more* was.

"She's become a good friend to me as well, Chief. I should be the one thanking you for the opportunity to get to know her. This last month has been one of the best months of my life," I said carefully. I pushed the envelope back toward him slowly.

Surprise filled his face as he stared at me.

I continued, "Sir, at first I thought I would simply act as a security guard around your house, but that's not how things progressed. We did become friends, but my feelings for her are much stronger than that now."

He leaned his elbows on the desk in front of him, supporting his weight. Clearly, he had not been anticipating this statement. He opened his mouth twice before any words came out.

"And what *are* your feelings for my daughter?"

"I'm in love with her, sir."

There might have been a nervous undertone to my previous statements, but not to this one.

This I knew.

Loving Charlie was like blood to my body, oxygen to my lungs. There was no doubt in this truth I claimed.

The Chief's eyes never left mine—nor did they blink. Only the sound of our breathing filled the office for what felt like an immeasurable amount of time. Finally, he broke the silence and stood, facing me.

"Charlie is a very unique woman, Briggs, but there is a history to her that you couldn't possibly-"

"She told me about the adoption, sir—and about her mama," I interrupted.

His eyebrows shot up, as if he was more shocked by that fact than my declaration of love for his daughter a minute prior.

"She…she told you?"

"Yes, we've talked quite a bit during these last four weeks," I replied.

He turned then toward the window and stared out. I remained seated.

"What is it you want, Briggs?" His voice was low, but stern.

"I want your blessing to date her. My intentions are honorable, sir, I can assure you. I have never felt this way for anyone…and I can promise you that I would cut off my own arm before I would hurt her in any way."

He seemed to consider my words before crossing his arms over his chest. He kept his eyes focused on something in the distance.

"Twenty-eight pounds."

"Excuse me, sir?" I asked, feeling like I must have heard him wrong.

"Charlie was twenty-eight pounds when she came to live with us—she was five." Emotion had crept into his tone, growing the knot at the base of my stomach. Charlie's neglect as a child made me physically ill to think about.

"When they went through the apartment she lived in…do you know what they found?"

I shook my head once.

"A half empty jar of peanut butter, a bread bag and an old box of stale Cheese-Its which mice had ravaged through. We've concluded that her grandfather was the one to drop off the food to her every other week or so, but she was severely malnourished and looked like she hadn't been bathed in a very long time, if ever. No one had cared for her, Briggs—no one before Julie and I. We were her emergency foster care placement. And even once she was safe in our house, she spent nearly two years sleeping under her bed. She didn't trust anyone, she had no reason to." He turned to me, a small lift at one side of his mouth, "I know this may be hard to believe, but she was a very quiet, withdrawn child. It took many hours of therapy before we realized that she was trapped inside a prison of guilt—believing that her mama's suicide was somehow her fault. "

I clenched my jaw over and over trying to rid my mind of the image of my beautiful Charlie as a broken, hurting child. I reminded myself that no one would ever hurt her in that way again. She was safe now; she was loved. Those reminders eased the pain in my chest momentarily.

I also knew that her adverse reaction to peanut butter wasn't an allergy.

Chief turned to me again, a new resolve filling his face.

"I cannot give you my blessing, Briggs."

The blood drained from my head, causing me to feel instantly disoriented as I struggled to comprehend his words. *No…no, this isn't right!*

"Sir, I know that I could never meet your standards for Charlie, I don't even pretend to meet my own standards for Charlie, but you must believe there is *nothing* I would deny her." I stood then, facing him head-on as my chest heaved with passion, "You were her rescue once—saving her from a fate worse than death. But she is my rescue *now*—breathing life into the places of my heart that were long ago dead. She *is* love to me."

He took a deep breath, staring down at his hands before making eye contact with me again. "Briggs…you are like a son to me. I have watched your life over this last year, and I feel nothing but pride when I look at you—when I think of how you've changed. So please, hear me when I say that this decision is *not* about you. This is about Charlie—what's best for her, and if you mean it when you say you love her, then you should want what's best for her, too." He pointed to the chair across from him, "Give me a chance to explain."

My heart was pounding as I took a seat for the second time.

"Alex was a wolf in sheep's clothing. I knew from the start that he would hurt her, but she wouldn't listen to me. I had never felt so helpless as a father—I was literally watching her self-destruct one day at a time. I wasn't surprised when he left her, but I was furious when he almost stole her future away from her, too. She doesn't have any more chances, Briggs—if she loses her scholarship, then she loses everything she has worked so hard for. Music is her future, it's her dream—I can't let her give up on that up now, not when she's so close…not even for you." He clasped his hands together before looking up at me again, "Have you heard her play?"

I nodded, my shoulders stiff with tension.

"Then you know what kind of talent she has. Alex almost ended that for her-"

"I. Am. Not. Alex!"

He lifted one palm in the air, as if to calm me, but I was far from calm.

"I realize that, but you must realize the distraction you would be to her, Briggs." He sighed. "What have you told her—about your feelings?"

I stared down at my fists. "Not much yet."

"Briggs…I think it's probably best that it stays that way."

I lifted my head up to meet his eyes again, "For how long?"

He took a deep breath. "Do you know why the Bible lists patience as the first virtue of love? Because it is usually the hardest one for us to endure. We always want what we want *right now*…but *now* is not always what's best for the other person. Charlie has three semesters left, can you really tell me that you would ask her to risk her talent and future elite opportunities because of your feelings? It takes hours and hours of daily discipline and focused dedication for her to master her skill. So you tell me, is satisfying your own desire to be with her *now* worth the sacrifice it could cost her later?"

I pushed my body back against the chair, raking my hands over my face and hair in utter frustration. *He's right.*

I hated how right he was.

"I'm not asking you to stop being her friend—she obviously values your friendship, Briggs, but encouraging anything else will compromise her heart…and yours."

"Mine's a lost cause already, sir."

"Then spare Charlie's."

I stood again, nodding as I turned to face the door behind me. A heavy hand fell on my shoulder as I grabbed the doorknob.

"I can't make you choose to do what's right for her, Briggs, but I hope you will."

A random thought occurred to me then. "I've asked her as my date to the wedding…"

He nodded in what seemed to be approval. "I don't want to control her life, Briggs, I only want her to preserve her future. "

"Yes, sir."

I might have nodded before closing the door behind me, but I couldn't be sure, all I knew was that in less than a minute I was in the gym. I pushed every thought away before dressing down into my shorts.

Thinking hurt too much.

I wrapped my knuckles on autopilot as I stood before the black leather bag. The only cope for this kind of pain was physical exhaustion, and that was exactly what I intended to get to.

Chapter Twenty-Two

Charlie

It was just after 1:30 when I arrived at the station. Briggs hadn't responded yet to my text about bringing lunch by today, but I figured he was out on a call. I could wait if that was the case. I had spent the morning working on some old compositions before helping my mom unpack and fold laundry. I was grateful to be out of the house for a bit.

And I missed Briggs already.

There were only a couple guys in the dining hall, one I recognized as Evan, the other I had only been introduced to once. I couldn't recall his name. After a short greeting, I made my way back to my father's office. His smile was warm as he hugged me. I put the bag of food down in front of him.

"Oh wow, thank you, sugar. I think after today though I need to go on a strict salad-only diet. My pants are fitting a little too snug these days…"

"I told you, Dad. Cruise food does that to the best of folks," I laughed.

"Do I get the privilege of eating with you today?"

"Uh…well, I was planning on seeing Briggs, too. I got him something from Fifth Street Café as well. He loves that place."

His face held an interesting mix of emotions when I mentioned Briggs' name. Last night he had seemed delighted by our friendship, but today I sensed something else. *Was it hesitation? Strange.*

"Is he here?" I asked.

He didn't look at me as he opened his to-go bag. "I am honestly not sure where he is at the moment. I know several trucks are out, but I'm not sure about Briggs."

I narrowed my eyes at him. *Is he acting weird? Or am I reading into something that isn't there?*

"Is…everything okay, Dad?"

He looked up at me then, a reassuring smile filling his face.

"Yes, darling. Everything is fine. Why don't you tell me more about the piece you composed for Kai's wedding while you're here? You never finished that story last night."

I felt something ease in my chest as I sat down to fill him in on the processional for Kai and Tori's wedding. I knew Briggs would eat this food no matter what time of day it was, so I felt alright about taking a few extra minutes to chat with my dad. He seemed pleased that I did. He thanked me for the all the work I had done in his absence, especially the ruthless data-entry and filing. It warmed my heart to hear the pride back in his voice again when he spoke to me. It had been quite a while since I had heard that.

It felt nice to be home with him.

Briggs

"I'm not in the mood, Kai," I said through clenched teeth as I did another sequence of uppercuts.

I had seen him standing in the far corner of the gym watching me, but I wasn't about to break concentration. If I didn't concentrate on this, it would mean having to concentrate on something else. I couldn't deal with that something else quite yet.

"It would appear that way," Kai said, "why do you think I'm standing *over here*?"

I didn't respond.

My combinations were second nature; the flurried punches would have made my old sensei proud.

One. Five. Three. One. Two. Four. One.

One. Five. Three. One. Two. Four. One.

One. Five. Three. One. Two. Four. One.

"What are you gonna do, Briggs?" Kai asked, his voice laced with concern.

I stopped the bag, breathing hard as I steadied my body. Sweat poured onto the floor from my face and arms.

"This better not be some kind of early intervention plan, Kai. I'm not going to start drinking again…or anything else, so can you just lay off me for five minutes?"

I started the sequence again.

He walked closer, "That's not what I'm asking and you know it."

With a powerful blow I sent the bag spinning. Kai caught it with both hands.

I crossed my arms and rested them on top of my head, catching my breath. My body throbbed from exertion, but I was not nearly exhausted enough to forget the knife that was lodging itself deeper into my heart with each passing second.

"Ultimately, he made the decision mine…but there is no choice. If I love her, then I have to choose her first. He's right about that. And choosing Charlie means..."

"That you won't allow her to choose you." Kai finished my sentence, rubbing the back of his neck with his hand, exhaling loudly. "So you're not going to tell her, then—not anything at all?"

I snapped my head back in his direction, "Don't you think I *want* to? It's all I've thought about for weeks!" I exhaled, "But he's right…it will only make things more difficult if I do. I don't know how she feels about me, but I don't want to lose her—even if friendship is all we have."

I could see a mirror of pain staring back at me. Kai understood this kind of pain; he had gone through it not too long ago himself. Only now he was on the other side of that great divide. I couldn't be sure a similar fate awaited Charlie and me. "Love is patient, Briggs. It waits for us, even when we can't see how it will."

I was beginning to hate that phrase, yet even as he said it, I could feel a tiny spark of hope.

"I don't think today could have gone any worse."

Kai chuckled at that, "Oh it could have, go read the story of Jacob and Rachel. That poor guy had to spend seven years doing slave labor for his future father-in-law to earn his blessing, only to be given the wrong sister on their wedding night. He then had to work another seven years to marry Rachel. At least we know the Chief likes you—and we also know that he doesn't have another daughter he wants to pawn off."

I felt a faint smile cross my lips as I pulled the bag from his hands to steady it back in place. Kai backed away at the start of a new a new sequence.

"I'm here for you brother."

"I know."

Charlie

As I walked out of my dad's office, I smacked straight into Kai.

"Oh…uh, hi Charlie," Kai said, looking quite surprised to see me.

"Hi," I laughed, awkwardly.

What is going on around here today?

"Were you headed in here?" I asked, gesturing toward the office door.

Kai nodded once, a strange look passing over his face as he took me in for the second time.

"Oh, okay. Well, do you happen to know where Briggs is? Is he out on a call?"

Another strange look—I knew I hadn't imagined it this time; something was off.

"He's uh…he's working out."

I stared at him, searching for some hidden meaning lurking behind his guarded words. I came up with nothing.

"Okay…is there some kind of *problem*?" I asked, cautiously. I suddenly felt the need to speak in a coded language.

"No?"

"Then why did you answer with a question?"

To see a lack of confidence in any of these men was rare, but the fact that he was reacting this way toward *me* was completely unsettling.

"To be honest Charlie, I don't know if you want to see Briggs right now. He's… having a bit of a bad day." A forced smile returned to Kai's face as he shrugged his shoulders, as if his explanation was the only one I would need.

It wasn't.

"Well, I would like to see him. He's my friend," I said a bit more passionately than the moment probably called for.

I won.

Kai led me through the far hallway to the workout room, and in no way was I prepared for what I saw. Kai put his hand on my shoulder. "You might want to stay back until he sees you…he wouldn't want you to get too close." He hesitated before walking away a moment later.

My jaw fell open at the sight of Briggs.

The music was turned up loud, the bass resonating in my chest like a heartbeat. When he said he was into fighting before, this was not what I had pictured—not even close. I had imagined some broken bar chairs and drunken men throwing aimless punches at each other, but *this*, was far from that.

I knew he was fit—that was obvious to anyone who had eyes to see, but *that* word did not apply to him. He was instead what some might call…shredded. Every contour of his abs and arms reflected in the lights overhead. His hair was completely soaked—beads of sweat flinging in every direction with each punch he threw. I could not take my eyes off him. It was like watching a performance. Because I was not particularly athletic, this kind of endurance was beyond mystifying.

His hits were hard. I could hear each impact as it pounded against the leather, even above the booming bass line of his music. I slid my body against the wall slowly, sinking to the floor, watching, wide-eyed. His back faced me, but every once in a while I could see the profile of his face. His eyes were focused, intense.

A trickle of uneasiness ran up my spine, igniting my mind.

I wondered if I hadn't trusted Briggs the way I did, if this sight would have frightened me. I wanted the answer to be no, but I couldn't be certain. This was the first time I had seen even the slightest glimpse of the Briggs he spoke of in his past—the hard Briggs, the fighter. But then I remembered, he was still the Briggs that I knew. He was the Briggs who had wrapped my wrist, the one who had held my hand and kissed my lips. He was my Briggs.

As the song died out, he stopped the bag to pick up his iPod. It was then that he saw me. He wiped his eyes with the back of his sweaty arm, and blinked.

Slowly, I raised my hand, giving him the smallest version of a wave I could, which seemed to confirm his suspicion: I was in fact, really here.

There was no emotion I could detect on his face as he stared back. I stood, unsure of what I should do next. This was a first for us—I was the one playing the role of *creepy-stalker* this time.

"I…I'm sorry. I texted you a little while ago to let you know I was bringing lunch by," I lifted the crumpled bag off the floor, "And then I got here, and you looked pretty…uh, focused. I didn't want to disturb you."

He blinked a few more times before walking over to a weight bench to grab his towel, wiping his face and hair. I tried to keep my eyes focused upward, it was a challenge.

"How long have you been sitting there?"

"I'm not sure," I said, feeling the slow rise of panic in my chest at the cold tone of his voice, "Do you…want me to leave?"

There was no immediate answer—no reassuring smile to ease my doubt. There was just a blank face on a beautiful man-body, one that looked completely spent. I could see his arms shake slightly as he stood before me catching his breath.

I swallowed hard, realizing Kai had been right. I shouldn't have come back here.

"I'll go," I said softly, placing the lunch bag near the back door. "This is for you."

My chest heaved with the weight of rejection bearing down on it.

"Charlie…wait."

I stopped, turning back to him slowly.

"Can you give me ten minutes? I need to shower."

"Sure," I squeaked.

Briggs

I stood in the cool stream, letting it revive the body I had just beat to a pulp. My knuckles, despite the wrapping, were cracked and bleeding already.

I banged my head against the wall.

Why did she have to come today?

After I had dried off and put a new uniform on, I found her sitting outside the station on a bench seat, to-go bag sitting in the spot next to her. My heart seized as I watched her tuck a rebellious strand of hair behind her ear.

How can I live without her?

She faced me when she heard the door close behind me.

"I'm sorry if intruded on your personal space, Briggs. I should have-"

"Stop, Charlie. You didn't intrude, I should have seen you there." I picked up the bag on the bench, thanking her. I was starving.

"You were, uh, really hard core in there."

I looked up at her briefly, taking a large bite of the chicken and rice.

Did I scare her? I focused back on my plate.

"It was…amazing, I've never seen anything like that before," she said.

This time I looked up, meeting her eyes so I could gauge her response.

"Were you afraid of me?"

She thought for half a second before responding. "No. I'm a bit in awe of you, though," she laughed, "I wish I could learn some moves like that. Maybe you could teach me someday. My piano hands aren't quite athletically gifted." She held her hands out as if inspecting them in the sunshine.

"Your hands are perfect the way they are, Shortcake," I said.

She gasped then and reached out for me, seeing my knuckles for the first time.

"Oh my gosh, Briggs…that looks horrible!"

She grazed the outline of my knuckles with her warm fingers. I could feel her touch more than the burning of my cracked skin.

"It's just superficial. I'll clean them up in a bit," I said.

"Uh…I'm no paramedic or anything, but that doesn't look superficial to me," she said.

I winked at her, but kept eating.

"So are you going to tell me why you're having such a bad day?"

I shook my head *no* instantly, my mouth still full with my last bite.

"Does it have to do with Angie or Cody? Please tell me if there is something going on with them Briggs."

Urgh! Why does she have to be so dang compassionate all the time?

"It doesn't, Charlie. I just have to figure some stuff out, okay? I'm sorry that I'm not very good company today."

"I don't care what kind of company you think you are today…we're *friends. Friends* have bad days sometimes. You've seen plenty of mine. And…I'll have you know I'm a pretty good figure-er outer," she said, puffing herself up with pride.

"Is that right?" I laughed.

"Yep," she said, smiling.

"Well, I'll keep that in mind then," I said, smiling at her.

I love when she smiles like that.

"Briggs?"

"Yeah?" I put the container back inside the bag, smashing it down before throwing it into the trashcan a couple feet away.

"Why did you stop fighting?"

Her hand moved to rest on my knee softly, her eyes filled with sincere curiosity. My chest ached at the sight. I had every intention of telling her someday, but today was definitely not the day I had imagined for such a heavy conversation.

And yet…

I made the decision as I stared down at her hand. If I couldn't tell her the truths I wanted to say—the words that filled up my heart and poured over into my soul, then I would tell her my other truths, the ones that haunted me most, the ones that couldn't be shaken off or forgotten.

The ones that would dissuade whatever affection she might have for me.

I had plenty inside of me that was unlovable. Maybe it was time for Charlie to know that part of me, too. There was no benefit to her loving me—not if the end result would ultimately rob her of the future she should have.

I kept my voice low, even, steady; though my heart raced a thousand beats a minute.

"Because I almost murdered a man." She went very still, but I continued on, undeterred. "I told you that Angie and I moved here when she was pregnant, to get away from her ex-husband, but there is more to that story. He found her, a couple years later—staked out the house, waiting for me to leave. I did, only I forgot my wallet. When I came back, Angie was lying on the ground in a pool of blood, Cody was screaming."

Charlie's hand moved to her mouth, "No…no, how awful."

"I had trained for years as a fighter, my sensei drilling into my head how important it was to remain in control—to not give away my power, my mind or my body to any opponent, but something snapped in me that night—a rage like I had never known. I charged him, while listening to the screams of my nephew in the front seat of his truck. I could hear the sirens in the distance and I knew I had to make a choice…go to my sister, or stop Dirk from taking Cody. I chose the latter, and when I did, I had already decided that I was going to kill him. I wanted to make him suffer for every hurt he had caused her, I wanted his death to be painful."

Charlie's breathing was so soft beside me. I refused to look at her, I didn't want to see the revulsion in her eyes. "When the ambulance and police arrived after responding to the neighbor's call, I was covered in his blood, and in a daze."

"Did he die?" She asked.

I shook my head staring down at my feet, "No, they revived him. Angie was touch and go for seven days, though. I thought I was going to lose her."

She was quiet for several seconds. "I'm so sorry, Briggs. I can't even imagine the horror of that night. Angie is so lucky to have you as her brother—you saved her son."

I looked up at her face incredulously, "Don't sugar coat it, Charlie. I was far from heroic—I was out of control! If the police hadn't arrived when they did, I would likely be in prison right now—serving time right alongside Dirk."

She furrowed her brows slightly, "So what, you stopped training because you were afraid it could happen again, the rage feeling? Is that why you changed—the reason you decided you wanted to live differently?"

If only.

I could feel her gaze hot on my face as the acid drip of shame ran down the back of my throat, "That was the end of my training and fighting, but it was far from the end of my destructive wake. You might think that going through something like that would cause me to reflect on my life—search for answers—find God, but that wasn't what happened. I went in the opposite direction," I laughed, though there was nothing funny about my next statement. "When I wasn't at the station, I was usually drunk—I can't even count the number of times Kai picked me up after a night of drinking, or how many girls he saw me go home with."

Charlie tensed, physically recoiling at my words. Her reaction made my stomach sick, but I wasn't done yet. "I lived that way for over a year—drinking, partying, sleeping with any girl that showed interest in me…" I stopped, the words on my tongue refusing to come out.

"What?" Her voice was a whisper. "What happened, Briggs?"

"I walked out to my truck one morning after work and a woman was standing there, waiting for me. She looked vaguely familiar, but I didn't know why." I stopped again, sliding my elbows to my knees while raking my hands through my hair. "She asked me if I remembered her. I told her I didn't, but when she started to cry I knew that my selfish decisions had finally caught up to me. She told me her name was Brenna, and I waited for her to drop the pregnancy bomb on me, but that wasn't why she had come. She was angry, cussing me out as she cried, telling me that I was just like her father—a drunk who cared about no one but himself. She ranted about how she would never put a child of her own through that kind of life, and that if I had been a better man she wouldn't have had to make the decision that she did. And that's when I realized that she wasn't telling me she was pregnant, she was telling me that she had just had an abortion."

Neither of us spoke for several seconds, but my words continued to play over and over in my mind…the shameful truth that was mine to own. All the pain and rejection I had tried to forget as a child, all the grief and fear I had experienced over Angie's assault, and all the murderous rage I had felt the night I attacked Dirk, had finally come to a head that morning.

An innocent life had paid the penalty for my sin.

I turned my face toward Charlie, the silence weighing heavy between us, like a thick, itchy blanket.

Her eyes glistened as she spoke. "That's a lot to deal with."

It *was* a lot for her to deal with. She had every right to think differently of me now. I had never been fool enough to believe I deserved her in the first place—friend or otherwise.

"It is, I just think it best you know what's in my past, as dark as it is-"

"What? No," she said, shaking her head, "I didn't mean it was a lot for *me* to handle; I meant that it must be a lot for you to wrestle with—even now. I know there's nothing more difficult than stepping out from the shadows of our past into the light, but you've already taken that step—and *many* more after it. You told me once that you never wanted to be that man again, and I see nothing of him when I look at you now." She held my gaze as words failed me. "I *see* you, Briggs, and I am lucky to call you my friend." A tear slid down her cheek as she said the last word, shredding my heart.

"You are not the lucky one, Shortcake."

She smiled, as she skimmed her finger over my knuckles, "And *you* are not your past."

I closed my eyes, willing myself to move away from her touch, while everything in me screamed in protest. "I should get back inside."

"Okay," she said softly, standing up from the bench a second later.

"Okay," I said, following her lead.

She smiled, "I hope your day gets better."

You make everything better.

"Thanks for bringing me lunch."

She nodded, waving as she walked on the path that led to the front parking lot.

As I watched her go, the ache inside my chest intensified. My plan to diminish the spark between us had not only failed, it had backfired with epic proportions. She wasn't supposed to accept the shameful secrets of my past…but she had.

And if it was possible, I loved her even more than I had an hour ago.

"I can't make you choose to do what's right for her, Briggs, but I hope you will."

In that moment, any wavering in my resolve disappeared. I had made too many decisions in the past for my benefit alone, and Charlie wasn't in my past. I would choose what was best for her, even if it meant she wasn't in my future, either.

Chapter Twenty-Three

Charlie

Thursday morning I met Tori for coffee at my favorite used bookstore in the University district. I brought an old pile of books in with me to sell for store credit while I waited for her to arrive. It was just after ten when I saw her.

"Good morning!" Tori said as she approached.

"Good morning to you, too." I hugged her.

We ordered our drinks and scones as she filled me in on the latest wedding drama. There was no stress in her voice when it came to the wedding, just when it came to the coordinators.

"I swear I might go insane if I have to be in on one more meeting where I hear about the different uses of chiffon verses organza, or the argument about twinkle lights verses Chinese lanterns. I don't know how else I can possibly say, *I don't care,* but I feel I am losing the battle with those three."

"Three?" I asked her.

"Yes, Mom, Stacie and Betty—the official coordinator."

"Yikes, you're a bit out numbered."

She laughed and rolled her eyes as we went found a table to sit down at. "Well I am done talking about all that," She waved her hand in front of her face as if to dismiss the conversation. "I will be so happy when the wedding part is over so I can just focus on being married."

I smiled at her, thinking of the perfect match Tori and Kai were.

"Well, I'm very excited for you, Tori, both for the wedding and for your marriage. Kai seems like such a great guy…you two are really an inspiration." My throat grew thick with emotion.

The two of them reminded me why love was such a gift. I had forgotten that truth over the last six months. I had recently begun to question if I had even known it at all. There was a dramatic difference between my relationship with Alex and what I saw between Tori and Kai.

"Thank you, Charlie. We weren't always an inspiration though, I can assure you. In fact, there were many months that I doubted we would end up together at all. That was a very difficult time…for both of us."

My face must have registered a look of shock, because she smiled sincerely at me before taking another sip of her coffee. I waited for her to continue; I wanted to hear more.

"There is a long history to our story that I will have to tell you another time, Charlie, though I promise you I will. It would likely take up our entire time this morning if I tried to attempt it now. But yes, in short, there were about three months that I thought it was over, for good. I was very stubborn," she said, smiling. "I had actually made plans to go to Africa for a year with a mobile medical team. Our time apart was by far the most difficult time in my life…Kai would say the same," Tori said.

"But how did it work out? What happened?" I asked.

"The crux was I had to let go of a lot before I could let him back in. There wasn't room for Kai to be in my heart amidst all the other baggage I carried."

"I never would have guessed that…" I said, letting my voice trail off.

"Everyone has a past, Charlie." She took another sip as I thought about her words.

My mind wandered down a trail leading to Briggs, and the secrets of his past that he had trusted me with. The conversation had been a painful one, but it had also filled in a lot of gaps for me. His honesty had made me respect him even more. Briggs was likely the most honest man I knew apart from my father. My heart warmed at the thought.

Tori's voice brought me back to the present.

"So what has it been like—being back home?"

I bit my lip, thinking. I would have answered that question so differently a few weeks ago, but now, so much had changed.

"Surprising," I said, "I was so angry when I first got here—broken, but I don't feel that way anymore."

"Why is that?" Her smile was contagious.

I laughed, "Well, it's multi-faceted, but yes, I'll say it...Briggs is one of the reasons."

As if on cue, her phone buzzed on the table.

Briggs

Tori laughed, "His ears must have been burning. Do you mind?"

I shook my head, heat flushing my cheeks.

Within ten seconds of Tori answering the phone, she was laughing. I couldn't help but laugh as well, knowing the man on the other end like I did. She would listen and gasp and then listen some more. Finally, I saw her reach for her purse to grab a pen, writing down an address on her pastry napkin.

"Okay, so you'll text me about an hour before to make sure? Alright, but you think roughly around noon? Sure, yeah. Well...I will not be held responsible for any part of this, but I am more than happy to watch! See ya then. Bye."

She hung up, shaking her head, a look of mischief in her eyes.

"Dare I ask?" I laughed.

"Charlie, what are you doing around noon on Saturday?" She raised her eyebrows in expectation.

"Is the right answer, whatever you're doing?"

"Yes. I'll pick you up at eleven."

Briggs

I hadn't seen Charlie since Tuesday at lunch, and I was certain I was starting to lose my mind. The weekend had been reserved for Kai's bachelor party, but I had a hard time justifying why I shouldn't be able to see her today—Friday. The line between friendship and *more than friendship* needed to be redrawn for me. Everything I thought or did in regard to Charlie now had a new tag line attached to it, "*Is that what a friend would do?*"

Charlie texted me before I could answer.

Miss Strawberry Shortcake: Did you fall off the face of the earth? Should I call out a search party? If so, you'll want to remove any traces of bacon from your clothing. I hear the dogs can get pretty vicious, and I've seen the way you eat breakfast.

Me: Thanks for the warning, though I can't help but feel insulted—I eat breakfast just fine, thank you very much. What are you up to?

Miss Strawberry Shortcake: Just finished practicing and had to reply to a few emails from my professors—big day so far! Haha! I'm starting to go a little stir crazy.

I felt myself twitch with indecision. I did have to pick a few things up to take with me to the cabin Saturday night. Would running errands together be okay? *Is that what a friend would do?* I hated that question.

I picked my phone back up, ignoring the whisper of caution in my head.

Me: Feel like going on a covert mission for bachelor party supplies?

Miss Strawberry Shortcake: Do I get to wear camo and combat boots?

Me: No.

Miss Strawberry Shortcake: Geesh, grumpy much?

Me: I have a feeling that your version of camo and combat boots wouldn't quite be up to military standards, Shortcake. I'm banning whatever plan you have for a camo mini-skirt comeback right now.

Miss Strawberry Shortcake: You have no vision when it comes to fashion. And for the record, it wasn't going to be that mini.

Me: Do you need my definition on the purpose of pants again? See ya in an hour?

Miss Strawberry Shortcake: No, once was enough! An hour is good.

I smiled at her cheekiness. Charlie was many things, but dull would never be one of them.

I stopped at the bank before picking her up. I hoped that I wasn't making a mistake by spending a few hours with her today, but it had to be better than the alternative.

At least, that's what I told myself on the drive over.

Charlie

I took a deep breath. The worry I had been feeling for the last two days was finally dissipating as I exhaled. These texts today had finally felt like *us* again. He had barely texted with me on Wednesday, and Thursday his funk had still not lifted entirely. I was starting to wonder if I had done something wrong, but a flood of relief filled me when I saw his truck pull up out front.

Things are normal; we are normal. Whatever that means.

He came inside and gave my mom a hug as I headed to meet him at the front door.

"Briggs, it's so nice to see you. Max said he thanked you for us both at the station the other day, for staying here while we were away?" Mom asked him.

Just briefly I saw a look of surprise pass over his face, but it vanished quickly. He raked a hand through his hair, and cleared his throat.

"It was my pleasure, Mrs. Julie," Briggs said, glancing in my direction.

"Good…well, don't make yourself a stranger around here. Charlie told me what a great chef you are," she continued.

I felt myself flush. *Thanks, Mom. Why don't you just tell him that I talk about him non-stop while you're at it.*

"Well, growing up around your kitchen, I'll take that as a high compliment," Briggs said.

"You're too kind. She also said-"

"Okay…thanks Mom. We gotta run," I interrupted.

Mom smiled at us and nodded. Briggs laughed as he waited for me to step outside, shutting the door behind us.

“Glad to see you’re in jeans. Makes my heart happy,” he said, tapping his chest dramatically.

“Whatever I can do to make your life easier,” I laughed.

“If only…” He mumbled something under his breath as he opened my door.

“What was that?”

“Nothing, ready for the errand run of your life time, Shortcake?”

“You betcha.”

Briggs

My rules for maintaining a friendship-only status with Charlie:

1. *Stay in DENIAL of all non-friendship feelings. If it doesn't fit into the platonic box, it doesn't belong in my head.*
2. *Do not make eye contact for longer than 5 seconds at a time.*
3. *Do not breathe through nose when she is near—peaches are a powerful scent.*
4. *Never get closer than six inches in proximity to her, but twelve is preferable. This will help with #3.*
5. *If any of these are broken…retreat immediately.*

The day went smoothly as long as I kept my list at the forefront of my mind. Only once did I inhale too deeply, her scent carving into my heart like a knife, but I recovered by sticking my head into the dairy freezer.

We filled up several carts of groceries and supplies for the cabin at Lake Owens. The chief had offered it to me with no questions asked, of course this meant he was also extended an invite, but he would have been invited regardless. Over half of his men would be attending and he wouldn't want to miss out on at least a couple of the activities Jack and I had planned. I was in charge of *part one* of the weekend, while Jack was in charge of the second half.

I smiled as I headed down an aisle looking for a blindfold.

"What is this for?" Charlie asked, holding up the bandana I had thrown in the cart.

I grinned.

"You know you look creepy when you do that, right?"

"Yep."

She laughed and threw it back into the cart again. The damage at the register was high, but oh, it was going to be so worth it. Kai was only getting married once, so it had to be done right. There wouldn't be a second chance.

Tori had given me her permission, I needed nothing more.

As we made our way through the parking lot, Charlie turned to me, "I've been thinking about when I came to see you at the station on Tuesday."

I stopped dead, suddenly giving her all my attention. "Yeah?"

She smiled faintly, "I think you should teach self-defense."

"What?" I laughed, jumpstarting my heart again.

"I'm serious, Briggs. You're really skilled. I know you gave up fighting, but you don't have to throw away all your years of training, too. What would you say if I told you I was going to give up my music?"

I stopped laughing. "Don't ever give up your music, Charlie. Not for anything."

She pushed my arm, "It was just an *example*—relax, but I do think you should really consider it."

"Consider *what*, exactly?" I said, opening the tailgate of my truck.

She huffed, "Teaching self-defense classes. Think about a room filled with women like your sister…you could really help people, Briggs."

I looked at her, breaking rule #2 as the seconds ticked by, "You've really put some thought into this, haven't you?"

She nodded, her eyes bright with enthusiasm, "I may have even found you a class that needs a new instructor at the Women's University." She shrugged, tilting her head.

I couldn't help but laugh as I tossed another package of water bottles into the back, "You might have been given a little too much ambition."

"So? Will you do it?"

"I'll look into it, Charlie…it sounds like something I should consider."

She jumped up, clapping her hands as if she had just won The Price Is Right.

"Good, 'cause there's just one more thing?"

"What's that?" I said before I grabbed a bottle from the last pack and uncapped it, pouring it into my mouth.

"I want you to teach me, too."

I spit the contents onto the asphalt, narrowly avoiding Charlie's shoes.

I hope she's joking. But her look told me otherwise—she was serious.

****

As we drove back to her house I had hoped the conversation had ended with my volcanic eruption of water in the parking lot, but no such luck. Charlie was convinced she wanted to learn a few moves—from me.

"Why are you being so obnoxious about this? I'm not asking you for a new pony, I'm asking you to show me a couple of moves…for just in case."

"There won't be a *just in case*, Charlie...I wouldn't let anything happen to you—ever. Just stay out of those stupid clubs you love and you'll be fine!"

"You won't always be with me, Briggs! Think about what you're saying…"

I looked at her, knowing my arguments were dying a slow and painful death. I wanted her to be safe—more than anything, I just didn't know if I could handle being that close to her…touching her. But she was right. I wouldn't always be with her. I *hated* that thought.

"Your wrist, Charlie-"

"Is fine!" She said bending it in an exaggerated fashion to prove her point.

I sighed heavily as she grinned in the seat next to me, "Fine."

"Is that a promise?" She asked, holding out her hand to me.

"It's a promise." With one hand on the steering wheel, I shook her hand, breaking rule #4.

And despite her gloating face, I was reminded of a question I wanted to ask her earlier.

"Hey…so how is everything back at school?"

She narrowed her eyes at me in suspicion.

I laughed. "What's *that* look for? You said you were returning emails to your professors earlier, is everything okay?"

She shrugged, taking an extra few seconds before replying—which made *me* suspicious. "Yeah…things are fine."

I glanced at her out of the corner of my eye, "Why do I get the feeling that there's something you're not saying?"

"Why do you *always* suspect that's the case?"

"Because I'm usually right."

She sighed, "Jessica McClaren's brother just passed away from cancer, and she was the lead pianist for the University's summer music tour…they've asked me to replace her."

My stomach dropped, twisting itself into a knot. I was not prepared for that.

You're not suppose to leave me yet…

But as soon as the thought crossed my mind, I gave myself a mental kick. I wasn't guaranteed anything when it came to Charlie.

"What are you gonna do?" I asked, refusing to look her way this time. I focused only on the road ahead.

"I don't know yet. To be honest, I'm surprised by the invite. I didn't exactly leave on good terms, but Professor Wade loves me...I think I could set the dorms on fire and he would still hold a place for me in his classroom."

I nodded. I knew the feeling.

"The tour starts June first—it's six weeks long. They go through ten states on a charter bus and perform at all sorts of venues. If I did it, it would help me make up a lot of the credits I missed in this last term…"

Is it getting warm in here? I turned up the a/c. I needed air—I suddenly couldn't breathe.

"And then what?" I asked, "You would stay until fall term starts?"

"Well…I'd probably just stay on campus, yes. Fall term would start just five weeks after I got back from the tour. I could probably make up the rest of my work in that time—Lord knows I have plenty to do."

The internal battle within me was waging war. I told myself to be a grown up—to remember the resolve I had made for Charlie's sake, pouting was not an attractive behavior on a twenty-six year-old man. But I couldn't even comprehend how it would feel for her to leave so soon…

I pulled into her driveway as dusk had begun to settle in for the evening.

"Aren't you going to tell me your thoughts on any of this?" She asked after a bout of silence.

No. I'm about the least objective person in the world at the moment.

Tightening my hands on the steering wheel I broke rule #2 again, and looked into her Caribbean-blue eyes. I remembered instantly why that rule had been so important, only now I didn't care. That was the danger in creating your own rules; they were easy to break.

I knew she would hate me for my answer, but there was nothing else I could say.

"I think you should talk to your parents about it."

I saw her visibly stiffen, as if a metal rod had just been shoved down her spine.

"Do you really think I'm that much of a child? I wasn't asking you as the manny, Briggs…I was asking you as my…*friend.* Of course I was planning on talking to them about it, but I hoped their opinion wasn't the only one that mattered," she said, opening her door and stepping out into the driveway. Her next words were spoken softly, but their blow was as crushing as if she had screamed them, "Apparently, I was wrong."

I was out of the driveway before the front door closed behind her.

Rules or no rules…this sucked.

Chapter Twenty-Four

Charlie

"So when are you going to tell me where we're going?" I asked Tori. We had been driving for nearly thirty minutes already. The longer we drove, the farther out of the city we seemed to be heading. My curiosity was growing, steadily.

She smiled, "Well, would you rather know now, or be surprised?"

"How much longer till we get there?"

She laughed, "I bet you're a thrill to take on road trips, Charlie."

I laughed. I hated road trips, actually. Though I loved to drive, I did not enjoy days on end of living on the road. The irony of the six-week tour I had just been invited on had not slipped my mind in the slightest. I hadn't given them an answer yet, but I needed to soon. They were waiting on me.

If I said yes, I would need to leave soon after the wedding so I could learn the music before hitting the road.

A heavy sadness sunk into my chest. *Why had Briggs responded that way to me yesterday, as if he didn't have an opinion? He always had an opinion. Did he really not care if I left?*

"We'll be there in about fifteen minutes. Briggs just texted—looks like everything is on time."

And then another kick to my gut, I was going to see Briggs today.

Great. This day isn't going to be awkward at all.

"Hey, I forgot to tell you, Stacie bought you a gown. She got you two different sizes cause she wasn't sure…but she is *certain the coloring will be perfect for your hair and skin tone*!" Tori said, doing her best impersonation of Stacie. That got me out of my head for the moment, it was pretty funny.

"She didn't have to do that, I was planning on getting something," I said.

"No, you don't understand. Stacie needs to go to fashion rehab. She is a freak about this stuff. Getting your gown was probably the highlight of her week."

I laughed again. I was excited to see it.

"I'll bring it by the house next week."

We pulled into one of the largest fields I had ever seen, and then I saw the tarmac…and the plane.

And three bodies I distinctly recognized climbing aboard it.

Oh dear Lord, what has Briggs done now?

Briggs

Kai had been a good sport about the blindfold until the last five minutes of our hour-long drive. I was honestly surprised that he'd lasted that long. His guesses had included: hunting, shooting, golfing (laughed at that), white water rafting, and every sporting event known to mankind, but he had not guessed right.

Even with our scheduled appointment time, we would likely be waiting for a while. I had cleared my plan with Tori first, more afraid of her reaction than Kai's, but she had been great about it—as usual.

Kai yanked at his blindfold when Jack's Jeep came to a stop. We both stared at him, gauging his reaction.

"What the…?"

We watched as he sorted out his surroundings—putting two and two together.

"You're taking me sky-diving?"

Both Jack and I started laughing hysterically at the shock on his voice, after a only a few seconds, Kai joined in. "Dude…no way! I can't believe you guys did this! I would have never guessed…" He looked around again in disbelief.

"Are you…alright with this?" I asked.

He smiled—that was all the assurance I needed.

As we got out of the Jeep he hit me on the back, laughing again. "This is gonna be awesome…nothing like taking the plunge before I take the plunge," Kai said.

"Hey…that was supposed to be my line!" I yelled over the noise on the tarmac.

Jack and I had both jumped tandem before, but this would be Kai's first time. We had talked about doing this together years ago, but never got around to it. I was glad now that we had waited for such a memorable occasion.

"You're gonna be hooked after this, Kai. It's like nothing I can even describe," Jack said.

We walked into the office and checked-in. After watching the mandatory instructional video and signing our lives away, we waited.

I texted Tori to let her know my best guesstimate on our jump time, that part I was keeping a surprise. Kai would be thrilled to know that she had watched.

She texted me when she arrived, right on time.

Perfect.

Our names were called.

This is it.

Charlie

"Oh my gosh, that's them! They're going to jump out of an airplane, Tori!" I yelled, nearly bursting out of my skin with nerves. I covered my mouth, watching the plane ascend higher and higher into the horizon.

I felt sick to my stomach.

"I know, awesome, huh? I kinda wish I was up there with them; Kai is going to love it. He is such an adrenaline junkie…well, so are Jack and Briggs for that matter. They're really a pretty scary trio when I think about it," she laughed.

I laughed too, only it was of the high-pitched hysteria variety. I could actually feel my face start to crack from the spasms going through it. My eyes watered, unsure of what emotion they should be preparing for. I looked at Tori again; she represented everything calm and serene, I was pretty much the opposite side of that spectrum.

If I wasn't so busy freaking out, I would likely be embarrassed of myself.

She's a trauma nurse—she gets paid to be calm.

I didn't know what to do with my body, my hands, or my mouth. I was one big nervous ball of energy. I started bending at the knees over and over, fixating my eyes on the plane above. Tori turned her head to me then, eyeing me suspiciously, but thankfully she didn't say anything. I didn't need a medical diagnosis to tell me that I was acting like a lunatic. I may only be a music major, but I was pretty sure I could diagnose myself. That fact did not deter my crazy antics in the slightest though.

Briggs is up there. Briggs is up there. Briggs is up there.

The heat in my chest was a constant flow of hot lava. I was certain it had to be doing permanent damage to my insides; my esophagus was likely charred already.

And then…I saw the black specs.

One.

Two.

Three.

I was screaming, but I didn't know it until Tori asked me if I was going to be alright. I had to stop my loud soprano hair-dryer noise in order to answer her, but as I did, I kept my eyes fixed on their falling bodies in the sky. I thought I would vomit in the sixty seconds it took for each of their shoots to open, but I didn't. I made it. I pulled through.

Seriously? You are not the one who just jumped out of an airplane!

Their bodies finally hit the ground.

Without so much as a word to each other, Tori and I were running toward them, both thinking the same thing. My emotions were wildly insane, but I didn't care.

I couldn't wait to see Briggs, my concerns of yesterday no more.

Briggs

How do I describe free fall?

BEST. SIXTY. SECONDS. EVER!

And then I saw Charlie.

And I was falling again.

Charlie

We yelled their names—okay, I might have yelled quite a bit louder than Miss Composure over there, but it did the trick. They saw us. Kai was the closest one to us on the field where they had landed, and was completely taken by surprise at the sight of Tori. He ran to her, lifting her up, and kissing her in mid-air.

I slowed my run the second I made eye contact with Briggs, my heart slamming harder against my rib cage with every step I took toward him. He closed the gap between us quickly; his bulky jumpsuit and straps hanging off his body. I could feel the adrenaline coming off of him in waves.

It was intoxicating.

I want you.

I knew the thought was mine, yet I knew with absolutely certainty that it was his, too. I could see it in his eyes. I could hear it in his mind. I could sense it from his body.

He lifted me up like I was the size and weight of a paper doll and spun me around. I threw my head back and laughed, wrapping my arms tightly around his neck. I had never wanted his kiss more than in that moment. My spine tingled as I felt his breath on my neck, and then on my cheek, and then on my mouth.

I was drowning in want.

I begged for it with my eyes—pleaded even, but with a pained look, he simply slid me down his body instead, until my feet hit the ground again. His breathing was labored; as he lifted his hands to my face, and touched my cheeks.

He held my gaze for days…weeks…months…

And then, I was left wanting.

Briggs

Blindsided.

There was no other way to put it.

I had just jumped out of an airplane! It was fair to say my defenses were down. When I saw Charlie running toward me a minute after I had landed, my first reaction was not to stay away from her. The words were written across her face, they were in her eyes, and on the lines of her mouth.

I want you!

I couldn't tell where her want ended or where mine began. The words were burning a hole inside my chest before I had even reached her.

And then…

I ALMOST KISSED HER!

I set her down, actively reminding myself of why I couldn't have her; of all the reasons she couldn't be mine. An eternity passed before I was strong enough to drop my hands from her beautiful face.

I saw confusion flash in her eyes as I pulled away, and then I saw something even worse: Rejection. I scrubbed my face hard enough to take off the first couple layers of skin.

"Charlie, I don't-"

"Hey! So, how was it?" Tori asked, walking toward us, hand in hand with Kai.

I couldn't take my eyes off Charlie, she was hurt…and I was the reason.

"It was great." My response fell flat, drawing the attention of both Tori and Kai as they looked between Charlie and me.

"Okay…" Tori said.

Charlie turned then, walking back toward the parking lot.

My heart sank.

"Should I….uh?" Tori asked pointing at Charlie.

I nodded. Tori didn't hesitate; she was in stride with Charlie before I could have even verbalized the request. I wanted more than anything to be the one to comfort her, but I knew that was an impossible task. I was supposed to be creating boundaries, not confusion. I was failing miserably.

I looked at Kai, trying to distract from my latest Charlie blunder, "Best fall of your life?"

He smiled wide, Jack joining us a second later. "Pretty darn close, man."

Kai refocused his gaze to rest on Tori's back as she walked with Charlie through the field, his meaning clear.

There was no competition with falling in love, or being fallen for.

Chapter Twenty-Five

Charlie

I was beyond mortified.

Briggs had come over to my window before we pulled out of the parking lot, but I could hardly face him. I didn't know how to fix what had just happened, mostly because I didn't know *what* had just happened.

All I knew was that I wanted to crawl in a hole and never come out—ever.

How could I have been so wrong?

For a brief moment I had been certain, certain that he felt what I had been feeling for weeks. That, apparently, was not the case.

I was so tired of acting like a fool for the sake of love. *What had I been waiting for?* Whatever it was, it wasn't coming. He didn't hold back his thoughts—ever. He had expressed his feelings of friendship to me, and nothing more. Whatever our kiss had meant the night I told him about my past, there was no future to it.

Briggs had made that clear today.

I felt a tear slip down my cheek as I looked out the window of Tori's car, my chest aching with each breath I took. I could handle the pain of mistaken love. I could even handle the rejection of an unwanted kiss. But I could not handle losing Briggs.

I'd take a permanent friendship status over nothing at all.

Whatever I needed to say to fix the awkwardness I had caused, I would.

He was worth it.

Briggs

I will not be a kill joy. I will not be a kill joy. I will not be a kill joy.

The cabin was already booming with life by the time we entered. We still had about three hours before sunset. Luckily Evan and Thomas had already gone out ahead and set up the paintball course. Everyone had chipped in, so the amount of ammo, guns and barricades we had at our disposal was obscene.

Chief was manning the grill, as the food and drinks I had purchased the day before seemed to be making their way through the crew. While Kai was bombarded with questions about his skydiving experience, I made my way to a back bedroom and pulled out my phone. I had to connect with Charlie before this weekend could continue.

No signal? You have got to be kidding me!

"Is my life a joke?" I threw my phone on the bed.

"I have wondered that same thing about your life…many times," Evan said, smiling as he walked by in search of the restroom.

"Very funny," I mused.

He laughed as I heard a door close down the hallway.

This was going to be one very long twenty-four hours without mending what had happened earlier. *How could I have been so stupid? Of course she was hurt! I was a millimeter away from kissing her…and then I suddenly shifted gears and put her on the ground like I couldn't decide what I wanted!*

But that was the cruelest joke of all, there was no question as to what *I wanted.*

I had to figure this out, I had to figure out how to have Charlie *without having her.*

I couldn't lose her.

Chapter Twenty-Six

Charlie

The tiny green pills were scattered on the table beside mama's bed. I knew never to swallow one, but not because anyone had told me. Somehow, I just knew. The morning had been cold—really cold, and I could feel the wind coming in from under the door and through the gaps in the windowpane. I shivered.

Mama had been asleep for a long time. Though my fingers ached from the bitter cold, I picked up each pill I could find, and put them back inside the brown plastic bottle. I stared at her body, wishing I could be closer to her. Jenny had given me a hug before; she was full of hugging and kissing, even though I knew there was a lot of sadness inside her home, too.

I wanted my mama to hug me and kiss me like that, to make me feel warm, to make me feel safe. I shook her body lightly with my hand. There was no response. Her breathing was quiet and soft like it always was when she slept, so I carefully climbed onto her mattress and pulled her quilt up to cover me too. Little by little I inched my body closer to hers till my front was facing her back. I made no sound.

I closed my eyes, secretly wishing I could crawl to the other side of her and lay under her arm. I wanted to be held that way—just once, but that was too great a risk. If I had learned anything, it was to be thankful for any moment of good. And right now, lying next to my mama, life was good.

****

I sat up in bed, rubbing my eyes as they roamed my dark bedroom. I lifted my phone, checking the clock. It was 4:49 a.m. I didn't want to go back to sleep, that dream had been much too real—probably because it wasn't a dream, it was a memory, a vivid one. I could recall colors, smells, and textures like it had happened only yesterday. That routine of mine I had executed countless times when mama had been too drugged to know I was even present at all. I had been so desperate for touch, so desperate for comfort and love, but she never knew my needs.

She never knew me.

She was severely depressed, mentally unstable—you can't blame her for that.

I threw the blankets off my legs, too exhausted for that internal debate at the moment. *Why won't these memories just vanish already?* It was the question I had asked for years while in my therapist's office. Hadn't I done my work? Hadn't I spent the time? What could possibly be left to rehash? My mama was dead, yet somewhere inside me, the lost, unwanted little girl, just couldn't let her go.

I put on a long-sleeved shirt, and slipped on my shoes before making my way through the house to the porch swing. I knew playing the piano at this hour would wake my mother, so I opted for the next best thing: Watching the sunrise.

My dad was already at the station. He started every Monday with an early circuit-training workout.

I hadn't asked him too many questions about the big bachelor weekend last night when he came home, but he did say that Briggs and Jack had thrown quite the party. That little factoid had answered the question that had gnawed at me all weekend: *What had Briggs thought about our awkward moment in the field on Saturday?*

I had been miserable during the last thirty-six hours, and shamefully, I had half-hoped he would have felt the same way, that maybe I wasn't alone in my feelings. But it wasn't only my dad who had confirmed that my wishful thinking had been in vain, Briggs had as well, in his own words. I sighed, picking up my phone to stare at the text again—the one I had already committed to memory.

The hottie who lives above your garage: I'm sorry it's so late, but I didn't have coverage up at the cabin. I know things feel weird with us right now, and I am completely to blame for that. I want to be your friend, Charlie. I'm hoping I haven't screwed that up…can you forgive me for being a moron?

And there it was in black and white—written proof.

I want to be your friend, Charlie.

Wasn't it Briggs who had joked that texting was like writing under oath? I set the phone down, mentally berating myself again. True to his character, he was trying to protect me, let me down easy, point the finger of blame at himself instead of at me. But I was the one seeing things that weren't really there.

My attraction to him had muddied my vision of reality.

It was me who had hoped for something more, me who had acted like an idiot by misreading his kindness toward me over and over again. This particular life lesson seemed to be stuck on repeat, and I was definitely ready for God to choose another. *Anything else* would be fine.

I pushed the swing silently, the toe of my shoe straining to make contact with the deck as I watched the beginning of the sunrise.

The last six-weeks had stretched me, challenged me, and forced me to think in ways I never had before. I was no longer the angry girl who needed to feel justified—or the broken girl who had built her life on quicksand. Instead, I was a girl who had finally let herself be known.

And Briggs had been the one to crack me.

I picked up my phone again as the sun broke out into a brilliant display of orange and red.

I would be thankful for this moment of good.

Briggs

After a long night of cleanup at the cabin, I finally made it back to my apartment just after midnight. I was completely exhausted, but my desperation to reach out to Charlie took precedence. I told myself she most likely wouldn't see it till the morning, but it hadn't stopped me from checking my phone every other minute while I unpacked my truck.

After a much needed shower, my body had finally succumbed to the pull of sleep.

I woke up with a start, my bedroom still dark except for the grayish-blue hue coming through my window. It was nearly sunrise. I picked up my phone and checked for a message from Charlie: Nothing. I swung my legs over the side of the bed, resting my elbows on my knees as I rubbed the sleep from my eyes.

I sighed, my mind fully engaged despite the early hour. There would be no use in trying to go back to sleep now.

I threw on a t-shirt and jeans, and headed out the front door. After jogging down three flights of stairs, I started to walk. The spring air was warm, bringing with it temperatures in the mid to high eighties at the peak of the afternoon. A reddish-orange hue had slowly crept up on the horizon as I followed the path to the fountain. The fountain, which was nothing more than a glorified piece of twisted metal (a modern art project crafted by local university students) had been dropped off in the center of the dog park I lived near. Consequently, it was the only place that served for quiet meditation within the vicinity.

I sat on a bench, facing east. There was not another soul in sight. The radiant glow of the sun caused the fountain's water to shimmer as it flowed over the obtuse angles. I clasped my hands together loosely, hunching over.

Though I had spent the better part of two years working through the aftermath of my past, learning how to cope without my usual vices, the last six-weeks had thrown me on a new course entirely. It was like running in the dark…with vertigo.

I hadn't been expecting it. I hadn't been looking for it. I hadn't been waiting for it.

Yet it came and found me anyway—or rather love had, breaking me, softening me, molding me. I stared into my hands, considering the callouses that had only recently scabbed over the tender skin beneath them. Yet, unlike my hands, which were familiar with the splitting, cracking, bleeding and the eventual re-healing process, my heart was not.

I took a deep breath, hesitating. Though I believed in prayer, I knew no fancy words. I wasn't a professional at speaking to God, and I certainly didn't pretend to be. I didn't know if there was a right or wrong way, but I did know that having something to believe in was a thousand times better than going through life with only myself to depend on.

I closed my eyes, listening to the wind as it blew through the trees. Birds chirped and sang in the branches overhead, and in that moment I felt peace. I didn't speak aloud; instead, I spoke with God as if He were an extension of my soul.

Before I opened my eyes, my phone buzzed in my pocket.

Miss Strawberry Shortcake: Though I usually relish in calling you a moron, this time, that label does not fit the crime. I'm sorry, too. P.S. You'll always have a friend in me.

I looked up to the skyline.

"Thank You."

Charlie

"Sugar, why are you pacing?"

I stopped dead in my tracks. I *was* pacing. I closed my eyes and took a deep breath. Briggs would be here any minute to pick me up for the rehearsal dinner at the Sales Estate. It had been six long days since I'd seen the man. Between work, practice, wedding escapes with Tori, and Cody cashing in on his trip to Six Flags, the week had been full.

"Oh, I just…needed to walk a bit. I'm playing my piece tonight at rehearsal, just have some nervous energy I guess," I said, lying through my teeth.

He eyed me suspiciously.

These nerves had nothing to do with piano.

"Well, you'll do great, as always. Your mom and I are looking forward to hearing it tomorrow at the ceremony."

I smiled. Never had they lacked in their support for me, especially when it came to my piano. They had willingly paid for all my spendy tutors, sat in hard bleachers at my school talent-shows, and had arrived early to every boring recital I played in, and they had never complained. Without them, I would have probably stopped at Chopsticks when I was six.

There was a knock at the door.

He's here.

My dad went to the door while I raced back upstairs, remembering the purse I had traded out to go with my dress earlier.

As I approached the entryway where they stood, I heard just the tail end of their quiet exchange.

"…I gave you my word, sir. Nothing's changed," Briggs said.

My dad's hand rested on Briggs shoulder lightly as I heard him say, "You're a good man, Briggs."

Briggs nodded to him once, and then abruptly stepped away from him when he saw me enter. Though I didn't have any context for their words, I didn't need it. Their lack of eye contact, along with the sudden uncomfortable silence, filled in the gaps for me. I didn't have to be Nancy Drew to deduce that their pow-wow was meant to be private. I felt a rush of heat creep up my neck, warming my cheeks with embarrassment.

Maybe it wasn't about me…

My dad flung the door open as Briggs gently touched my back to lead me out. He said nothing to me.

Not. One. Word.

Urgh…was awkwardness our new normal?

"Bye, Dad," I said calling over my shoulder.

"Bye, sugar."

Briggs opened my door, making eye contact with me for the first time. When he did, my knees practically gave out. I was grateful for the seat directly behind me. I took a deep breath, reminding myself of my new *Friendship Creed.*

When he got into the truck he seemed to relax a little, smiling at me briefly before starting the engine.

"You look great tonight, Charlie," he said, softly. "I'm sorry about that back there…we just had to finish up a conversation from earlier."

I nodded, hoping again that it had nothing to do with me.

Stop being so narcissistic!

"No, that's fine, I understand," I said, staring at his hand on his lap.

How easy it would be to reach over and…

"I've been looking forward to this all week. Texting is fine, but it's good to see you," he said. I knew what he meant, and I agreed wholeheartedly. It was easy to reconcile over text, but the true test was in seeing each other face to face for the first time after the awkwardness.

Like the running-into-his-arms-begging-to-be-kissed kind of awkwardness.

I smiled, "I've been looking forward to it, too."

He reached over to pat my knee before bringing his hand back over to his own again. A tiny spasm rippled in the base of my belly.

Everything is going to be fine.

We can be friends, normal friends.

Briggs

I didn't need a reminder of what I had agreed to with Charlie. That reminder came to mind as frequently as the breaths I took, but I swallowed down my pride and answered Chief anyway. I knew he only wanted to protect her—a common goal between us.

But my heart stopped cold when she had entered the room.

I silently prayed that she hadn't been close enough to hear his question to me, but I couldn't bring myself to look at her face for confirmation. I knew if she had heard, she wouldn't hold back. Charlie was too much of a spitfire to let something like that go. I waited for her explosion, but it didn't come, much to our relief.

If Charlie had walked in five seconds earlier…

I didn't want to think about that. We were on the road to starting over—as friends, with boundaries in tact. To reveal my feelings now would only compromise that. And even if she felt the same way, I knew I couldn't be the one responsible for pulling her away from the future she had worked so hard for. I wouldn't be able to live with myself.

While she had walked with me in driveway, my eyes finally took her in. Her pink sundress and heels, her white sweater draped over her arm, she was a vision. I sorted through a mental list of compliments that seemed *safe*.

I patted her knee briefly, denying my desire to hold her hand.

Just like I was denying my desire to hold her heart.

Chapter Twenty-Seven

Charlie

I had been involved in several weddings before this, but nothing—and I mean nothing—could have prepared me for the chaos that was *this* rehearsal. I saw Tori right away, cornered by at least five women who were all talking at her in shrill voices at the same time. As Briggs joined the other groomsmen, I felt a rescue was in order for my new friend, the bride.

"Hey Tori, don't you have some special instructions for me before I head over to the piano?"

I raised my eyebrows at her so she would understand what I was really asking, and with a look of sheer desperation, she broke away from the posse.

She grabbed my arm and whispered, "You may have just saved my life, Charlie—or theirs!"

I laughed. "Maybe I should just hide you until you're actually needed?"

She sighed, "I think everyone is finally here, so hopefully we can start this whole production soon. Betty was just going over her final notes, you know, the ones I've heard about four hundred times."

I looped her arm through mine as we walked over to where the band would be playing. A stage had been set up not too far away from where the ceremony was to take place. Twinkle lights and lampposts were everywhere. The entire yard—if one could call acres of land a yard—looked like Cinderella's Castle had emptied itself onto it.

There were crews of men and women everywhere I looked. Some of the crews were on the grass, some on ladders, some knee-deep in the koi pond, and some on the deck, each busily working away.

It was stunning to watch the transformation that was happening here.

"Well, I will be your protector from all these crazies tonight," I said firmly, continuing to glance around.

With that, Miss Calm-and-Collected herself started to giggle. I had never heard Tori laugh like that—it was quite contagious. In a matter of seconds I was giggling too. She caught her breath and wiped at her watering eyes.

"Charlie…you are…the smallest person here! That…is the funniest thing…I've heard all week!"

Tori had caught the attention of several others, and soon we had a group around us, the exact opposite of my protect-Tori-plan. Kai and Briggs were among them, asking what the joke was. I pressed my lips together, refusing to admit the reason for her explosion of giggles. Tori, however, couldn't resist. She explained how I had rescued her from the *Mom and Coordinator Mafia*, and offered to protect her for the night.

Briggs literally choked on his laughter.

Sure, I was short alright, but really? *Really?*

"Geesh…y'all act like I'm as useful as an Oompa Loompa! I can hold my own, really I can!" I said, putting my hands on my hips, trying to keep the smile from my lips.

Briggs dropped his arm on my shoulders, "Oh yes, you are a certified mini-ninja if ever I saw one."

Briggs

Walk like this.

Stand like this.

Turn like this.

Exit like this.

Weddings were a bore, but at least the ambiance was excellent. While we were pushed and pulled by Betty-the-Brute, I got to watch Charlie play. She rehearsed her song several times as we practiced the walk-in over and over. Each time, she captivated me with her grace.

Would she ever stop leaving me breathless after she played?

Probably not.

And I didn't want her to.

Charlie was assigned to a different table than me during the dinner, *a non-wedding party table.* Betty-the-Brute had seen to that. However, that fact did not keep me from texting her under the table all night. I felt like I was in the fourth grade again writing notes in my desk, only now the risk/reward odds played heavily in my favor. The only thing better than texting with Charlie, was watching her read my texts. That, was an added bonus.

Me: This is lame sauce. We should ditch…you in?

Miss Strawberry Shortcake: You are quite possibly the worst best man ever! You should be expelled from your position for even suggesting such a thing ☺. Although, I can think of hundreds of things I'd rather be doing than listening to Betty drone on about tomorrow's schedule…

Me: Don't even get me started on that. I think a fork to the eye would be better than this.

She laughed out loud and then clasped her hand over her mouth. I looked away, innocently, doing my best to keep a straight face. She was gonna hate me for that.

I hoped I could get her to do it again.

Miss Strawberry Shortcake: Jerk! You did that on purpose.

Me: What? Never.

I smiled at her. She shook her head at me, smiling too.

Miss Strawberry Shortcake: You know, you need to come up with a new contact name on my phone…this "hottie who lives above your garage" one no longer applies to you.

Me: Well it better not apply to anyone else either, or we might have an issue when I drop you off tonight.

She bit her lip, trying to conceal her smile.

An all-too familiar ache radiated in my chest, bringing with it a choke-hold of loss around my heart. Her smile faded as she stared at me from across the sea of tables between us. I turned my head away, doing my best to hide what I knew was written all over my face.

You've wrecked me, Charlie Lexington, and your love is my only fix.

Chapter Twenty-Eight

Charlie

The big day had finally arrived.

Due to our different roles in the wedding, Briggs and I had agreed to drive separately today. He had to be *on site*—as Betty had put it—for pictures a few hours before I needed to arrive. As it turned out, the extra time at home was filled rather quickly as Professor Wade called for the second time in twenty-four hours.

I had run out of excuses, he needed my answer.

As I slipped into the champagne-colored gown that Stacie had picked out for me, I was in awe as I walked toward the mirror. I had tried it on for fitting purposes, but with my hair and makeup now done, it didn't seemed like the same dress. It was positively the most beautiful thing I had ever put on my body. The long, silk slip dress was floor length, even with my heels on. The neckline scooped just under my collarbone, leaving my shoulders bare as the thin spaghetti straps crisscrossed behind my neck, down to my mid-back. My hair I wore in a loose up-do, soft curls cascading down from the crown of my head, leaving the ends to brush the nape of my neck.

After one final glance at my reflection, I grabbed an ivory wrap from my closet to take with me just in case. I was fairly sure I would be fine without it, considering it was in the high eighties today, but I would rather be on the safe side when it came to Texas weather.

With that, I was out the door and headed to the wedding.

****

The stage that housed the piano and the rest of the hired-out musicians, was only a few yards from the bridge where Kai and Tori would say their vows. It was the same bridge where they first met, when Tori had first moved back to Dallas. I had gushed profusely when Tori had told me that.

Their story was a beautiful one. As a method of distraction after the whole skydiving fiasco where I had made a complete and utter fool of myself, Tori had decided it would be a good time tell it to me. I think she had figured out pretty quickly that I wasn't going to be much of a talking companion on the ride home that day. She had given me space, not pushing me to *explain my feelings*, and I had been grateful since I couldn't even define them for myself.

Tori was by far the least invasive person I knew, yet it was that same quality which continued to assure me that I could trust her with anything. Her motives were never self-seeking, and that in and of itself was refreshing.

I smiled again at the thought of this special day; I couldn't wait to see her as a bride.

Perfection was everywhere I looked as I made my way onto the stage. The crews of chaos that had covered the outdoor space in droves yesterday were no more. Instead, an enchanted sense of wonderment and peace filled the property. Beauty was all around me.

The ceremony was set to start in just over an hour. Tori had asked if I would play while her guests were seated in addition to the processional piece I had composed. Of course, I had obliged. I sat down on the bench, smoothed out my dress, and started to play.

Briggs

I didn't see her until it was time to walk in for the processional, but I had heard her playing for some time before that. As people around me commented on how beautiful the music was, I secretly reveled in the fact that I knew the soul who played it. But as I walked in with Stacie on my arm, nothing in this world could have prepared me for what I saw on that stage.

Charlie looked positively angelic.

Once in my assigned position, I was pleased to discover I had an unobstructed view of her at the piano. When the song changed, indicating the bride's entrance, I had to peel my eyes away from Charlie.

Tori was a gorgeous bride, no doubt about it. Her eyes were focused on Kai as she made the long walk down nature's aisle, her dad at her side. I glanced at Kai, feeling a strong sense of pride swell in my chest at the thought of him as a husband. There was no better fit for either of them.

This union was right, in fact, it was as perfect as they came.

I fought the desire to watch Charlie throughout the entire duration of the ceremony, but since she already thought me a lousy best man, I did my best to focus during the vows.

Finally, it was time for the kiss.

The cheers and claps from a few hundred guests rang out as Kai dipped his bride low, planting a kiss on her mouth. And that was that. My two best friends were married. The band started to play an upbeat song as we made our way back down the aisle, exiting just as Betty-the-Brute had instructed.

The ceremony may have been over, but the massive crowd was causing some major interference with my Charlie-radar. After a few dozen photo-ops, and several formal introductions, I was ready to find my date. It proved an easy task.

Charlie

I loved weddings.

The fact that I now held the baggage of an ex-wedding date along with an ex-fiancé did not deter my love for what this day represented for my new friends. I listened to every word spoken, took in every detail, and even shed a few tears when Kai dipped Tori and kissed her, sealing their union. I think I could do this every weekend and never tire of it.

I had lost sight of Briggs a while ago as the wedding party was instructed to re-group for yet another round of pictures. I laughed when I heard the announcement from Betty, knowing that Briggs was more than likely groaning in misery somewhere.

I walked over to the reception tent as the band continued to play. The evening's cocktails and appetizers were currently being served as I milled around, looking for a table. In the process I found my parents, who in turn, complimented me tirelessly in front of their friends before I could break away.

I was thankful that there wasn't a seating chart tonight; I hoped that meant I'd actually get to sit with my date—my friend date. I was handed a glass of white wine by one of the waiters when he walked by me. I sipped it slowly, heading toward the edge of the tent, my earlier mission of table hunting momentarily forgotten.

The setting sun was too beautiful a distraction for me to ignore.

I stood watching it in awe. It was moments like these that I knew I could never doubt the existence of God: Sunsets couldn't be by chance. Art wasn't made without an artist; just like creation wasn't made without a master Creator. My skin prickled immediately when I heard the familiar voice behind me.

"Ya know, it's not very nice to compete with the bride on her special day, Shortcake."

My stomach flipped.

Friend or not, he was still a flirt.

I smiled, turning to face him as my words slipped away in an instant. Briggs had looked good from afar, but up-close? *Whoa.* I cleared my throat, forcing myself to reply.

"You look...nice."

Really, Charlie? Lame.

He laughed. "Come on, let's go find a seat. Dinner is about to be served."

I nodded, feeling his hand brush against my lower back as we made our way back through mob. Once we sat, I was grateful to finally focus on something other than the nearness of him. For the next half an hour or so we talked with the other guests at our table, swapping stories of how we had come to know the bride and groom. I enjoyed this conversation immensely, though I could feel Briggs' eyes on me throughout the majority of it. I wished I could stop trying to read more into his looks than what was actually there.

Dinner was served soon after that.

As the dessert tray made its way to our table, I felt myself start to retreat. Nerves, which had been easily sidetracked by the many events of the evening, had finally found their way back to me. I touched the stem of my second glass of wine and twirled it over and over with my fingertips. The later the hour became, the less time I had to delay the inevitable conversation that was to come.

I picked up the glass of wine then and tipped it back quickly. I needed to get this over with. A low, radiating warmth spread throughout my belly as I caught Briggs' eyes on me. I told myself it was the wine; I almost believed it too.

Briggs

Charlie was a bubble of delight when it came to meeting people. She not only knew how to ask the right questions to make a conversation flow, but she actively participated in it as well. Nodding, laughing, commenting, there was nothing she missed…and nobody missed her. She was simply captivating.

Not only was she the most stunning woman in the room—the only possible exception given to the bride—she was the most coveted as well, a fact that did not escape me in the slightest. I had already warned off several brave attempts by young males who had tried to approach our table, but luckily, my non-verbal threats to them had been lost on Charlie.

I watched her throw back an entire glass of wine after hardly touching her dinner, realizing her talkative streak had suddenly come to a halt. I caught her eye then, as Kai and Tori finished their first dance together as husband and wife.

"I have a promise to keep," I said, baiting her to remember.

She looked at me puzzled, shaking her head in confusion. I nodded to the dance floor and her eyes lit up in understanding.

"Dancing?" she asked.

"Yep. Can't let you make a liar out of me, I promised you a dance…and tonight I'm gonna cash it in," I said.

"Oh you are, huh? That is some way to ask me, ya know, it really is a wonder that you're still single," she said.

I threw my head back and laughed, the corners of her smart little mouth turned up as I did. Standing, I held out my hand to her.

She took it without a second of hesitation.

Chapter Twenty-Nine

Charlie

I shivered as he drew me close. Holding my right hand in his and my other on top of his shoulder, I felt dazed. There was nothing that went unnoticed by me in those few moments. My world had melted into one giant, soundless collage of colors. My focus was suddenly very concentrated.

All I could see was Briggs standing before me.

All I could feel was his touch, burning into my hand and hip with equal intensity.

All I could hear was the quickened beat of my heart in my ears.

He only wants to be your friend, nothing more. That reminder was like ice on a sunburn.

I turned my head away from him to stare out into the dark night that was intertwined with every kind of twinkle light known to man. I felt the effects of the wine then, as the lights began to blur together into one large ball of fire. I gave my head a shake, trying to clear my double-vision.

"You okay?" he whispered, bending closer to my ear.

"Yes, fine. You?" I asked. I swallowed hard.

"Why did you go all quiet back at the table?"

He of course, had ignored my deflection.

I took a deep breath, "I talked to my Professor today…I'm going on tour."

Other than the tightening of his grip on my hip, he did nothing, said nothing.

"Did you hear me?" I asked quietly, although I knew that he had.

"Good."

I stopped moving and looked at him. His face was hard, his eyes intense as they focused. It seemed a strange word choice, one that didn't match his expression at all.

"Good?" I repeated.

"That's the right choice, Charlie. It's the best thing for you."

He led me to move again to the music as I pondered his response, my heart plummeting with each shuffle of our feet.

What had I expected him to say?

It's a great opportunity, he knows that.

His voice startled me back into the present as we swayed, "How come you've never told me about your dreams, Charlie?"

"My dreams?"

"Yes, what are your dreams for the future?"

You.

I cleared my throat, pushing down the word that had almost escaped me.

Note to self: No wine before talking with Briggs about anything involving the future.

"I'm not really sure anymore," I choked out.

This time he was the one to stop dancing.

Briggs:

"I find that hard to believe, Charlie," I said, "Someone as annoyingly tenacious and ambitious as you can't be aimless for long. It goes against your nature."

She just shook her head, as if refusing to say more.

"What was your dream before there was an *anymore?*" I asked her softly.

She took a deep breath. "To be in concert, to travel to different venues and play for anyone who would listen, to use my music as a ticket to see the world, I guess."

A spasm shot through my chest at her admission, but I didn't let it deter me. I had made a promise, I would honor it.

"I believe you will then. What's to stop you? You're young and talented. When opportunities knock, you need to answer them, Charlie. You're special; you belong on stage more than anyone I've ever known. Don't let anything distract you from that...it's your destiny."

I felt her stiffen in my arms as she looked up at my face. Her eyes said so much, yet I couldn't decipher any of it.

What is that look?

Acceptance. It was the look of acceptance.

Good, I hope she hears me.

She needs to run after her dreams, accept them with open arms and not look back.

For nothing.

For no one.

Charlie

And there it was.

"It's your destiny," Briggs said.

To someone else those words might have meant warm-fuzzies, or feelings of blissful purpose and hope, but for me, they served only as a reminder—one that was etched in my mind like a tattoo.

"But there are other instruments, which were only ever meant to stand alone, to solo."

I had been discarded as a child, rejected as a girlfriend and imprisoned in a sea of want in this permanent friendship with Briggs. And though my parents loved me as a daughter, they had not separated who I was from the talent I possessed. Instead, they had pushed me to run toward the dream and life of a concert pianist, which up until recently, I thought was the only future I could ever have.

Alex had watered that weed of loneliness and fear in me, but Briggs had been the one to cut me loose from its grasp—until tonight. Despite how much I had wanted to believe, despite how much I longed for Briggs to see me differently, he had not.

He saw me as everyone else always had: As a solo act.

He may have believed he was encouraging me to pursue my dreams and desires, but my heart could only envision distance, solitude, and isolation. The life of a traveling concert pianist was anything but a social one. My music would be my only companion, and for the first time it didn't feel like enough. Yet hearing him say the words, hearing him speak so highly of the future I was currently second-guessing, gave me pause.

Maybe *I* was the one who couldn't see myself clearly.

Maybe it was time to accept what was and stop fighting against what might never be.

"Yeah, maybe it is." It was not just a response; it was a resignation. My head fell to his chest as I closed my eyes, willing away the tears that wanted to fall as I breathed him in. I wouldn't let him see me cry tonight. He believed I was strong, and tonight, I needed to believe that too.

He wrapped his arms around my shoulders, hugging me, oblivious to the couples that were in constant motion all around us, "Just don't forget me when you're rich and famous someday..."

His joke fell flat, neither of us laughed.

Of all the things I had begged God to help me forget, Briggs was one thing I always wanted to remember.

****

It was early, but that fact didn't seem to bother Briggs the way it bothered me. I yawned and rolled my neck as I watched him saunter across the field in his workout clothes. The spasm in my stomach increased as he neared.

This was the third morning we had met since the wedding. Briggs had suddenly taken a new interest in teaching me self-defense, and since I was leaving for Austin this coming Friday, our time together was limited. I had been more than just a little surprised when he had made the offer.

"Morning." He smiled as if he had been awake for hours.

I nodded and gave him a wave, the loose bun on top of my head sagged to the left as I did.

"Okay, quiz time first," he said, clapping his hands once.

I rolled my eyes—so far these "sessions" had been filled with far more talking than training. I was growing tired of his pop quizzes. I spouted off the mantra that Briggs had drilled into my head.

"Eyes, ears, mouth, throat," I paused, counting the seven in my head. "Groin, fingers, toes."

"Good. And what's my first rule?"

"Do anything and everything I can to get away first."

"ERRR!" Apparently my answer was wrong.

I put my hands on my hips, "But you said-"

"The *first* rule is don't be stupid. Don't put yourself in a risky situation, Charlie." He eyed me as if we both knew exactly what situation he was referring to.

"Okay. Fine. Moving on," I said smiling. He gave me a lopsided grin in response.

He threw out several scenarios: choke from behind, bear hug around the waist, hair grab from the side. Then, he waited for me to tell him what I should do in each one. I complied, but grew increasingly irritated as I did.

"Briggs, shouldn't I be practicing each of these rather than just talking through them?"

His face became like granite. "If you don't know them here"—he said pointing to his head—"than your first response won't be to defend yourself, it will be to freeze. You must be proactive, Charlie. There is no *wait and see what feels right in the moment.* Self-defense is not about reacting, it's about *acting*, and staying in control, reading your attacker."

"Okay," I said, heat creeping up to my cheeks.

"Okay." He turned and walked two steps before reaching out and grabbing hold of my left wrist.

"Oh!" I yelled, struggling against him.

"What do you do, Charlie?" Briggs asked, his hand still tightly clasped over my wrist.

And then I knew. I made a fist and rotated my arm inward in a scoop motion before whipping it up into a block, forcing him to release his hold.

He smiled. "Good. Again."

We practiced this move several times on each wrist before moving on. Fingers were a key part to any self-defense strategy I learned. If I could grab ahold of a finger, I had control of the hand. There wasn't much an attacker could do if I had his finger bent backward.

For the first time, my small size didn't matter. I felt confident as each move I had described in detail came to life as we practiced. I loved heel strikes the best—much to Briggs' dissatisfaction. I had come a little too close on a shot to his nose once. Luckily, it had only bled for a few minutes.

"Not too shabby for a little Leprechaun."

"Haha," I said, rolling my eyes.

"Come on," Briggs draped his arm across my shoulders as we walked through the parking lot. "Here, hand me your phone…it's time I updated my contact name."

I complied, watching him edit the old one with his free hand.

"So…does this mean you're gonna teach a class at the University?"

He looked at me out of the corner of his eye, "Did I ever have a choice—really?"

I smiled, "No."

"Yeah, I didn't think so. I start next month."

We stopped in front of my car as I clasped my hands together in front of my chest. "Awesome! That makes me so happy, Briggs."

He stared at me, a heavy silence falling between us for longer than felt comfortable.

He patted the wild nest of hair on top of my head, "Then that's enough for me."

"What's enough?"

"Your happiness, Shortcake. I'd do almost anything for it." He squeezed my shoulder before walking to his truck and saying goodbye.

As I slumped into my car, my chest pounded with an intensity I hadn't felt since our dance together at the wedding. I might have just spent the last two hours learning how to keep my body safe, but my heart was far from protected. There was no self-defense when it came to my feelings for Briggs. I had already broken rule number one.

I had put myself at risk, and I had lost.

Briggs

Tomorrow.

Charlie was leaving tomorrow morning.

That reality was about as painful as stepping on a tack while barefoot. With every text that we shared, the urge to beg her not to leave had grown increasingly strong. My self pep talks were failing at an alarming rate.

Sweat dripped off my forehead as I ran down Wilton Street, the late night air still very warm. I had been running for nearly an hour, listening to nothing but my own thoughts. I didn't want music tonight. I needed to think—make a plan.

I wasn't a quitter, or a liar, or a failure, but all three titles sounded better to me than being without Charlie. Maybe we could figure out a way make it work. I could give her whatever time and space she needed to practice—whatever she needed in order to complete her assignments and compositions…

"What was your dream before there was an anymore?"

"To be in concert, to travel to different venues and play for anyone who would listen, to use my music as a ticket to see the world, I guess."

Charlie's plans didn't include living in Texas, her dream was to travel the world. That took the idea of a *long-distance* relationship to a whole new level. Every time I heard her voice replay that line in my head, it was a slap to the face. Practicality took priority over any romantic notions I had of leaving my life behind to follow Charlie on her future tours. As much as I would love to be with her, watch her play, explore the world with her…there were too many anchors holding me here.

How would I work? How would I provide for Angie and Cody if I didn't have sufficient income coming in? Would I really be okay with not seeing my nephew for a year at a time? No. I couldn't leave Cody and Angie behind—they were the only family I had left.

I stopped suddenly, realizing where my feet hand taken me while my mind had escaped to the land of problem solving. I was a block away from Charlie's house—Chief's house.

Even when my mind was saying no, my heart was saying yes. I fished my phone from my pocket.

11:30pm.

I took my shirt and wiped the sweat off my face, making a decision—one I knew I'd likely regret come morning.

Me: You awake?

If she responds I tell her everything tonight.

Immediately, the phone buzzed in my hand.

Strawberry Shortcake: Yep. Leave it to me to be doing laundry at midnight…procrastinator. You home from work?

My fingers shook as they hovered over the keys. I was now only a few houses away, walking quickly before I could change my mind. My heart was beating at a faster rate than it had been during my run.

Me: I'm actually in front of your house…talk?

Strawberry Shortcake: Um…yes. Hang on.

It was official, I was going to be the first man who's heart shot right out of his chest due to anxiety. The drumming was so loud in my ears that I swore the neighbors across the street could hear it. A minute later, her front door opened and she stepped off her porch, turning on the infamous floodlight I had grown to love.

Her hair was up, her makeup scrubbed away, and she was barefoot, but she couldn't have been more beautiful to me. I charged toward her,

her eyes growing wider with my every step. I couldn't wait one more day, or one more minute, or even one more second.

I didn't have any new answers for how it was going to work.

I didn't know of any new formulas that would make the distance between us bearable.

I didn't even know how Charlie would respond to what I was about to unload on her…

But there was *nothing* that was going to stop me.

"Briggs—are you okay? Is something wrong?" She stood in the driveway, light illuminating her like a spotlight from heaven.

"No, nothing is wrong-"

"Why are you all wet? Is…is that sweat?" She asked, scrunching her face up.

Fifteen feet. She was fifteen feet away.

"I was running."

"Why were you running? It's almost midnight…are you *sure* everything's okay?"

I closed the gap, my body shaking with adrenaline.

"It is now," I smiled, taking in each detail of her face. "I need to say some things to you before you leave."

She nodded, staring at my lips while I spoke. It was everything I could do not pull her to me and kiss her in a way that would make up for every moment I had lost with her during the past few weeks, but I needed to speak first. I had to speak.

"Okay..." she breathed.

I took a breath, my mind trying to catch up to speed with my heart. "I've waited…I've waited for what feels like forever, Shortcake, and I know that you leave tomorrow for school and I'll do everything I can to support you in that choice, but you have to know…you *must* know that my feelings are not-"

"Briggs? Charlie? What's going on out here? It's almost midnight."

I froze.

Charlie froze.

Chief walked over to us both, squinting as he made his way out of the shadows to the well-lit stage where I was about declare my undying love for his daughter. The hot adrenaline surge I had felt only a second earlier, was now a cold, slow molasses, working it's way out of my veins with each pump of my heart.

He stared at me.

Even in his sleepy state, I saw the question in his eyes.

What are you doing, Briggs?

And then I remembered his words on a Tuesday in his office, not long ago.

"I can't make you choose to do what's right for her, Briggs, but I hope you will."

My body deflated like a popped balloon.

"Briggs was just telling me, goodbye, Daddy. Everything's fine, really. Sorry the light woke you."

Chief never broke his gaze from mine.

"Is that all?" Chief asked, knowing I would understand what his question really implied.

I took several seconds before responding, Charlie's eyes burning into me like fire. "Yes, that's all, sir."

"Okay…I'll leave you to it, then. Goodnight." The words left his mouth, but his body took longer to catch on to what he had just said. Finally, Chief headed back toward the porch.

We both stood silently, watching him retreat back into the shadows.

My rush was gone; my reality was back.

Charlie stared at me, waiting for me to say something more.

"Charlie, I-" I shook my head, staring at the ground.

"Your feelings are not, what?" Her voice was strained; I couldn't bear to see her eyes.

I squeezed my hands into fits at my sides.

Say something!

"My feelings for you are not…temporary."

"What?" she asked.

What? What does that even mean?

"What does that mean, Briggs? I don't understand."

I don't either!

"It means…it means…" I lifted my head, "It means that no matter where you are…you will always have a friend in me." I scratched my head, willing my brain to think of something platonic to say that didn't involve the word *love*. "I *need* you, Charlie. I *need* your friendship, your humor, your ability to tell it to me like it is. Tomorrow your life will switch gears again—with school, homework, music, practice, touring…but I will still be here for you. I'm only a call away, a text away, a postcard away…please don't forget that, *please*." My throat grew thick as I said the last word, a rush of emotion threatening to drown me where I stood.

I struggled to keep my head afloat.

Her eyes glistened. "I could never forget you, Briggs. I need you, too. You're the best friend I've ever had."

My heart ached—no, my heart shattered.

"This isn't goodbye."

She shook her head. "No, this isn't goodbye."

"Okay."

"Okay."

I stared at her for a few more seconds more before she finally turned and walked back inside. As I heard the front door close, the last fragment of my heart—the only piece that had remained so I could finish out this conversation, fell away.

And for the first time since the night of my sister's stabbing, tears blurred my eyes, mixing with the sweat on my face as I ran back home.

Home.

Did such a place even exist anymore?

The answer was too unbearable for me to acknowledge.

Charlie

The second I closed the front door, I slid down it into a heap on the floor, my knees finally giving out on me.

No! No! No!

I banged my head against the door, closing my eyes as I felt my heart rate return to a steady rhythm once again.

"I need you, Charlie. I need your friendship, your humor, your ability to tell it to me like it is."

I sobbed silently into the darkness, his words looping through my mind again and again. He had looked so raw when he said them, so completely vulnerable, yet they were not the words I craved his lips to speak.

"I need you too, Briggs…more than you'll ever know."

****

The next morning when I left for Austin, there was a text waiting for me.

Manny knows best: This isn't goodbye.

My eyes watered as I smiled. *No, this isn't goodbye, Briggs.*

I wouldn't have been able to leave if it had meant saying a real one.

I drove to school in the sunshine, convincing myself not to stop until I arrived. I needed the distraction of new compositions and tour performances and Professor Wade to help me remember why I had fallen in love with music in the first place.

Because maybe in that, I could uncover the secret of how to fall *out of love* with Briggs.

****

One week later, I loaded into a charter bus with twelve other seniors, and hit the road.

Chapter Thirty

Briggs

"Got another one, Briggs," Evan said while holding a stack of mail and walking through the dining hall.

I couldn't help but smile.

True to her word, Charlie had not only sent me a postcard from every state she had been in, but every city as well. And true to Charlie, all were some obscure and usually hilarious representation of said location. I had kept them to myself at first, pinning them to the inside of my locker, but after about number fifteen, I decided I would share them. She never wrote anything too personal on the back, so I felt okay about tacking them up to the bulletin board in the hallway. The Charlie shrine had become quite a spectacle—the guys loved them, almost as much I loved getting them.

She was on her last week of tour, heading back down to the southern east coastline toward Austin. I busted out loud when Evan handed me this latest post card. On the front of the postcard was a picture of a billboard—one that stood next to an old, beat-up highway, farmland all around it.

The words on the billboard read:

***Please...*Neuter your pets**

&

Your *weird* friends and relatives, too!

Evan laughed with me as I tacked it up next to the rest of them. She would be in Atlanta one more night before moving into Alabama tomorrow. We usually texted numerous times a day, talking on the phone whenever possible, even if that was only for a few minutes. I couldn't describe what hearing her voice did to me, but it was almost enough to squelch the pain that was now a constant part of my reality, *almost*. Living on a charter bus, however, had left little to no privacy for Charlie in the evenings, so we often resorted solely to texting.

Eight weeks had passed since I last saw her. *Eight. Long. Weeks.*

At first I had tried to pretend that *time* might somehow make missing her more bearable, but that, in short, was a load of crap. There was nothing *bearable* about not being with Charlie. I had learned a few new tricks since that first awful month without her. I might never be able to lessen the sting of her absence, but I could at least try to manage it.

The pain at first had been a sharp and twisted kind of torture. The kind that made me lose sleep, pacing while others slept peacefully in their beds, the kind that spurred on seemingly endless workouts, and created a perpetual state of adrenaline (otherwise known as appetite suppression).

It was that same pain that served as my daily reminder: I had *willingly* watched the love of my life walk away from me. It went against my nature. I was *not* the type of man to surrender; I was a fighter.

But not this time. Not with Charlie.

I'd been in the midst of a downward spiral of self-pity and depression when Kai decided he was done watching my misery unfold. I couldn't really blame him. Being miserable and watching someone be miserable were fairly close to each other on the scale of awful.

He had been right; it was time.

I had to find a way to manage without her.

Managing, as it turned out, looked a lot like being an anal-retentive busybody. But hey, it worked. I kept myself on a tight schedule, no longer living the life of spontaneity I had once loved. Unaccounted hours didn't serve me well. In addition to keeping active in the gym, I taught classes at the Women's University twice a week, along with finding odd jobs to do around the station when I wasn't on rotation.

And I watched a lot of sunrises at the dog park.

Charlie

Just three more days…

Whoever said that life on a tour bus was glamorous, was probably the same person who thought Spam was a good idea. Apart from having no privacy—something I didn't know I was privy to before this little adventure began—it was also uber-claustrophobic. Because there were twelve of us on board, we were usually allowed a night in a hotel room twice a week. We also stopped for daily showers at different locations on our route since the cramped on-board bathroom couldn't accommodate our incessant demands. If it wasn't a *hotel night*, we slept in our tiny bunk bed compartments. There were fifteen of those compartments in total, and nothing but a five-foot sliding curtain separated one sleeping pod from the next.

I would never again complain about sharing a dorm room—ever.

The music part of the tour had helped make up for some of the more annoying aspects of the six-week trek across the U.S., and overall, I was grateful for being chosen to participate. I had made some good friends—one in particular I had felt an instant connection with, Camille Thompson. I had recognized her from around campus.

Camille was an exceptional violinist; she was also a pretty amazing person. While the others went out and partied in the evenings, we had decided to find alternative methods of entertainment. Sometimes her boyfriend, Trey, would come with us, too. He was a pretty fun guy to have around, though definitely the nerdy-poet type. They were a great match.

Though I missed the dancing, I no longer felt the need to *escape* inside a club. I was pretty much over that whole scene. There was also the fact that I would get yet *another* safety lecture about the dangers of *booty-call clubs* from Briggs if I went. In the end, it just wasn't worth it. I could hear that lecture in my sleep now.

Camille had been talking to her mom on the phone outside when I got a text from Briggs.

Manny knows best: So, what's going on tonight…you're still in Atlanta, right?

Me: Yes. Camille and I are going to go to a coffee house, I think. Live Jazz…should be pretty sweet.

Manny knows best: Is Trey going with you girls?

I rolled my eyes.

Me: No. We are taking a cab. Stop worrying, Grandma.

Manny knows best: Ha…never gonna happen. How'd your show go this afternoon?

Me: Was actually pretty great, made a few new contacts. There was a ton of potential students that came from the local high schools too. Professor Wade loved that.

Manny knows best: Cool. I gotta run, have a call. I'm at the station tonight, I'll check in with you later. Don't do anything stupid, and wear pants—my definition.

He almost always ended with those same closing words.

Me: Ditto.

Manny knows best: Don't be cheeky. I'm serious.

Me: Me too ☺

I stared at the screen for several minutes after his last text had come through, pushing down the feeling I always had when our communication was over. I missed him more than I had ever missed anyone, and every day I wished the ache would cease. I sighed and slid my phone back into my pocket.

"What time do you want to catch the cab? I think the show starts at eight," Camille asked, practically skipping over to me. Her short auburn hair was cut in a pixie-style, which accented her giant blue eyes. She was actually pretty stinkin' adorable, but the best part about Camille was that she was almost as short as I was.

"Maybe seven would be good, then," I said absently.

She put her hand on her hip, tilting her head as she scrutinized me.

"Were you just out here texting with your *non-boyfriend*, again?"

Her tone was full of teasing, but I still stiffened at her word choice. "Why do you ask?" I deflected, like usual.

"Because every time you're done talking with him—either via text or call—you look like someone just stole your favorite toy and set it on fire in front of you."

There was probably some truth to that statement, not that I would ever agree out loud.

"Don't be ridiculous. He was just asking about our show today."

She smiled, "Whatever you say, Charlie. I'm no fool to the look of love…I denied it with Trey for nearly two years. I feel ya sister, I really do."

With that, she walked back onto the bus to grab her purse. We had gone round and round with this conversation over the past six weeks, and I had grown weary of explaining how things were between Briggs and I. My *friend argument* was getting as hard for me to say as it was for my heart to believe. Still though, I pushed it all down.

I knew I was actively living in bull-face denial, but what were my options, really? It was either be happy with the way we had it…or don't have it at all.

The latter I simply refused to accept.

****

The coffee house, *Black Diamond*, was located in the heart of historic downtown Atlanta. It was a beautiful three-story vintage colonial with small white lights illuminating its perimeter. Camille and I both wore summer dresses and heels, which were a far cry from the University's polo and khaki uniform we wore at every tour venue we had played at. It felt good to look feminine again—it had been a while.

My eyes took a bit to adjust to the dim atmosphere inside, but the jazz band was out of this world. It was no wonder the place was completely packed. We managed to snag a small table in the very back, but figured out real quick that we wouldn't be able to have much of a conversation; it was too loud.

About an hour into the evening, after downing two large coffees, the band took a fifteen-minute intermission.

I was on my way back to use the ladies room when I heard it: A voice from my past; the one I wished I could delete from my mind.

But there it was…calling my name.

I turned, all the blood draining from my face when I saw him. My head felt like I was on the tilt-o-whirl ride at the fair. I wanted to cry and vomit, all at the same time.

"Alex?"

Oh my…

His grin was exactly as I had remembered it—maybe with a dash more predator than polish. He swore under his breath as his eyes roamed my body. "Charlie? I can't believe it—it *is* you. You look *amazing*," he said smoothly, tucking a piece of his jet-black hair behind his ear casually. He leaned against the wall in the hallway, as if this were the most natural place in the world to have a post-breakup run-in.

I want to punch your smug face.

"Me neither," I said, searching for words. *What did I just say? Does that even make sense?*

He smiled, as if he knew the internal warfare going on inside my head. I looked away from his eyes. He was like Medusa's male equivalent.

"Why are you in Atlanta, Charlie? Not that I'm complaining…time's been nothing but good to you darlin'." I could feel his eyes perusing my body again. I felt sick.

I swallowed hard, trying to remember how to speak.

What did he just ask me?

"Uh…I'm here on a summer music tour—with the University."

He nodded, and then he reached out and touched my bare shoulder. His touch, as nauseating as it was, caused my mind to re-focus. In that brief second, I felt myself stand-up straighter as I held his gaze for the first time. I crossed my arms in front of me.

A look of surprise passed over his face, he seemed to smile at me with amusement.

I'm not your pet anymore, Alex.

"I always knew you were good enough for the big stage, Charlie. I hope you don't hold any hard feelings about how things *ended* between us. You must know I was right, though, don't ya darlin'? We were both meant to stand out…on our own."

His thumb had rubbed a blazing circle of fire into my shoulder before I shrugged off his entire arm at once. He laughed, but kept his hands to himself.

"Don't touch me." I scowled at him. "You *were* right, Alex. Thank you for saving me from making the biggest mistake of my life." The words dripped with every ounce of animosity I had felt toward him for the past seven months.

He stared at me intensely, slowly raising the side of his mouth into a lopsided grin. He leaned in closer, his hot breath reaching the flush of my cheeks.

"You don't have to play hostile, Charlie. The engagement ploy was your idea if I remember correctly. It's too bad we had to ruin a good thing just to suit your guilty conscience. I never wanted marriage." He moved closer to me, our bodies practically smashed together in the tight space. Awareness buzzed in my head as I heard Briggs' words scream through my mind like a freight train. Alex lifted his hand to my face, tracing my jaw, before trailing a finger down my neck.

I jerked back, "Don't touch me."

He chuckled at me and reached out again for my face, this time, I grabbed his finger, wrenching it back, reveling in the startled cry that came out of his mouth. The look he gave me after he yanked his hand out of my grasp was one of shock and amazement—not exactly what I had been going for.

"I said, *don't* touch me!" I backed up a few more steps, staring straight into his face. "I am not the same stupid, naive girl, you used to know, Alex."

He didn't miss a beat, "Ah, come on now…you weren't *that* naive, darlin'. I have a very good memory." He flashed a sinister smile at me, and this time I actually felt the bile in my mouth. Clamping his hand on my arm, just above my wrist, he pulled me toward him. Leaning down close to my ear he whispered, "I'd be up for a refresher course though. I'm the Agent for this band tonight, my hotel is just down the street, why don't we-"

I didn't let him finish. Though Alex was twice my weight, and towered over me, I did the move I had practiced with Briggs a hundred times in the field. I scooped my arm inward, whipping it up into a block while I turned my free hand into a heel-strike, making contact just under the side of his rib cage. The release was immediate. He stumbled backward, colliding with the wall.

"It's like you said, we were both made to stand out…*on our own.*"

I turned just as Camille came around the corner, relief flooding her face when she saw me—until she looked closer.

"Charlie…are you, okay? Did something happen?" She looked down the hallway, her eyes growing huge with panic as she looked from Alex to me.

I gripped her arm, pulling her to me as I forced my shaky legs to walk. "I will be—let's get out of here."

Chapter Thirty-One

Briggs

Once I was back at the station, I reached into my back pocket for my phone. It was just after midnight, which for Charlie meant just after one in the morning. It had become an unspoken rule between us to text *goodnight*—no matter what craziness had been in our day, or how limited we were on our talk-time.

We hadn't missed a single evening—until tonight.

Me: You asleep, Shortcake?

I stared at the screen, hoping she wasn't. The unsettled feeling in my gut wasn't going to rest until I heard from her, I could tell. An instant later my phone buzzed in my hand.

Miss Strawberry Shortcake: No. Sorry…I forgot to text. Goodnight.

Me: Is everything okay?

Two minutes went by before she replied. I knew the answer before I even looked at my phone. Something was wrong.

Miss Strawberry Shortcake: Don't freak out…but I saw Alex tonight. He was at the coffee house.

Charlie

Not even a full second went by before Briggs was calling me. I silenced the vibration immediately as I was already curled up in my tiny cocoon aboard the bus. I answered with a harsh whisper, ignoring the groans of several exhausted students around me.

"Briggs…I can't talk, people are asleep."

"Well that's too dang bad. Figure it out, Charlie. I'm not getting off this phone until you tell me what happened…and I mean what *really* happened."

"Just a second."

I rolled my eyes in hopeless frustration and climbed down the bunk ladder. Walking in the dark with only my sleeping boxers and tank top on, I made my way to the rows of seats near the front of the bus. I slumped down in one, resting my head against the window.

"Okay," I said, breathing out in a huff.

The good thing about it being mid-summer in Georgia, was that the generator on the bus had to work overtime in order to regulate the air-conditioning. This thankfully created enough of a noise diversion for me to speak without disturbing the others in the back, or worry too much about someone overhearing me.

"What happened?" His voice was hard, unwavering.

"He was there as the Agent of the band we went to see…he found me during the intermission," I said.

"I swear Charlie if he even laid a finger on you I'll-"

"I'm okay Briggs, I promise." I took a deep breath, debating on what I should tell him next. "I think I'm still just in a bit of shock."

"*Please*, tell me what happened, Charlie." There was an unmistakable plea in his voice that flamed a fire in the pit of my belly.

I took a deep breath. "Before tonight I thought I needed closure—to understand why he left me, why he walked out without saying goodbye. I spent months thinking of what I'd say to him if I ever got the chance. I thought if I could convince him to take me back, I would finally be happy again."

I could hear Briggs breathing on the other end, which was the only way I knew he was still there, listening to me.

"But tonight…it was like I was seeing him for the first time. I understand now why my parents acted the way they did when I was with him, and I realized something else, too."

"What's that?" Briggs was quiet, concern etched deep into his every word.

"I never loved him—not the way I know love to be now, anyway." I moved my legs to rest underneath me. "I was so desperate, Briggs. I tried to fill a void with him—one I realize now was never meant for him to fill."

Briggs was quiet again for a moment, and I was grateful. My confession didn't need commentary; it just needed to be heard. Tonight held more benefit to me than simply gaining closure; it had also provided a giant revelation of contrast.

Alex wasn't love, because Alex wasn't Briggs.

"I wish I was there with you right now," he whispered.

A warm tingle rushed over every pore of my body.

"I wish that every day." Emotion welled in my throat as my eyes pricked with hot tears. In less than two seconds, they were rolling down my cheeks.

"Are you crying, Shortcake?"

"No."

"Liar."

"Maybe just a little," I peeped, "but not about Alex."

"I know," he said softly.

"Briggs?" I asked, feeling a unique surge of bravery.

"Yeah?"

"You know the night before I left to go back to Austin?"

"Yeah."

"And you ran to my house at midnight?"

I heard him exhale. "Yeah."

"Did you really run all the way just to tell me the *this-isn't-really-a-goodbye* speech?"

Silence.

"I mean, it's fine if you did…it just felt like…before my dad came outside, like you might have wanted to say something different." My nerves were slowly taking over my whole body like an alien invasion.

Did *I REALLY just ask him that? Oh my—*

He sighed loudly into the phone, "Charlie."

I had never known my name to sound mournful—until this moment, until it left his lips and entered my ears. It was like a sorrow-filled dirge, penetrating my heart, and bruising my soul, all at once.

"Help me understand, Briggs…please. I need to know if-"

"You mean more to me than-" he stopped, several seconds ticking by, "You mean so much to me, Charlie. I needed you to believe that then—on *that* night—almost as much as I need for you to believe it now, *tonight*."

I swallowed, a steady stream of tears flowing once again, "I do believe that, Briggs, but…"

But what? But why can't you love me back the way I love you? But this sucks and hurts and feels like every time I hang up with you a little more of my heart decays?

"I'm so incredibly proud of you—of what you're accomplishing. I can't wait to watch you graduate and hear all about the offers you get. Maybe I can come to one of your concerts in Rome or Spain or Zimbabwe."

I laughed, wiping my face clean of tears and snot with the bottom of my shirt.

"I highly doubt I'll be playing in any concert halls in Zimbabwe, Briggs."

"Hey—don't limit yourself," he teased.

I relaxed into the seat, the tense moment vanishing with each new second that passed.

"Well…I know something else you'd be proud of me for."

"Oh yeah? What's that, Shortcake?"

"I used both a wrist release and a finger twist on Alex tonight—it worked like magic."

"Charlie! You promised me that he didn't-"

Uh oh. He was angry.

"Whoa…whoa…whoa…hold your horses, cowboy. I promised you that I was *fine*, and I am. But I thought you should know that our little field sessions worked. It was the most incredible feeling—you should have seen his face, Briggs."

"It's probably a good thing I didn't, Charlie. He wouldn't have gotten off with a simple wrist-release or a *finger twist* as you so sweetly called it."

I smiled, "I miss you."

"I miss you, too." He sighed, "We should probably call it a night. Do you think you can try to avoid any more run-ins with your ex before you get back to campus?"

I laughed, covering my mouth as I remembered the late—or rather, early hour. "I think I can, yes. Goodnight, Briggs."

"Goodnight Shortcake."

Chapter Thirty-Two

Briggs

The months seemed to compound one after the other once Charlie got back into her school routine. We still connected daily in some way—even if it was only a text goodnight, but her schedule had become much more demanding, as had her practice time. She had been receiving offers left and right as prospective agents came to listen to her play. With each one, I created a new boundary to stand behind. I didn't want to sway any decision she made—no matter what the ramifications were for me. It was her choice. *Her* future.

Whether consciously or not, there had been a shift in our interactions since the "Alex encounter" in mid-July. We had teetered too close to the edge of *something more than friends* that night, and I knew I wouldn't be strong enough to handle it a second time. I didn't need to test that theory.

Instead, I did everything in my power to keep us from having another one like it.

That, however, may have been the wrong tactic.

Me: So what did you decide? Turkey day is just two days away…when are you rolling in?

Miss Strawberry Shortcake: Camille really wants me to meet her family, and I only have three days off. I'm just gonna stick around here. I told my parents earlier today…they're gonna visit my Aunt in Tulsa now.

Charlie and I had been counting down to Thanksgiving weekend for months. Not only was I dying to get to see her (on something other than a phone screen or laptop), but I was going to get to be near her, for days. I had even planned to take her to Angie's on Black Friday for leftovers and game night. To say I was disappointed with her change of plans would have been the understatement of the century. It was difficult to be understanding when I couldn't shake the feeling that this decision was personal—not logical like she wanted me to believe.

Me: Wow…that's a bummer, Charlie. I was really looking forward to seeing you. It's been months…

Miss Strawberry Shortcake: I was just there, Briggs…Labor Day, remember? Please tell Angie and Cody "Happy Thanksgiving" for me.

Me: Just here? That was three months ago! And of the two whole days you were here…I saw you for maybe two hours of it, with your parents!

I was fuming as I saw her reply, she knew exactly what she was doing…and so did I.

Miss Strawberry Shortcake: Need to go…I'm late for class.

I stared at the phone in my hand like it was my mortal enemy.

Instead of being the vessel that connected us, it felt more like the barrier that separated us.

Charlie was slipping away from me more and more each day, and I was powerless to stop it.

Charlie

It hadn't all been a lie.

Camille had asked me to go home with her to meet her family over the holiday weekend, conveniently they only lived twenty-minutes away from school. I may have only had three days off, but that turn-around time would never have stopped me from coming home in the past. And it wasn't the reason I had chosen to stay back now. Neither distance nor time bothered me, but the status of my heart did.

That bothered me very much.

The difference was slight at first, almost as if I had imagined it. We would talk, text, email, video-chat, like everything was fine—like we were fine. But really, we weren't. Something had changed.

I could sense it in his word choice, I could hear it in his voice, and I could see it in his face during our Wednesday morning coffee dates online. The only problem was, my heart wouldn't conform to this change.

Even though I knew he was pulling away from me, my will to fight it was stronger than my ability to let go.

Hadn't that always been the case? Yes.

I had gone over our conversations in my head countless times, searching for the cause of our regression. I always came back to that night in July, after my run-in with Alex. I had taken a risk that night, hoping for *something more than friends* to be the result. But like always, he had let me down easy, reminding me exactly what we were: Friends.

I wanted that to be enough, to tide me over for forever, but the track of denial only went so far. And my train was running out of steam.

I couldn't go home and face him. Pretending indifference over the phone was one thing, but having to keep up this act while being near him? That wasn't possible—not yet anyway.

I didn't know how to *un-love* Briggs, but I had to try.

I had to.

****

"What are you going to do with this? Ever going to finish it?" Camille asked, holding up the composition I had started a year ago—the one I still hadn't finished.

She lay on my bed, rifling through my old music binder as I typed an email reply to my mom. She was always so good at keeping me updated on everything going on back home, no matter how small. This made the big stuff—the Briggs stuff for instance—feel like less of the giant life-sucking complication that it was. Somehow hearing about the neighborhood holiday bizarre, which was right around the corner, was just what I needed right now.

That was the kind of information I could process. It was simple, concrete, solid.

I sighed. "I don't know. I just can't seem to finish that one," I replied.

"Why is that? It's the only one that's not completed, out of this entire book…"

I shrugged, clicking out of my email.

Camille had moved into my dorm nearly two months ago now. After Sasha was expelled for drinking on campus (again), I requested Camille as my new roommate. She proved to be a great match—not that there was any doubt about that. She had become a great friend to me. In addition to my texts and occasional phone calls with Tori, Camille had quickly become the strongest female influence in my life—outside of my mother.

I knew that if not for my time at home during spring term, my fate would have likely mirrored Sasha's. It was bittersweet for me to think of that season of my life. On the one hand, I was grateful for what my time home had shown me—how it had grown and shaped me, reminding me of the importance of my faith, showing me hope and love, but on the other hand…

I stood and rubbed my palms anxiously on my pants. Winter break was almost here. Avoidance was not going to be an option for me much longer. I couldn't skip Christmas like I had skipped Thanksgiving—four weeks was hardly a three-day weekend.

"You have to talk to him when you go back, Charlie. He deserves to hear it, as much as you need to say it."

I was startled by the change in subject matter.

I sighed. "I'm not saying anything, Camille. We've been over this a thousand times…you're really starting to get on my nerves." I rolled my eyes.

"But what if you're wrong? What if there's a reason he hasn't said more…what if he's waiting for some reason?"

I spun around, my hands coming up to my hips defensively.

"I'm *not* wrong, and even if I were…there is no reason he would keep feelings like that inside. He doesn't work that way. Briggs says everything he thinks—believe me, he is *not* shy. I've been on the receiving end of many an uncomfortable conversation because of that fact. If he..."

I couldn't even say the words, it hurt too much to hope that they could be true.

"If he *loves* you…then what?"

"Then he would have said so already. Opportunity has not lacked between us, Camille…we talk every single day. There is no reason, there is no excuse, there are just facts—the same ones I have told you over and over. He doesn't love me, not the way I…not the way I love him. Please, I can't keep having this conversation. It's not helping."

"I'm sorry…I guess I'm just a hopeless romantic." She shrugged apologetically. "I just want to see your fairytale ending."

I shook my head sadly, "Take it from me, Camille, there is no such thing as a fairytale ending."

Briggs

The chief insisted on Christmas lights.

Today was December first, and today, like every other year that had come before it, was "light day". I groaned inwardly as I stared at the three giant Rubbermaid containers in front of me. I hated this job…that was no secret. But this year, I seemed to hate it even more.

This year I was finding it hard to get into the holiday spirit at all.

Charlie was coming home in five days, and though I should feel ecstatic, the only thing I felt at the moment, was confused. It wasn't only the emotional distance she had wedged between us in these last few weeks that worried me; it was also the way she had been responding to me as of late.

I could squeeze more warmth from an ice cube than I could from Charlie right now.

If there was another way to ask her *what was wrong*, I certainly didn't know it. Apart from asking her in Pig-Latin, I could honestly say that I had tried everything.

The chief walked out, greeting me and carrying yet another box in his hands. He laid it at the base of the hydraulic ladder—the one I was just about to step onto. He stretched his arms above his head, rotating his shoulders.

"Here's one more, Briggs. And one of those larger ones over there should have the Santa sleigh and the Nativity scene for the side yard inside it, I think," he said smiling.

"Does it also have the Easter bunny in it, too? Or that Leprechaun guy from Saint Patty's day?" I grumbled.

"No, but I think I just found the Grinch." He folded his arms over his chest, but continued to watch me—an odd look crossing over his face.

"I'll look for them in a bit, sir, sorry." I pulled the first long strand of lights out, and climbed into the lift's cage.

He walked a bit closer, putting his left hand on the lift's rail as if trying to get my attention. I had just grabbed the staple gun when I met his scrutinizing gaze for the second time. I stood upright, waiting for him to speak his mind.

"Have you spoken with Charlie recently?"

A pang shot through my heart at the mention of her name.

"Yeah, just texted lately though. Why—is something wrong?"

I leaned on the back rail, hanging the staple gun onto my belt loop.

He rotated his shoulders again, shrugging slightly in the process. "I think something might be going on with her."

My brows furrowed as my heart rate increased, "Like what?"

I was not in the mood to be accused of anything, especially when it came to her. I had done everything that had been asked of me, kept every promise I had made to the man. It was most likely those very promises that had me second-guessing our relationship right now.

"Relax, Briggs…this isn't an interrogation. I know you've been nothing but honorable when it comes to her, but her mom and I think…"

"What?"

If I hadn't been talking to my chief—a.k.a Charlie's Dad—I would have demanded him to speak faster, but I held my respect in check, and waited for him to continue.

"We think she's trying to avoid something…it's what she does when she's anxious or stressed. It was odd for her to change her plans so last minute at Thanksgiving, and now with winter break almost here, she doesn't even seem…excited about coming home."

I knew exactly what he was talking about, maybe even more than he did.

"Yeah." I nodded in agreement, pulling on my neck.

"Ever since she got back to school after the tour…she hasn't seemed like herself. Her grades are excellent, and she's received several invitations to go abroad after graduation, but yet, there's no passion in her voice when she talks about it," Chief said, raising his arm off the lift and stretching it across his body, massaging his shoulder in the process.

"I've noticed that too, sir. I don't know what I can say to help, though…I've tried to ask her, believe me," I said, shaking my head.

"But that's just it, Briggs. What I'm trying to say, is that Julie and I think her lack of passion is somehow connected to you."

Ouch.

"Is this supposed to be a kick-me-when-I'm-down-conversation, sir?"

"Not at all…I think maybe I'm gaining some new perspective. I think you did more for her than what I may have given you credit for." He paused, shifting his feet as he held my gaze. "Briggs…do you still love my daughter?"

I stared at him, desperately trying to believe that what I was hearing was real—hoping to God that this was not just my sad attempt at a daydream.

"More than my own life," I said firmly.

He nodded, but as he did, he staggered forward a step…and then another.

"Sir—sir, are you okay?"

He clutched his chest as I jumped out of the lift, staple gun falling to the ground with a loud clang.

"I think…I'm having a heart attack."

****

One might think it *lucky* to have a heart attack surrounded by a bunch of paramedics and firemen, and maybe that was true, but it didn't change the fact that our chief was currently being rushed into surgery.

Mrs. Julie had just walked in a few seconds before, followed by Kai, as we piled together in a private waiting room. It had seemed like years had passed with the amount of worry that saturated the air, but in reality, it had been no more than twenty-minutes since the chief had spoken his last words to me.

I knelt beside Mrs. Julie, just one thought reverberating inside my head.

Charlie.

"Mrs. Julie, have you spoken with Charlie yet?" I asked softly.

She shook her head slowly, her face dazed in shock.

"I'd like your permission to go pick her up and bring her back here, but I think it would be best if no one calls her until I'm with her. I'm afraid if she hears about this now, she will get on the road regardless of what anyone says, and I don't think that would be safe. Do you agree with me?"

She took my hands in hers. "Yes, I do. Just bring her home to me safely, Briggs. Please have her call me as soon as she's with you."

"I will, ma'am, I promise."

Kai and Evan were at my side the second I stood up. I grabbed Kai's shoulder, pulling him close. "Nobody calls, Charlie," I said through gritted teeth, "Nobody."

"But it's gonna take nearly four hours to get to her," Evan said.

Kai shot him a warning look, he knew what was coming.

I pointed my finger at his chest. "When you love a woman the way I love Charlie Lexington…you will do whatever it takes to keep her safe—even if that means keeping her safe from herself. She can't drive with this in her head. So, I will say it one more time Evan, nobody calls her!"

Kai stepped between us. "You have our word, Briggs. We'll make sure of it, and I'll keep you updated with the latest on Chief."

"Thanks."

And with that, I was gone.

Charlie

There were few things in life that could transcend beyond the confines of time, space, culture and language. One such thing was the look of bad news, a look that I had known far too intimately as a child—I couldn't possibly forget it.

Why I didn't doubt his presence in the doorway of my music hall, or at my school, or even in my city, remained a mystery to me. But even if I had, the look on his face was enough to smack me with reality.

Bad news.

I seemed to float weightlessly to where he stood. The air around me was thick and fuzzy; it hurt to breathe it in. I focused on his lips, as if they held in them the balance of good and evil. I waited for his words, bracing myself for their impact.

Out of everything he said, I heard only three words.

Just. Three. Words.

Dad.

Heart Attack.

The next few minutes I don't remember very well. I have only snapshots and glimpses that they even existed at all.

Snap Shot: Dorm room. Camille packing my suitcase.

Snap Shot: Strong arms. Walking through a parking lot.

Snap Shot: Truck door. Cold leather at my back.

"Tell me what happened," I said—or at least I think I said. The voice didn't sound like me. It was foreign, too far away.

Briggs took a deep breath and grabbed my limp hand from my lap. I couldn't squeeze back, nothing seemed to be attached to me. I was breaking from the inside out.

"Call your mom first, Shortcake…here. I just spoke to Kai a few minutes ago, and your dad is still in surgery. Your mom needs to know you're safe," he said.

He gave me his phone, my mom answered on the first ring. It was then that my world began to crash.

Dad could be …

I wouldn't think it.

"Charlie?"

"Mom? Oh Mom…," The tears came, wetting my face for the first time.

"He's still in surgery, his heart…he needed a triple bypass."

I heard the shake in her voice, she was scared. I had never heard my mother like that—not ever. She had sweet southern charm, yes, but she was never weak. Listening to her speak, the lack of strength in her tone, was more frightening than the words that she had said.

"Oh, Mom…" I whispered.

Would I get there in time? Would he even know me if he did wake up from this?

"I need to go…Aunt Jo just got here. I'll call you when I know more. I need you, Charlie."

"I need you too, Mom."

I laid the phone down on my lap and sobbed. I didn't care that I wasn't alone. I didn't even care that it was Briggs who with me. I brought my knees up to my chest and turned my head toward the window, pushing the top of the seatbelt under my chin. Everything burned and twisted and sliced. There was not just one source of pain; it was all muddied up together. My sobs became rhythmic, time seemingly irrelevant.

I wanted sleep to come, to take me away from this nightmare, so that I could trade it in for a different one—one that didn't hurt my family.

But sleep wouldn't come.

I felt Briggs touch my upper back, rubbing warm circles on the outside of my sweatshirt. It was then that I was glad that he was with me. He had come for me. He had known this pain would cripple me—just like it had when I was five years-old.

I had felt this pain once before.

I tried to speak, but my words were soundless. I tried again, but a sob escaped instead. He just kept rubbing my back and driving. We still had two hours left—I recognized the road signs. I unbuckled my seatbelt, and slowly scooted next to him. Immediately, he pulled me closer, grabbing the end of my buckle to click it into place around me. I laid my head on his chest, his arm the anchor that held me in place.

I closed my eyes and breathed him in.

I never wanted to move again.

"He's strong, Charlie, one of the strongest men I've ever known, and he loves you very much. I don't know what will happen, but I do know that."

I nodded against him, feeling my tears overwhelm me once more.

Then a deep voice filled the cab once more.

Briggs was praying.

Briggs

It had only taken me three hours and ten minutes to get to Austin. Kai, true to his word, had kept me updated during my drive, though his status hadn't changed.

Chief was still in surgery.

It wasn't until I had pulled onto campus that I realized I didn't have the foggiest idea how to find her. I parked near the admin building, hoping someone could help me, when I nearly ran into a sign pointing to the Music Hall. I took a chance, taking the steps two by two as I went inside.

Not even ten seconds later, I saw her.

Her back had faced me as I entered the room, she was speaking to a young woman with a violin on her lap. For half a second, I forgot why I had come. My memory had not done her justice. I fought the urge to run at her, flatten her against the wall, and kiss her until there was no more air left in the room.

But as her eyes found me, I remembered.

I remembered why I was there.

She had stumbled toward me, as if already expecting the news I was about to deliver. Within seconds, the girl with the violin was at her side, knowing my name before I gave it. She was Camille…Charlie had told me all about her, too. Camille led me to their dorm room, packing a bag for Charlie with superhuman speed.

As I led her to my truck, Charlie was non-responsive; she was in shock. I saw that face multiple times a week in my profession, and I knew it well.

I had only one goal: Get Charlie to the hospital safely, and in time.

Chapter Thirty-Three

Charlie

He was out of surgery when we arrived, but no one had been allowed to see him yet. He was still in recovery—stabilizing. My mom and Aunt Jo were huddled together on a couch in the waiting area, and that's when sob-attack number fifty-seven came over me.

Apparently, even when you've convinced yourself that you can't possibly cry one more tear, you can.

Though I wasn't completely aware of his presence, I knew Briggs was there, hovering nearby—always. An hour later, my mom and I were ushered back into my dad's room by a nurse to meet his doctor. Seeing as my mom was so fragile-looking as we entered, I wrapped my arm around her waist. I knew it was time for me to be the strong one.

"Mrs. Lexington, as you were informed earlier, your husband needed a triple bypass, and though the surgery was routine, there are several precautions we need to take in terms of his recovery—it will be *very* slow. It's a good thing he was brought in when he was. We will be monitoring him in the ICU tonight and..."

The rest was a blur. I couldn't hear him anymore.

A triple-bypass? Precautions?

I leaned around the doctor to look at my dad through the window. The sight made my stomach churn, until I realized…it wasn't him. *This* man was an imposter…a man who only *resembled* my dad. My dad was too strong to be lying in a hospital bed with cords and machines attached to him. My dad was too healthy to be here.

They had it wrong.

"That's not him," I said, interrupting some new detailed rant from the doctor.

"Charlie," my mother crooned as she kissed the top of my head.

"No, Mom. That's not dad, look at him!" I demanded.

Instead, they both looked at me.

"Maybe you should go get some rest, sweetheart," mom said. "It's been a very long day for all of us. I'll meet you back out in the waiting room, alright?"

A bubble of laughter seemed to come from some unknown depth within me, shocking everyone nearby, even myself. My laughs were sharp, intense, and high-pitched, but mostly they were just unstoppable.

This isn't real.

I am not really here.

I was at school, and it was five days before winter break.

Camille was just telling me about her date with Trey last night.

Mom had just written me an email about an ornament exchange.

None of this was real…finally, something made sense.

Briggs

"Are you Briggs?" A short older nurse asked me.

Turning around quickly I nodded at her, "Yes?"

"Can you come with me? You're needed."

I followed her back through the waiting room, down the hall to the cardiac recovery unit where Mrs. Julie stood. A doctor was next to her, and sitting on the floor by their feet, was Charlie.

And she was…*laughing*?

No…she was hysterical.

I approached the scene cautiously, looking from the doctor to Mrs. Julie, seeking out answers from their body language. Mrs. Julie looked slightly embarrassed, but the doctor simply looked perturbed. Charlie's reaction was obviously cramping his style.

"What's going on here?" I asked.

"Charlie's not…I think she should go home and get some rest before she can come back," Mrs. Julie said.

"She's seems to be experiencing a mild psychotic break…due to stress"—the Doctor looked from me to Mrs. Julie—"she may need to be hospitalized tonight if this continues on, Mrs. Lexington. It's not necessarily an uncommon reaction, but-"

"That won't be necessary. I'll stay with her tonight. She just needs some time, it's been a long day, and this is all a lot to take in," I said, scowling at the doctor.

I ignored his glare, looking to Mrs. Julie. She smiled weakly and nodded. I didn't hesitate. I picked Charlie up off the floor as she continued laughing on my shoulder. I walked toward the elevator area, and purposely avoided the waiting room. Charlie didn't need to feel humiliated the next time she saw any of those people.

****

I slipped her keys out of her purse and unlocked the door to her parent's house. Charlie had been quiet for some time, but I could sense she was still under a significant amount of stress. I supported her into the house, and turned on the main light. She wiggled out from underneath my arm, and headed to the restroom on the first floor. I went to the fridge, searching for something she could eat. I felt like an idiot for not thinking of that before now. It was well after midnight, and I'd been with her since early afternoon. Though I had snacked on several protein bars during my time in the waiting area, I hadn't seen Charlie eat or drink a thing in all that time.

I walked into the front room where she sat on the couch, her head resting on the arm.

"Charlie, you need to eat and drink something before you fall asleep-"

Too late.

I set the plate and cup down on the coffee table, and carefully removed her shoes. She didn't budge. I watched her, having a hard time believing that I was actually standing in a room with her again. It'd been so long—*too long*. Before I could question it, I slipped off my jacket and carefully stretched out beside her, covering us both with the blanket that rested on the back of the couch. She melted back into the groove of my body, never waking.

I listened to her quiet, rhythmic breaths, eventually finding sleep of my own.

I didn't need to dream about Charlie tonight; this was my dream.

Charlie

I woke with a start as a light saber sliced into my eyelids, painfully.

What the—the sun?

Why is the sun waking me up?

Something heavy lay on top of my arm, and my hip ached with stiffness. I pushed myself up into a sitting position, and that's when I saw him.

Briggs.

My mind screamed at me to remember. *Why am I sleeping on a couch in my parent's house—with Briggs?* I pounded my head with my fists. *Work. Work. Work.*

It did.

"No," I breathed.

Briggs sat up in that instant, rubbing his eyes.

"Good morning, Shortcake," he said, groggily.

I stood, my stomach knotting as a rush of dizziness came over me. I stared at his face, watching him grow steadily more alert with each passing second. I shook my head.

"It's real?" I asked breathlessly.

"Yes, Charlie. It's real."

I nodded, trying to take in a full breath. My throat was closing in, and my lungs were leaking out bit by bit. Oxygen was scarce.

I can't breathe.

I can't breathe.

I can't breathe.

"Charlie, sit down!" Briggs demanded.

I didn't move. He pulled me down next to him and forced my head between my legs.

"Breathe. There you go. Just breathe, focus on each exhale," he said.

When my panic finally subsided, I sat up and looked at him.

"I need to go back, my mom needs me."

"I know. I have your bag in the truck—Camille packed it for you. Go take a shower and we'll head back over there together. I'll make you some breakfast and call your mom."

I followed orders, having no desire to argue.

Briggs

Charlie didn't move for the next two days.

Every time I went to the hospital, which was several times a day, Charlie was sitting in the same chair—the one next to her dad's hospital bed. Mrs. Julie had been in and out with her sister Jo, and so far, Chief had been in and out of consciousness since surgery, but mostly out. The doctor said his vitals looked good, but his body still needed a lot of rest.

Charlie talked to her dad as if he was actively listening to her, though he wasn't, he was sleeping. She told him stories of being on the road during her tour—most of which I had already heard before. She told him about Camille and her funny Irish family. She told him about Professor Wade's latest muse—an old cast-iron hen, and she told him why she liked Christmastime in Texas.

All the while, she held his hand in hers.

Tori and Kai had been up to see the Chief last night. They had brought us all dinner, but Charlie didn't touch hers. I knew she was trying to be strong, trying to make up for what she felt was an *embarrassing display of weakness* on that first night in the hospital, but I worried about her.

Strength she had, but her stubbornness often overruled her common sense.

I pulled a chair over from the corner of the room to sit next to her. Mrs. Julie and Jo had just gone to get something to eat in the hospital cafeteria. Charlie had refused to leave, of course.

"You know your body still takes fuel to function, right?" I asked, pushing a lock of strawberry hair off her shoulder.

She kept her gaze on Chief Max.

"So you keep telling me, ever so annoyingly I might add," she said.

I smiled, at least she wasn't catatonic anymore, I could work with this side of Charlie.

"Tell me what sounds good to you and I'll go get it…even if it's something crazy like avocado ice-cream or pumpkin pancakes," I said.

She looked at me, a soft, tired expression settling into her features. My heart nearly stopped.

"I don't want anything, Briggs, but thank you."

I searched her face, my eyes landing on her lips. I stared at them. I was desperate to feel them against my own again—*desperate.* I leaned in by a few inches, tempting myself beyond restraint.

"You're so beautiful."

She questioned me with her eyes, but didn't pull away. I brought my hand up to her face, touching her cheek with my thumb.

"I've *missed* you so much, Charlie. You have no idea what it feels like to be this close to you again…after all this time," I continued.

She closed her eyes, leaning into my palm and opened her mouth to speak. But instead of words, the loud shock of beeps and buzzes came from every angle of the room. We jumped to our feet, as two nurses and a doctor rushed into the room, pushing us out into the hallway in the process.

Mrs. Julie and Jo were there with us before I could blink.

And then everything happened so fast…

Chapter Thirty-Four

Charlie

"Where are you taking him?" I yelled after the pack of white coats that were wheeling my dad away. I ran after them, but to no avail. Briggs was at my back all too soon, pulling me to him. I thrashed against his chest, breaking out of his hold as anger radiated through my body for the first time since I'd been at the hospital.

"What happened…where are they taking him?"

My mom was crying again, and Jo was comforting her—a sight I had become way too familiar with over the last seventy-two hours. I was sick of it. I was sick of everything.

I want answers!

"The doctor said he's having a complication from the surgery Charlie, they're going to try and…"

I shrugged his hand off my shoulder. I didn't want to be touched, not right now. The grenade pin had been pulled, and it was just a matter of time before it exploded. I raced down the hall to the stairwell, running down four flights of stairs toward the exit door. I could hear the drumming of feet behind me, but I chose to pretend I didn't.

I gasped, the cold, December air filled up my lungs as I paced in the darkness. Two streetlights stood in the distance beyond me, their glow failing to reach the shadow I claimed as my own.

Until that moment, I hadn't even realized it was night.

"Charlie, it's freezing out here, let's go back inside," Briggs said.

"This can't be happening!" I threw my hands in the air. "Do you even know the last thing we talked about? The last conversation I had with my father? It was when I told him I wasn't coming home for Thanksgiving."

He looked at me with confusion.

"But that's not the worst part…I knew that it made him sad, but I said it anyway—like I didn't care about his feelings at all," I said, shaking my head.

"Charlie, you can't start blaming yourself for-"

I whipped my face back toward him, sharply. "You're absolutely right, Briggs…and I don't—not solely, anyway. I blame you, too."

"Me?" he choked.

I walked closer to where he stood, pointing my finger at him, feeling a rage inside me that was fighting for release.

"*You* are the reason I didn't come home, Briggs. You! Whatever *this* is," I said, pointing between him and me, "It's over. I can't do it anymore! I can't be your *friend*…it's too exhausting. I don't have the energy to worry about one more thing, so I'm finished—done!"

His eyes grew huge as I stared at him mercilessly.

I continued, undeterred, "I knew if I came home at Thanksgiving, I'd be forced to deal with some things I wasn't quite ready to let go of—primarily *you*, and because of that, I don't have a *goodbye memory* with my dad. I don't have a last hug, or a last kiss. The only thing I do have, is the memory of his disappointment after I told him that I wasn't going to come home and see him…because of *you*!" I shook my head, my voice calming momentarily. "I let you steal those moments from me once, and I won't give you any more."

A tearless sob rolled off me as I crossed my arms over my chest.

He took a step toward me, his hand outstretched. "Charlie, I know you're upset right now, you have every right to be, but you don't mean those things," he said.

My head snapped up in attention, "I have never meant anything more in all my life. Do not follow me, Briggs. Do not call me, do not text me…I don't need you!"

I stalked back into the building, and this time no one followed me.

Briggs

Truth be told, I had taken many blows in my life.

I'd taken hits that had knocked me unconscious, hits that had left me crumpled in a pile of blood and broken bones, hits that had taken me weeks to recover from. But none of those came close to the level of power that Charlie had packed into her punch. The girl knew how to fight.

As I stared at the backside of the hospital, watching her leave, I told myself she didn't mean it.

I told myself that she was tired, hungry, stressed, and scared. I told myself that if not for the man lying on an operating table for the second time this week, I would have ignored her outburst and ran after her. But there was a shred of truth in her argument, and that's what stopped me. There had been too many missed opportunities in the past, too many unspoken words and moments. I understood that concept more than anyone.

This night was bigger than me, or her, or even us.

Charlie needed to focus on her dad, and I needed to let her do that.

Charlie

My dad always said that pride was the ugliest part of humanity.

Not only did it aid us in hurting those we loved, it told us we were right, justified in our hurts. It kept us from saying sorry. It kept us from offering forgiveness. It kept us isolated and alone. Pride was ugly.

When my dad woke up from his *complication*—also known as a life-threating pulmonary embolism—I was there, sitting in the chair by his bedside. The days following were painful to watch as he struggled to talk or move, but the nurses assured us that his responses were normal.

Normal.

Would anything ever be normal again?

The men from the station had staggered their visits over the last few days, and though I had seen Briggs several times in passing, we had not spoken a word to each other.

The guilt I felt was nearly unbearable.

I had felt so much anger that awful night, but as my therapist would say, "*anger is only a surface emotion*". Underneath my anger was fear; I had been scared out of my mind. My frustration over my ever-shifting relationship with Briggs had been the big, blinking target.

I had shot to kill.

I cringed thinking of the things I had yelled at Briggs—*horrible* things, maybe even unforgiveable things. Sorry wasn't enough, but what else was there?

The dust may have been settling on my dad's medical drama, but I knew that I couldn't go back to being *just friends* with Briggs. As much as the thought of life without him caused me physical pain, I couldn't keep doing life with him either, not the way we had been doing it. I couldn't sit back and watch him date or marry someone else while I was off on tour abroad—alone.

Neither of us could move on with our futures if we didn't let go of each other now.

I hated that my rational mind was back; I almost preferred *crazy* on days like today.

****

"Go home Charlie, you need to sleep in a real bed and eat a real meal. Mom's here, and I have several of my guys coming here soon, anyway," dad said.

I rolled my eyes. This argument of his was wearing me down, and he knew it. It was hard to fight a man in a hospital gown.

"You know I'll go and then just come right back, Dad. I can't just sit at home when I could be here, with you," I replied.

"Charlie, it would be good for you to go stretch your legs. Go for a walk, shower, eat, take a nap, and then you can come back, okay?" My dad leaned over, whispering, "Maybe you can even slip a coke in your bag for me."

"I heard that, Maxwell." My mom scolded.

"No caffeine," I repeated.

"You girls are going to be the death of me."

"Better us than another heart attack, right?"

"Funny…now get out of here before I call security," he said.

"Fine, but I won't be gone too long."

"Well, you're not getting back in here for at least four hours. I'll post a guard if I have to."

I stared at him, but he was always better at these staring contests than I was. I may have learned from the best, but my talent was still not equal to his. I threw him a smile before exiting the room. I could hear him laugh as I closed the door behind me.

Briggs was waiting on the other side.

My throat was suddenly void of all moisture.

"Hi, Charlie."

"Hey," I managed to croak out.

He placed his hand on the door handle as I scooted around him. I could hear the words screaming like a siren in my head, they were begging for release.

Say it, just say it!

I'M SORRY!

I'M S-O-R-R-Y!

He pushed the knob, knocking twice as he entered. The sadness in his eyes had held me prisoner as I watched him disappear behind he door.

It was true: Pride was an ugly, ugly thing.

Briggs

"Briggs, it's nice to see you, son," Chief said, pointing to the chair that Charlie usually occupied. I sat down. He had texted me an hour ago asking me to come, telling me he was going to make Charlie take a break. If I hadn't just seen it with my own eyes, I wouldn't have thought it possible.

"I think I'll go get some coffee…do you need anything Max?" Mrs. Julie asked.

"A Coke?" Chief asked.

"You're beating a dead horse, Maxwell. I'll be back soon, call if you need me."

"I will sweetheart."

Chief turned to me after the door clicked shut.

"I heard what you did for Charlie," he said.

I wasn't quite sure what he was referring to. A lot had happened since the day of his heart attack.

"Driving to get her from school," he continued.

"Oh, yes," I said, looking anywhere but his face. This conversation was quickly turning painful and it had only been a few seconds in length so far. I wasn't sure I was up for a talk about how I could help him fix Charlie—apparently, she still believed I was the reason for her distress.

"Thank you for doing that, it means a great deal to me—to Julie and I both, actually." He took a deep breath, drumming his fingers soundlessly on his lap. "I never got to finish the conversation I started with you before…the old heart had other plans, I suppose."

He tapped his heart like the Tin-man on The Wizard of OZ. It was a funny gesture, though my smiled was short-lived.

"Well, Chief, it might be pointless to try and continue it now since she's not speaking to me. I doubt I can be of much help to you, although I did find out the reason she didn't come home for Thanksgiving. It was because of me, she told me that much," I said.

He nodded, as if the information I had just shared with him wasn't a surprise. Maybe she had told him that. I hadn't been around for too many conversations lately—or any, for that matter.

"And you're feelings for her haven't changed?"

I laughed humorously. "Hardly."

"Good."

I stared at him. "I don't see how that's *good*, sir. She's barely spoken a word to me since-"

"She can be stubborn, Briggs, but Julie and I believe she's just trying to protect herself."

"From what?"

"You."

What does that even mean?

"Something happened when she was home last spring…it *changed* her. She'd been so distant and defensive prior to that term that when I came home from my trip, I hardly recognized her. She was so *joyful*." He paused. "But in my excitement to have my daughter back, I think I overlooked a vital part—or person—who helped in that transformation of her heart." He pointed to me. "*You*, Briggs."

I shook my head, dumbfounded. "What? But you just said you think she's trying to protect herself from me."

"I do." Chief said again, nodding. "Charlie has always tried to escape hurt and pain by doing whatever she could to avoid it—all of us do that to some degree, but with her it's a little different. Charlie has always had the same weakness Briggs, do you know what it is?"

In an instant, the answer was there, in my head and on my lips.

"She's never felt wanted."

Tears welled in his eyes as he spoke, "I have spent many years praying that Charlie would grab ahold of her second chance. When Julie and I realized her talent, we both believed that piano was the vehicle she needed to leave behind her past." He shook his head slowly, "There is no question that Charlie is gifted, but her accomplishments in piano will never overshadow what she needs the most. I can't say what she will choose for her future, but I hope you're in it, Briggs. I'm convinced your love for my daughter runs as deep as my own for her does. You've waited a long time, and I don't want you to have to wait any longer. You have our blessing, Briggs. I hope the two of you can figure out your future…together."

My mouth hung open.

"But Chief, Charlie…" I couldn't finish the sentence. I'd waited nearly eight months for his approval, and now that I had it, Charlie would barely look at me.

The slap of irony stung.

"Go, Briggs. Charlie will want to hear what you have to say."

I nodded, thanking him as I made my exit.

I didn't need to be told twice.

Chapter Thirty-Five

Charlie

After showering and eating—yes, I made myself a ham sandwich—I sat down at the piano. I couldn't remember the last time I had played. With all that had gone on, it felt lower on the scale of importance now. Camille and her brother had dropped my car off yesterday, along with my music binder. I ran my hand across the front of it before turning to my unfinished composition. I stared at the blank lines and spaces at the end, and suddenly, I knew the notes to fill it.

I poured my heart into that melody until there was nothing left inside it. Every last hope, every last thought, every last dream it held, I played, note by note. And just like that, the piece that had challenged me the most, the piece that had avoided an ending for so long, was finished.

I picked up my pencil, scribbling the notes down with lightening speed so I wouldn't forget them—ever.

And then I added a simple title, which was anything but simple: *BRIGGS.*

The only thing waiting to be written in our future was an ending.

Briggs

I pulled up to Charlie's house, overcome by the reality of the moment that lay ahead. After waiting so long, it hardly felt real. I knocked lightly on the front door, but like countless times in the past, there was no answer. I was certain she was either asleep or playing the piano. I cracked the door and listened. Sure enough, the sounds of heaven met my ears.

I wanted to rush in and beg her to hear me out before she had the chance to erupt again, but more than that, I wanted to give her the ability to choose.

This decision needed to be hers alone.

When I saw her phone sitting on the coffee table, I had an idea. I was in and out in just under a minute.

Charlie

I reached for my keys on the table and picked up my phone, scrolling through my missed texts. *I'm not bringing you a Coke, dad.* And then I saw it. I blinked over and over again, trying to understand how and when Briggs had gotten to my phone.

Truth or Dare: If you choose to accept this dare, I promise to give you nothing but the truth. I'll be on a bench near the pond on the south side of the hospital at 7 tonight. Please come. We need to talk.

Thirty minutes. I grabbed my jacket and scarf, and headed out to my car.

It was time to have this conversation; it was time to complete our composition.

Briggs

I didn't realize how nervous I was until I saw her on the path, walking toward me. Her nose and cheeks were pink from the chilly night air. She had her hands tucked into her red coat and a thick scarf wrapped her neck. I couldn't take my eyes off her.

She came.

I walked toward her, unwilling to wait another minute.

"Charlie, I-"

"Briggs, I-"

Apparently, I wasn't the only who had something to say.

Charlie looked up at me, her voice soft. "May I speak, *please*?"

I nodded, noticing for the first time the space she had placed between us—she stood just outside of my reach. A pang hit the pit of my stomach, hoping that the distance was not as symbolic as my mind was leading me to believe it was.

"I came to tell you I'm sorry. You are not to blame for any of the decisions I made, Briggs. I was cruel to suggest that you were. I hope you can forgive me-"

"Of course, Charlie-" I took a step closer, reaching out for her hand as she slipped it away from my grasp while retreating several steps back, leaving a wider gap between us.

Everything stopped in that moment—my words, my breath, my heart.

Her eyes were full of silent torment, but she held my gaze nonetheless. "There's more I need to say to you." She took a breath, "Although I'm ashamed of how I treated you after all you've done for my family this last week, I can't do *this* anymore—I can't do *us* anymore.

I used to believe that I could love you enough to stay your friend, but I don't just love you enough Briggs, I love you *too much*." She put her hand over her heart, her voice strained with emotion, "I've been drowning in denial for too long, and it's time we finally say a *real* goodbye, it's time we let each other go. I'll never forget you, Briggs. Goodbye."

She turned away from me without another word, walking quickly down the path. I had watched her leave one too many times, and it wasn't going down that way tonight.

Not again.

"I'm in love with you Charlie Lexington!"

She stopped immediately as I jogged to catch up with her.

"The first time you called me your manny I was ruined, and I've loved you *too much* ever since." My heart pounded wildly as she faced me—the face of the woman I wanted more than anything else in the world.

"What did you just say?" She whispered the question; her eyes were huge with shock.

"Charlie, you are everything I *want*, and yet nothing I deserve. All the months I've waited for this moment have proven only one thing to be true over and over again. I am hopelessly, miserably, and so out-of-my-mind desperately in love with you." I cupped her face, warming her cheeks with my hands.

Though her face still held the look of utter disbelief, she didn't flinch at my touch.

"You've...you've loved me for months?"

"Many."

"I don't understand, Briggs, you said-"

“I know, Shortcake,” I shook my head. “Until you, I never believed I would fall in love, much less desire a future with a woman long-term, but you changed all that for me. I wanted to tell you how I felt Charlie—*believe* me I did, but I needed to do it the right way, for you. When I told your dad my feelings for you last spring, I wasn’t sure I would ever get his blessing…until tonight. I never wanted to hurt you or confuse you—I only wanted to love you in the way you deserve to be loved.”

She opened her mouth twice before any sound came out, “My dad? You waited all this time for *his blessing*?”

I smiled in response to her squeaky voice and leaned in close, “Yes, but I don’t think I can wait one more second to do this.” I pressed my lips to hers, claiming her mouth with mine as my hands moved from her face to her hair. She wrapped her arms around my neck as our kiss deepened. This kiss was worth every minute of agony I had struggled to endure over the last eight months, and by the way Charlie was kissing me back, I hoped she felt the same way.

As we broke apart Charlie laughed, breathlessly. “I just can’t believe it...”

“Believe it,” I said pulling her close again, and kissing her temple. “And whatever this means for your dreams and your future in music, I will support you, Charlie. I don’t want you to give anything up for me.” I wrapped my arms around her.

She shook her head, “I’ve learned something recently: Dreams are as fluid as time. If they don’t adapt with us, they fail to remain. I used to think I couldn’t live without piano, until I thought I was going to have to live without you. There was no comparison to which sacrifice would be worse—all my dreams are meaningless if you’re not in them. I love you, Briggs.”

I kissed her again. “I love you, and you don’t have to worry…I’m not going anywhere.”

I tightened my grip as she said, "Do I have your word on that?"

"Shortcake, you have my heart, I hope that ranks higher on that screwy point system of yours."

She laughed, "Oh it does…no doubt."

Charlie

I put my hand on my hip and stared at my dad, "I can't believe he talked to you eight months ago?"

He pushed himself upright, sitting with his back against the headboard.

There was a huge part of me that wanted to be furious with him. All this time he was the one who had held the key to end my misery, and yet, the last hour I had spent with Briggs had easily been the best minutes of my life. My emotions were in a tug-of-war.

"Come here, sugar." I went to him, sitting down on the edge of his bed as he took my hand in his.

"The day you came to live with us—the day you became my daughter, I vowed I would protect you at all costs. I made it my life's mission to keep you safe, to push you toward a path that would lead you far away from heartache's door." He stopped, clearing his throat before continuing, "But you did get hurt again, Charlie…and I felt like I had failed you."

I knew instantly he was referring to Alex.

"Daddy, I brought that heartache upon myself. You and mom did your best to warn me, but I was still the one who chose, and I chose wrong," I whispered, feeling my throat thicken with emotion.

Tears pooled in his eyes. I had never seen my dad cry until this moment.

"When Briggs came to me, I was scared for you, Charlie. I didn't want to lose you again, or watch you throw your dreams away. I have loved Briggs like a son for years, and though I never doubted he was a good man, I did doubt the timing of it. You had just been through so much, but now, as I look at you, I can hardly believe how much you've grown over this last year. And I have never been more proud of you than I am right now. I love you, sugar."

I watched two tears roll down his cheeks, and my heart warmed with love for him.

Just outside the door was the man who was my future, but sitting here in front of me, was the man who had redeemed my past. I hugged him.

"I love you too, Dad."

I heard a soft knock just as our hug released. Briggs stepped inside, smiling as our eyes met. My heart fluttered in response.

Maybe life wasn't a fairytale after all…maybe it was better.

Epilogue

Briggs

The night I told Charlie I loved her was the night my countdown began.

These past five months had meant dozens of road trips to Austin, countless video chat hours, and a lot of long-winded texts. And she was worth every minute.

I would have waited forever for Charlie.

As I entered the auditorium with her parents, my heart swelled with pride at the thought of her walking across that stage. We took our seats, Chief patting me on the back as I scrubbed my hands over my knees.

The countdown was finally over.

Tonight was it; tonight was the night I would ask Charlie to be my future.

Several hundred students filed in, but I didn't see her. Even after the Dean's welcome speech to the friends and family of the graduates, I still had not zeroed-in on her strawberry locks, which were usually quite easy for me to spot. When Dean Thomas took a step back from the microphone and introduced Professor Wade, I re-focused my attention to the podium.

He was Charlie's favorite professor.

"It's true that every one of my students is talented, and each one of them can give an extraordinary performance, but sometimes it's not about either of those things. There is a lot to be learned in music, lots to be practiced, memorized and understood, but there is one thing we cannot teach: Passion. Passion can inspire, it can transform, and it can create, but it *cannot* be learned in a classroom. I've been lucky enough to have a student who has reminded me time and time again that music begins in the heart. Charlie Lexington, can you please take the stage?"

What? Charlie?

I looked at Chief who seemed equally as befuddled. Charlie floated across the stage, her eyes focused on the piano straight ahead, which sat off to the side, only she stopped several feel short of it. Every hair on my neck stood at attention as she adjusted the microphone on the podium.

I couldn't breathe.

"Good evening, my name is Charlie Lexington." She paused, taking a deep breath before looking out into the crowd. "I was extremely honored when Professor Wade asked me to play one of my compositions tonight. But before I make myself at home on the piano, there are a few things I'd like to share with you first. Like so many of us here, music has been a constant companion to me, a source of strength, comfort and security—attributes that were far from what I knew as a young child.

"I was five years old the first time I heard the notes of a piano, yet I didn't realize then just how significant that moment was to my future. The memories I have of my early childhood are not pretty, and they are not easy to talk about, but they are apart of me nonetheless.

"The day that music found me, was the same day my mama committed suicide—a day marked by abandonment, rejection and fear. Every certainty in my life became uncertain and every known became unknown. Yet, as lost as I was that day, I couldn't let go of the sound I had heard, a sound I'm now convinced was my light in the darkness.

"I didn't understand all the trials I would face, or the heartache I would experience due to my mama's choice, but God gave me a family who did. My parents—Max and Julie Lexington—are not only responsible for taking me into their home and caring for me like their own, but for cultivating my talent and passion as well. Their sacrifice, love and devotion have been a constant example to me over the years, and the only reason I can stand here today is because they refused to give up on me. I love you mom and dad, thank you."

The auditorium broke into applause at her last statement, and then settled again, waiting for her next words.

"Music, like love, is a message from the soul, a divine gift that we are to cherish, nurture and express. Tonight, I'd like to do just that. The piece I'm going to play for you sat unfinished for several years, waiting for such a message to be received." Charlie's eyes roamed the audience until she found me. My heart stilled under her gaze. "It finally has. Thank you Briggs, for loving me enough to wait."

Tears welled in my eyes as she sat down at the piano, the applause in the auditorium quieting when her hands moved to the keys.

And then she played.

Every fiber inside me burned and pulled and stretched as her song overtook the room. I had heard Charlie play dozens of times before, but never like this. This melody was a story; I was reading her heart, line by line. Every word, sentence and phrase matched what I felt for her. By the time her last note resonated in the room, my cheeks were wet.

I couldn't possibly love her more.

Charlie

It was hard to focus on the speeches when I could see Briggs sitting out in the audience—waiting for me. It had been two full weeks since the last time we were face to face and I ached to be near him again. I had been looking forward to our drive home tonight for months—four hours alone with Briggs, life couldn't get much better than that.

It had been over a year since we had lived in the same town; I was definitely over being a long-distance girlfriend.

I had kept my performance a surprise, mostly because I loved to catch him off guard, but also because I wanted to be sure that I could go through with it. The second I saw him walk into the auditorium with my parents, my courage was strengthened.

This year, I learned what it meant to fully love and be loved in return. I had reached the impossible depth of my inability to feel wanted, realizing in the process that my mama's decision didn't diminish my worth. Years of therapy had finally been cemented in my heart the moment I chose to believe that as truth.

I no longer felt bound by the word that had owned my childhood, or the shame I had worn because of it.

The auditorium erupted with shouts and applause as my class made its way off the stage. I linked arms with Camille, grinning from ear to ear as we looked for our families in the crowd of people outside minutes later. I didn't have to look for long.

My feet were off the ground as I was wrapped in an embrace that sent my heart into a spastic fit.

"Shortcake," Briggs said, "You're amazing."

I kissed him, oblivious to the hundreds of people swirling around us.

"Ahem…"

We broke apart just in time to see my parents smiling at us. Briggs lowered me down again, so I could hug my parents.

"Charlie…" My dad pressed his lips together, swallowing hard, "We are so proud of you. Thank you for what you said—although I might have shed more tears than mom." He turned to my mom who was wiping her smiling eyes, "We love you, sugar."

****

"You sure this is everything?" Briggs asked, rolling his eyes at me. My convertible was stuffed beyond recognition with boxes and bags.

"Yes, as long as you can still fit, I have everything I need." I smiled my cheesiest grin at him and in a second flat, he was in front of me, pulling me close.

"I've missed you." He nuzzled his face into my neck, sending flames of heat throughout my body.

"Not nearly as much as I've missed you."

He laughed, "You will never win that argument—*ever*."

He opened my door for me, kissing me one last time before hoping in the driver's seat. He laced his fingers through mine as I reminisced. I had shed a few tears saying goodbye to Camille, but I knew it wasn't really *goodbye*, we were too close to stay apart for long. My smile was bittersweet as we headed out of the city. All in all, Austin had been good to me.

When Briggs turned onto a side road, I thought that maybe he was looking for a place to eat, but there were no buildings.

"What are we doing?"

He only smiled in response.

We drove for a few more minutes, my curiosity mounting as I stared at him. Whatever he was up to, he was keeping me in the dark, deliberately.

And then we stopped.

I looked around; there was no sound, or lights from the city—no people anywhere in sight. It was just us, in a large field lit only by the moon and stars, parked in front of an old, vintage gazebo. It looked to be weathered by time and exposure, but it was beautiful nonetheless. I moved toward it, touching the post and feeling the texture of the chipping white paint beneath my fingers as I started up the steps. I wanted to get a better look at the acres of farmland around us.

"Wow…this is really something, I didn't even know this was out here." I said, quietly.

When I turned around, Briggs was reaching into the car, tuning the radio. When he found the station he wanted, he started toward me. Immediately my heart began to race. His steps were purposeful, and his eyes were focused only on me.

"May I have this dance?"

"You may."

His hand pressed at the small of my back as he held me close, swaying to the music. The night was warm, but not stifling. It felt good to be close to him—it felt right. As the song ended, Briggs grip loosened, his hands moving slowly down my arms to my fingers as he dropped to his knee. I heard myself gasp—feeling instantly dizzy with elation.

"Charlie Lexington, I don't know how I lived without you for so long, but I can never go back—you've ruined me in the best possible way. Any day I spend with you is not long enough—I *always* want more. You are my forever, Shortcake. I love you. Will you marry me?"

"Oh Briggs, yes!" I dropped to my knees and threw my arms around his neck, kissing his face over and over, "I'm yours, forever. I love you."

He placed the ring on my finger, emotion bursting inside me as I stared at the sparkly symbol of our love. I looked up at him.

"I changed my mind about something."

"Well that was quick." He winked, as he took my face in his hands.

I shook my head. "No, no—never about you." He kissed my lips again. "About my name."

His eyebrows rose in surprise, "Your name?"

I nodded, tears pooling in my eyes. "You don't have to give up Shortcake, but I think it might be time to give Charlotte a second chance… don't you think?"

"*Charlotte.*" He smiled, the name like a sweet song on his lips. "I couldn't agree with you more."

THE END

1 Cor. 13: 1-8

Love is patient, love is kind. It does not envy, it does not boast, it is not proud. It does not dishonor others, it is not self-seeking, it is not easily angered, it keeps no record of wrongs. Love does not delight in evil but rejoices with the truth. It always protects, always trusts, always hopes, always perseveres.

Love never fails.

Special Thanks

Thank you, God.
You are my cornerstone.

Thank you, Tim.
You are my heart, forever.

Thank you to my boys, my family and my friends.
Your support and encouragement are never far from my mind.

Thank you to my Beta Readers:
Lara Brahms, Desi Brown, Nicki Davis, Bethany Deese, Helen Deese, Renee Deese, Kacy Koffa, Britni Nash, Kim Southwick, Aimee Thomas, Ashley Thomas, Rebekah Zollman.
You are all a HUGE part of my heart and this story.

Thank you Sarah Hansen @ Okay Creations.
Your covers are truly inspiring.

Thank you to my Editor, Renee Deese.
You are so much more than a red pen to me.
Without you I'd be nothing more than a sloppy-copy.

Books by Nicole Deese:

Letting Go series:

All For Anna

All She Wanted

All Who Dream *(available Oct. 2013)*

www.nicoledeese.com

Made in the USA
Lexington, KY
08 July 2014